"This anthology of science fiction stories is sure to delight fans of this genre."

That's how the *LIBRARY JOURNAL* began its review, and continued:

"Dickson has taken considerable care in smoothly developing his plots and characters. The reader is compelled to continue immediately from one story to the next . . . In each story *homo sapiens* is a direct threat to the survival of an extraterrestrial being, or to himself.

"The lead story, *Danger—Human,* sets the tone for the book when an alien race attempts to discover the unknown ingredient that makes the human race seem capable of surviving almost anything. In learning the answer, the aliens seal their own doom. Other stories are not as solemn, but are enjoyable comedies between beings, though with the same explicit warning: *Danger—Human!*"

Gordon R. Dickson

THE BOOK
OF
GORDON DICKSON

Original title:
Danger—Human

DAW BOOKS, INC.
DONALD A. WOLLHEIM, PUBLISHER

1301 Avenue of the Americas
New York, N. Y.   10019

COPYRIGHT ACKNOWLEDGMENTS

DANGER—HUMAN, *Astounding* December 1957, © 1957 by Street & Smith Publications, Inc.

DOLPHIN'S WAY, *Astounding* June 1964, © 1964 by The Condé Nast Publications Inc.

AND THEN THERE WAS PEACE, *If* September 1962, © 1962 by Galaxy Publishing Corporation

THE MAN FROM EARTH, *Galaxy* June 1964, © 1964 by Galaxy Publishing Corporation

BLACK CHARLIE, *Galaxy* April 1954, © 1954 by Galaxy Publishing Corporation

LULUNGOMEENA, *Galaxy* January 1954, © 1953 by Galaxy Publishing Corporation

AN HONORABLE DEATH, *Galaxy* February 1961, © 1960 by Galaxy Publishing Corporation

FLAT TIGER, *Galaxy* March 1956, © 1956 by Galaxy Publishing Corporation

JAMES, *The Magazine of Fantasy and Science Fiction* May 1955, © 1955 by Fantasy House Inc.

THE QUARRY, *Astounding* September 1958, © 1958 by Street & Smith Publications, Inc.

STEEL BROTHER, *Astounding* February 1952, © 1952 by Street & Smith Publications, Inc.

FIRST PRINTING, MAY 1973

1 2 3 4 5 6 7 8 9

CONTENTS

THE BOOK
OF
GORDON DICKSON

DANGER — HUMAN

The spaceboat came down in the silence of perfect working order—down through the cool, dark night of a New Hampshire late spring. There was hardly any moon and the path emerging from the clump of conifers and snaking its way across the dim pasture looked like a long strip of pale cloth, carelessly dropped and forgotten there.

The two aliens checked the boat and stopped it, hovering, some fifty feet above the pasture, and all but invisible against the low-lying clouds. Then they set themselves to wait, their woolly, bearlike forms settled on haunches, their uniform belts glinting a little in the shielded light from the instrument panel, talking now and then in desultory murmurs.

"It's not a bad place," said the one of junior rank, looking down at the earth below.

"Why should it be?" answered the senior.

The junior did not answer. He shifted on his haunches.

"The babies are due soon," he said. "I just got a message."

"How many?" asked the senior.

"Three—the doctor thinks. That's not bad for a first birthing."

"My wife only had two."

"I know. You told me."

They fell silent for a few seconds. The spaceboat rocked almost imperceptibly in the waters of night.

"Look—" said the junior, suddenly. "Here it comes, right on schedule."

The senior glanced overside. Down below, a tall, dark form had emerged from the trees and was coming out along the path. A little beam of light shone before him, terminating in a blob of illumination that danced along the path ahead, lighting his way. The senior stiffened.

"Take controls," he said. The casualness had gone out of his voice. It had become crisp, impersonal.

"Controls," answered the other, in the same emotionless voice.

"Take her down."

"Down it is."

The spaceboat dropped groundward. There was an odd sort of soundless, lightless explosion—it was as if concussive wave had passed, robbed of all effects but one. The figure dropped, the light rolling from its grasp and losing its glow in a tangle of short grass. The spaceboat landed and the two aliens got out.

In the dark night they loomed furrily above the still figure. It was that of a lean, dark man in his early thirties, dressed in clean, much-washed corduroy pants and checkered wool lumber-jack shirt. He was unconscious, but breathing slowly, deeply and easily.

"I'll take it up by the head, here," said the senior. "You take the other end. Got it? Lift! Now, carry it into the boat."

The junior backed away, up through the spaceboat's open lock, grunting a little with the awkwardness of his burden.

"It feels slimy," he said.

"Nonsense!" said the senior. "That's your imagination."

Eldridge Timothy Parker drifted in that dreamy limbo between awakeness and full sleep. He found himself contemplating his own name.

Eldridge Timothy Parker. Eldridgetimothyparker. Eldridge TIMOTHYparker. ELdrIDGEtiMOthyPARKer. . . .

There was a hardness under his back, the back on which he was lying—and a coolness. His flaccid right hand turned flat, feeling. It felt like steel beneath him. Metal? He tried to sit up and bumped his forehead against a ceiling a few inches overhead. He blinked his eyes in the darkness—

Darkness?

He flung out his hands, searching, feeling terror leap up inside him. His knuckles bruised against walls to right and left. Frantic, his groping fingers felt out, around and about him. He was walled in, he was surrounded, he was enclosed.

Completely.

Like in a coffin.

Buried—

He began to scream. . . .

Much later, when he awoke again, he was in a strange

place that seemed to have no walls, but many instruments. He floated in the center of mechanisms that passed and repassed about him, touching, probing, turning. He felt touches of heat and cold. Strange hums and notes of various pitches came and went. He felt voices questioning him.

Who are you?

"Eldridge Parker—Eldridge Timothy Parker—"

What are you?

"I'm Eldridge Parker—"

Tell about yourself.

"Tell what? What?"

Tell about yourself.

"What? What do you want to know? What—"

Tell about. . . .

"But I—"

Tell. . . .

. . . well, i suppose i was pretty much like any of the kids around our town . . . i was a pretty good shot and i won the fifth grade seventy-five yard dash . . . i played hockey, too . . . pretty cold weather up around our parts, you know, the air used to smell strange it was so cold winter mornings in january when you first stepped out of doors . . . it is good, open country, new england, and there were lots of smells . . . there were pine smells and grass smells and i remember especially the kitchen smells . . . and then, too, there was the way the oak benches in church used to smell on sunday when you knelt with your nose right next to the back of the pew ahead . . . .

. . . the fishing up our parts is good too . . . i liked to fish but i never wasted time on weekdays . . . we were presbyterians, you know, and my father had the farm, but he also had money invested in land around the country . . . we have never been badly off but i would have liked a motor-scooter. . . .

. . . no i did not never hate the germans, at least i did not think i ever did, of course though i was over in europe i never really had it bad, combat, i mean . . . i was in a motor pool with the raw smell of gasoline, i like to work with my hands, and it was not like being in the infantry. . . .

. . . i have as good right to speak up to the town council as any man . . . i do not believe in pushing but if they push me i am going to push right back . . . nor it isn't any man's business what i voted last election no more than my

bank balance ... but i have got as good as right to a say
in town doings as if i was the biggest landholder among
them. ...

... i did not go to college because it was not necessary
... too much education can make a fool of any man, i
told my father, and i know when i have had enough ... i
am a farmer and will always be a farmer and i will do my
own studying as things come up without taking out a pure
waste of four years to hang a piece of paper on the
wall. ...

... of course i know about the atom bomb, but i am
no scientist and no need to be one, no more than i need to
be a veterinarian ... i elect the men that hire the men that
need to know those things and the men that i elect will
hear from me johnny-quick if things do not go to my lik-
ing. ...

... as to why i never married, that is none of your
business ... as it happens, i was never at ease with women
much, though there were a couple of times, and i still may
if jeanie lind. ...

... i believe in god and the united states of america. ...

He woke up gradually. He was in a room that might
have been any office, except the furniture was different.
That is, there was a box with doors on it that might have
been a filing cabinet and a table that looked like a desk in
spite of the single thin rod underneath the center that sup-
ported it. However, there were no chairs—only small, flat
cushions, on which three large woolly, bearlike creatures
were sitting and watching him in silence.

He himself, he found, was in a chair, though.

As soon as they saw his eyes were open, they turned
away from him and began to talk among themselves.
Eldridge Parker shook his head and blinked his eyes, and
would have blinked his ears if that had been possible. For
the sounds the creatures were making were like nothing he
had ever heard before; and yet he understood everything
they were saying. It was an odd sensation, like a double-
image earwise, for he heard the strange mouth-noises just
as they came out and then something in his head twisted
them around and made them into perfectly understandable
English.

Nor was that all. For, as he sat listening to the creatures talk, he began to get the same double image in another way. That is, he still saw the bearlike creature behind the desk as the weird sort of animal he was, out of

the sound of his voice, or from something else, there gradually built up in Eldridge's mind a picture of a thin, rather harassed-looking gray-haired man in something resembling a uniform, but at the same time not quite a uniform. It was the sort of effect an army general might get if he wore his stars and a Sam Browne belt over a civilian double-breasted suit. Similarly, the other creature sitting facing the one behind the desk, at the desk's side, was a young and black-haired man with something of the laboratory about him, and the creature further back, seated almost against the wall, was neither soldier nor scientist, but a heavy older man with a sort of book-won wisdom in him.

"You see, commander," the young one with the black-haired image was saying, "perfectly restored. At least on the physical and mental levels."

"Good, doctor, good," the outlandish syllables from the one behind the desk translated themselves in Eldridge's head. "And you say it . . . he, I should say . . . will be able to understand?"

"Certainly, sir," said the doctor-psychologist—whatever-he-was. "Identification is absolute—"

"But I mean comprehend—encompass—" The creature behind the desk moved one paw slightly. "Follow what we tell him—"

The doctor turned his ursinoid head toward the third member of the group. This one spoke slowly, in a deeper voice.

"The culture allows. Certainly."

The one behind the desk bowed slightly to the oldest one. "Certainly, Academician, certainly."

They then fell silent, all looking back at Eldridge, who returned their gaze with equivalent interest. There was something unnatural about the whole proceeding. Both sides were regarding the other with the completely blunt and unshielded curiosity given to freaks.

The silence stretched out. It became tinged with a certain embarrassment. Gradually a mutual recognition arose that no one really wanted to be the first to address an alien being directly.

"It . . . he is comfortable?" asked the commander, turning once more to the doctor.

"I should say so," replied the doctor, slowly. "As far as we know. . . ."

Turning back to Eldridge, the commander said,

"Eldridge-timothyparker, I suppose you wonder where you are?"

Caution and habit put a clamp on Eldridge's tongue. He hesitated about answering so long that the commander turned in distress to the doctor, who reassured him with a slight movement of the head.

"Well, speak up," said the commander, "we'll be able to understand you, just as you're able to understand us. Nothing's going to hurt you; and anything you say won't have the slightest effect on your . . . er . . . situation."

He paused again, looking at Eldridge for a comment. Eldridge still held his silence, but one of his hands unconsciously made a short, fumbling motion at his breast pocket.

"My pipe——" said Eldridge.

The three looked at each other. They looked back at Eldridge.

"We have it," said the doctor. "After a while we may give it back to you. For now . . . we cannot allow . . . it would not suit us."

"Smoke bother you?" said Eldridge, with a touch of his native canniness.

"It does not bother us. It is . . . merely . . . distasteful," said the commander. "Let's get on. I'm going to tell you where you are, first. You're on a world roughly similar to your own, but many . . ." he hesitated, looking at the academician.

"Light-years," supplemented the deep voice.

". . . Light-years in terms of what a year means to you," went on the commander, with growing briskness. "Many light-years distant from your home. We didn't bring you here because of any personal . . . dislike . . . or enmity for you; but for. . . ."

"Observation," supplied the doctor. The commander turned and bowed slightly to him, and was bowed back at in return.

". . . Observation," went on the commander. "Now, do you understand what I've told you so far?"

"I'm listening," said Eldridge.

"Very well," said the commander. "I will go on. There is something about your people that we are very anxious to discover. We have been, and intend to continue, studying you to find it out. So far—I will admit quite frankly and freely—we have not found it; and the concensus among our best minds is that you, yourself, do not know what it is. Accordingly, we have hopes of ... causing ... you to discover it for yourself. And for us."

"Hey. ..." breathed Eldridge.

"Oh, you will be well treated. I assure you," said the commander, hurriedly. "You have been well treated. You have been ... but you did not know ... I mean you did not feel—"

"Can you remember any discomfort since we picked you up?" asked the doctor, leaning forward.

"Depends what you mean—"

"And you will feel none." The doctor turned to the commander. "Perhaps I'm getting ahead of myself?"

"Perhaps," said the commander. He bowed and turned back to Eldridge. "To explain—we hope you will discover our answer for it. We're only going to put you in a position to work on it. Therefore, we've decided to tell you everything. First—the problem. Academician?"

The oldest one bowed. His deep voice made the room ring oddly.

"If you will look this way," he said. Eldridge turned his head. The other raised one paw and the wall beside him dissolved into a maze of lines and points. "Do you know what this is?"

"No," said Eldridge.

"It is," rumbled the one called the academician, "a map of the known universe. You lack the training to read it in four dimensions, as it should be read. No matter. You will take my word for it ... it is a map. A map covering hundreds of thousands of your light-years and millions of your years."

He looked at Eldridge, who said nothing.

"To go on, then. What we know of your race is based upon two sources of information. History. And Legend. The history is sketchy. It rests on archaeological discoveries for the most part. The legend is even sketchier and—fantastic."

He paused again. Still Eldridge guarded his tongue.

"Briefly, there is a race that has three times broken out to overrun this mapped area of our galaxy and dominate other civilized cultures—until some inherent lack or weakness in the individual caused the component parts of this advance to die out. The periods of these outbreaks has always been disastrous for the dominated cultures and uniformly without benefit to the race I am talking about. In the case of each outbreak, though the home planet was destroyed and all known remnants of the advancing race hunted out, unknown seed communities remained to furnish the material for a new advance some thousands of years later. That race," said the academician, and coughed—or at least made some kind of noise in his throat, "is your own."

Eldridge watched the other carefully and without moving.

"We see your race, therefore," went on the academician, and Eldridge received the mental impression of an elderly man putting the tips of his fingers together judiciously, "as one with great or overwhelming natural talents, but unfortunately also with one great natural flaw. This flaw seems to be a desire—almost a need—to acquire and possess things. To reach out, encompass, and absorb. It is not," shrugged the academician, "a unique trait. Other races have it—but not to such an extent that it makes them a threat to their co-existing cultures. Yet, this in itself is not the real problem. If it was a simple matter of rapacity, a combination of other races should be able to contain your people. There is a natural inevitable balance of that sort continually at work in the galaxy. No," said the academician and paused, looking at the commander.

"Go on. Go on," said the commander. The academician bowed.

"No, it is not that simple. As a guide to what remains, we have only the legend, made anew and reinforced after each outward sweep of you people. We know that there must be something more than we have found—and we have studied you carefully, both your home world and now you, personally. There *must* be something more in you, some genius, some capability above the normal, to account for the fantastic nature of your race's previous successes. But the legend says only—*Danger, Human! High Explosive. Do not touch*—and we find nothing in you to justify the warning."

He sighed. Or at least Eldridge received a sudden, unexpected intimation of deep weariness.

"Because of a number of factors—too numerous to go into and most of them not understandable to you—it is our race which must deal with this problem for the rest of the galaxy. What can we do? We dare not leave you be until you grow strong and come out once more. And the legend expressly warns us against touching you in any way. So we have chosen to pick one—but I intrude upon your field, doctor."

The two of them exchanged bows. The doctor took up the talk speaking briskly and entirely to Eldridge.

"A joint meeting of those of us best suited to consider the situation recommended that we pick up one specimen for intensive observation. For reasons of availability, you were the one chosen. Following your return under drugs to this planet, you were thoroughly examined, by the best of medical techniques, both mentally and physically. I will not go into detail, since we have no wish to depress you unduly. I merely want to impress on you the fact that we found nothing. Nothing. No unusual power or ability of any sort, such as history shows you to have had and legend hints at. I mention this because of the further course of action we have decided to take. Commander?"

The being behind the desk got to his hind feet. The other two rose.

"You will come with us," said the commander.

Herded by them, Eldridge went out through the room's door into brilliant sunlight and across a small stretch of something like concrete to a stubby egg-shaped craft with ridiculous little wings.

"Inside," said the commander. They got in. The commander squatted before a bank of instruments, manipulated a simple sticklike control, and after a moment the ship took to the air. They flew for perhaps half an hour, with Eldridge wishing he was in a position to see out one of the high windows, then landed at a field apparently literally hacked out of a small forest of mountains.

Crossing this field on foot, Eldridge got a glimpse of some truly huge ships, as well as a number of smaller ones such as the one in which he had arrived. Numbers of the furry aliens moved about, none with any great air of hurry, but all with purposefulness. There was a sudden, single, thunderous sound that was gone almost before the ear could register it; and Eldridge, who had ducked instinctively, looked up again to see one of the huge ships falling—there is no other word for it—skyward with such unbelievable rapidity it was out of sight in seconds.

The four of them came at last to a shallow, open trench in the stuff which made the field surface. It was less than a foot wide and they stepped across it with ease. But once they had crossed it, Eldridge noticed a difference. In the five hundred yard square enclosed by the trench—for it turned at right angles off to his right and to his left—there was an air of tightly-established desertedness, as of some highly restricted area, and the rectangular concrete-look-ing building that occupied the square's very center glit-tered unoccupied in the clear light.

They marched to the door of this building and it opened without any of them touching it. Inside was perhaps twenty feet of floor, stretching inward as a rim inside the walls. Then a sort of moat—Eldridge could not see its depth—filled with a dark fluid with a faint, sharp odor. This was perhaps another twenty feet wide and enclosed a small, flat island perhaps fifteen feet by fifteen feet, almost wholly taken up by a cage whose walls and ceiling ap-peared to be made of metal bars as thick as a man's thumb and spaced about six inches apart. Two more of the aliens, wearing a sort of harness and holding a short, black tube apiece, stood on the ledge of the outer rim. A temporary bridge had been laid across the moat, protrud-ing through the open door of the cage.

They all went across the bridge and into the cage. There, standing around rather like a board of directors viewing an addition to the company plant, they faced Eldridge; and the commander spoke.

"This will be your home from now on," he said. He in-dicated the cot, the human-type chair and the other items furnishing the cage. "It's as comfortable as we can make it."

"Why?" burst out Eldridge, suddenly. "Why're you lock-ing me up here? Why—"

"In our attempt to solve the problem that still exists," interrupted the doctor, smoothly, "we can do nothing more than keep you under observation and hope that time will work with us. Also, we hope to influence you to search for the solution, yourself."

"And if I find it—what?" cried Eldridge.

"Then," said the commander, "we will deal with you in the kindest manner that the solution permits. It may be even possible to return you to your own world. At the very least, once you are no longer needed, we can see to it that you are quickly and painlessly destroyed."

Eldridge felt his insides twist within him.

"Kill me?" he choked. "You think that's going to make me help you? The hope of getting killed?"

They looked at him almost compassionately.

"You may find," said the doctor, "that death may be something you will want very much, only for the purpose of putting a close to a life you've become weary of.

Look,"—he gestured around him—"you are locked up beyond any chance of ever escaping. This cage will be illuminated night and day; and you will be locked in it. When we leave, the bridge will be withdrawn, and the only thing crossing that moat—which is filled with acid—will be a mechanical arm which will extend across and through a small opening to bring you food twice a day. Beyond the moat, there will be two armed guards on duty at all times, but even they cannot open the door to this building. That is opened by remote control from outside, only after the operator has checked on his vision screen to make sure all is as it should be inside here."

He gestured through the bars, across the moat and through a window in the outer wall.

"Look out there," he said.

Eldridge looked. Out beyond, and surrounding the building the shallow trench no longer lay still and empty under the sun. It now spouted a vertical wall of flickering, weaving distortion, like a barrier of heat waves.

"That is our final defense, the ultimate in destructiveness that our science provides us—it would literally burn you to nothingness, if you touch it. It will be turned off only for seconds, and with elaborate precautions, to let guards in, or out."

Eldridge looked back in, to see them all watching him.

"We do this," said the doctor, "not only because we may discover you to be more dangerous than you seem, but to impress you with your helplessness so that you may be more ready to help us. Here you are, and here you will stay."

"And you think," demanded Eldridge hoarsely, "that this's all going to make me want to help you?"

"Yes," said the doctor, "because there's one thing more that enters into the situation. You were literally taken apart physically, after your capture; and as literally put back together again. We are advanced in the organic field, and certain things are true of all life forms. I supervised the work on you, myself. You will find that you are, for all practical purposes, immortal and irretrievably sane. This will be your home forever, and you will find that neither death nor insanity will provide you a way of escape."

They turned and filed out. From some remote control, the cage door was swung shut. He heard it click and lock. The bridge was withdrawn from the moat. A screen lit up and a woolly face surveyed the building's interior.

The building's door opened. They went out; and the guards took up their patrol, around the rim in opposite directions, keeping their eyes on Eldridge and their weapons ready in their hands. The building's door closed again. Outside, the flickering wall blinked out for a second and then returned again.

The silence of a warm, summer, mountain afternoon descended upon the building. The footsteps of the guards made shuffling noises on their path around the rim. The bars enclosed him.

Eldridge stood still, holding the bars in both hands and looking out.

He could not believe it.

He could not believe it as the days piled up into weeks, and the weeks into months. But as the seasons shifted and the year came around to a new year, the realities of his situation began to soak into him like water into a length of dock piling. For outside, Time could be seen at its visible and regular motion; but in his prison, there was no Time.

Always, the lights burned overhead, always the guards paced about him. Always the barrier burned beyond the building, the meals came swinging in on the end of a long metal arm extended over the moat and through a small hatchway which opened automatically as the arm approached; regularly, twice weekly, the doctor came and checked him over, briefly, impersonally—and went out again with the changing of the guard.

He felt the unbearableness of his situation, like a hand winding tighter and tighter day by day the spring of tension within him. He took to pacing feverishly up and down the cage. He went back and forth, back and forth, until the room swam. He lay awake nights, staring at the endless glow of illumination from the ceiling. He rose to pace again.

The doctor came and examined him. He talked to Eldridge, but Eldridge would not answer. Finally there came a day when everything split wide open and he began to howl and bang on the bars. The guards were frightened and called the doctor. The doctor came, and with two others, entered the cage and strapped him down. They did something odd that hurt at the back of his neck and he passed out.

When he opened his eyes again, the first thing he saw

was the doctor's woolly face, looking down at him—he had learned to recognize that countenance in the same way a sheep-herder eventually comes to recognize individual sheep in his flock. Eldridge felt very weak, but calm.

"You tried hard—" said the doctor. "But you see, you didn't make it. There's no way out *that* way for you."

Eldridge smiled.

"Stop that!" said the doctor sharply. "You aren't fooling us. We know you're perfectly rational."

Eldridge continued to smile.

"What do you think you're doing?" demanded the doctor. Eldridge looked happily up at him.

"I'm going home," he said.

"I'm sorry," said the doctor. "You don't convince me." He turned and left. Eldridge turned over on his side and dropped off into the first good sleep he'd had in months.

In spite of himself, however, the doctor was worried. He had the guards doubled, but nothing happened. The days slipped into weeks again and nothing happened. Eldridge was apparently fully recovered. He still spent a great deal of time walking up and down his cage and grasping the bars as if to pull them out of the way before him—but the frenzy of his earlier pacing was gone. He had also moved his cot over next to the small, two-foot square hatch that opened to admit the mechanical arm bearing his meals, and would lie there, with his face pressed against it, waiting for the food to be delivered. The doctor felt uneasy, and spoke to the commander privately about it.

"Well," said the commander, "just what is it you suspect?"

"I don't know," confessed the doctor. "It's just that I see him more frequently than any of us. Perhaps I've become sensitized—but he bothers me."

"Bothers you?"

"Frightens me, perhaps. I wonder if we've taken the right way with him."

"We took the only way." The commander made the little gesture and sound that was his race's equivalent of a sigh. "We must have data. What do you do when you run across a possibly dangerous virus, doctor? You isolate it—for study, until you know. It is not possible, and too risky to try to study his race at close hand, so we study him. That's all we're doing. You lose objectivity, doctor. Would you like to take a short vacation?"

"No," said the doctor, slowly. "No. But he frightens me."

Still, time went on and nothing happened. Eldridge paced his cage and lay on his cot, face pressed to the bars of the hatch, and staring at the outside world. Another year passed; and another. The double guards were withdrawn. The doctor came reluctantly to the conclusion that the human had at last accepted the fact of his confinement and felt growing within him that normal sort of sympathy that feeds on familiarity. He tried to talk to Eldridge on his regularly scheduled visits, but Eldridge showed little interest in conversation. He lay on the cot watching the doctor as the doctor examined him, with something in his eyes as if he looked on from some distant place in which all decisions were already made and finished.

"You're as healthy as ever," said the doctor, concluding his examination. He regarded Eldridge. "I wish you would, though. . . ." He broke off. "We aren't a cruel people, you know. We don't like the necessity that makes us do this."

He paused. Eldridge considered him without stirring.

"If you'd accept that fact," said the doctor, "I'm sure you'd make it easier on yourself. Possibly our figures of speech have given you a false impression. We said you are immortal. Well, of course, that's not true. Only practically speaking, are you immortal. You are now capable of living a very, very, very long time. That's all."

He paused again. After a moment of waiting, he went on.

"Just the same way, this business isn't really intended to go on for eternity. By its very nature, of course, it can't. Even races have a finite lifetime. But even that would be too long. No, it's just a matter of a long time as you might live it. Eventually, everything must come to a conclusion—that's inevitable."

Eldridge still did not speak. The doctor sighed.

"Is there anything you'd like?" he said. "We'd like to make this as little unpleasant as possible. Anything we can give you?"

Eldridge opened his mouth.

"Give me a boat," he said. "I want a fishing rod. I want a bottle of applejack."

The doctor shook his head sadly. He turned and signaled the guards. The cage door opened. He went out.

"Get me some pumpkin pie," cried Eldridge after him, sitting up on the cot and grasping the bars as the door closed. "Give me some green grass in here."

The doctor crossed the bridge. The bridge was lifted up and the monitor screen lit up. A woolly face looked out and saw that all was well. Slowly the outer door swung open.

"Get me some pine trees!" yelled Eldridge at the doctor's retreating back. "Get me some plowed fields! Get me some earth, some dirt, some plain, earth dirt! *Get me that!*"

The door shut behind the doctor; and Eldridge burst into laughter, clinging to the bars, hanging there with glowing eyes.

"I would like to be relieved of this job," said the doctor to the commander, appearing formally in the latter's office.

"I'm sorry," said the commander. "I'm very sorry. But it was our tactical team that initiated this action; and no one has the experience with the prisoner you have. I'm sorry."

The doctor bowed his head; and went out.

Certain mild but emotion-deadening drugs were also known to the woolly, bearlike race. The doctor went out and began to indulge in them. Meanwhile, Eldridge lay on his cot, occasionally smiling to himself. His position was such that he could see out the window and over the weaving curtain of the barrier that ringed his building, to the landing field. After a while one of the large ships landed and when he saw the three members of its crew disembark from it and move, antlike, off across the field toward the buildings at its far end, he smiled again.

He settled back and closed his eyes. He seemed to doze for a couple of hours and then the sound of the door opening to admit the extra single guard bearing the food for his three o'clock mid-afternoon feeding. He sat up, pushed the cot down a ways, and sat on the end of it, waiting for the meal.

The bridge was not extended—that happened only when someone physically was to enter his cage. The monitor screen lit up and a woolly face watched as the tray of food was loaded on the mechanical arm. It swung out across the acid-filled moat, stretched itself toward the cage, and under the vigilance of the face in the monitor, the two-foot square hatch opened just before it to let it extend into the cage.

Smiling, Eldridge took the tray. The arm withdrew, as

it cleared the cage, the hatch swung shut and locked. Outside the cage, guards, food carrier and face in the monitor relaxed. The food carrier turned toward the door, the face in the monitor looked down at some invisible control board before it and the outer door swung open.

In that moment, Eldridge moved.

In one swift second he was on his feet and his hands had closed around the bars of the hatch. There was a single screech of metal, as—incredibly—he tore it loose and threw it aside. Then he was diving through the hatch opening.

He rolled head over heels like a gymnast and came up with his feet standing on the inner edge of the moat. The acrid scent of the acid faintly burnt at his nostrils. He sprang forward in a standing jump, arms outstretched—and his clutching fingers closed on the end of the food arm, now halfway in the process of its leisurely mechanical retraction across the moat.

The metal creaked and bent, dipping downward toward the acid, but Eldridge was already swinging onward under the powerful impetus of his arms from which the sleeves had fallen back to reveal bulging ropes of smooth, powerful muscle. He flew forward through the air, feet first, and his boots took the nearest guard in the face, so that they crashed to the ground together.

For a second they rolled entangled, then the guard flopped and Eldridge came up on one knee, holding the black tube of the guard's weapon. It spat a single tongue of flame and the other guard dropped. Eldridge thrust to his feet, turning to the still-open door.

The door was closing. But the panicked food-carrier, unarmed, had turned to run. A bolt from Eldridge's weapon took him in the back. He fell forward and the door jammed on his body. Leaping after him, Eldridge squeezed through the remaining opening.

Then he was out under the free sky. The sounds of alarm screechers were splitting the air. He began to run—

The doctor was already drugged—but not so badly that he could not make it to the field when the news came. Driven by a strange perversity of spirit, he went first to the prison to inspect the broken hatch and the bent food arm. He traced Eldridge's outward path and it led him to the landing field where he found the commander and the academician by a bare, darkened area of concrete. They acknowledged his presence by little bows.

"He took a ship here?" said the doctor.

"He took a ship here," said the commander.

There was a little silence between them.

"Well," said the academician, "we have been answered."

"Have we?" the commander looked at them almost appealingly. "There's no chance—that it was just chance? No chance that the hatch just happened to fail—and he acted without thinking, and was lucky?"

The doctor shook his head. He felt a little dizzy and unnatural from the drug, but the ordinary processes of his thinking were unimpaired.

"The hinges of the hatch," he said, "were rotten—eaten away by acid."

"Acid?" the commander stared at him. "Where would he get acid?"

"From his own digestive processes—regurgitated and spat directly into the hinges. He secreted hydrochloric acid among other things. Not too powerful—but over a period of time. . . ."

"Still—" said the commander, desperately, "I think it must have been more luck than otherwise."

"Can you believe that?" asked the academician. "Consider the timing of it all, the choosing of a moment when the food arm was in the proper position, the door open at the proper angle, the guard in a vulnerable situation. Consider his unhesitating and sure use of a weapon—which could only be the fruits of hours of observation, his choice of a moment when a fully supplied-ship, its drive unit not yet cooled down, was waiting for him on the field. No," he shook his woolly head, "we have been answered. We put him in an escape-proof prison and he escaped."

"But none of this was possible!" cried the commander.

The doctor laughed, a fuzzy, drug-blurred laugh. He opened his mouth but the academician was before him.

"It's not what he did," said the academician, "but the fact that he did it. No member of another culture that we know would have even entertained the possibility in their minds. Don't you see—he disregarded, he *denied* the fact that escape was impossible. *That* is what makes his kind so fearful, so dangerous. The fact that something is impossible presents no barrier to their seeking minds. That, alone, places them above us on a plane we can never reach."

"But it's a false premise!" protested the commander.

"They cannot contravene natural laws. They are still bound by the physical order of the universe."

The doctor laughed again. His laugh had a wild quality. The commander looked at him.

"You're drugged," he said.

"Yes," choked the doctor. "And I'll be more drugged. I toast the end of our race, our culture, and our order."

"Hysteria!" said the commander.

"Hysteria?" echoed the doctor. "No—*guilt!* Didn't we do it, we three? The legend told us not to touch them, not to set a spark to the explosive mixture of their kind. And we went ahead and did it, you, and you, and I. And now we've sent forth an enemy—safely into the safe hiding place of space, in a ship that can take him across the galaxy, supplied with food to keep him for years, rebuilt into a body that will not die, with star charts and all the keys to understand our culture and locate his home again, using the ability to learn we have encouraged in him."

"I say," said the commander, doggedly, "he is not that dangerous—yet. So far he has done nothing one of us could not do, had we entertained the notion. He's shown nothing, nothing supernormal."

"Hasn't he?" said the doctor thickly. "What about the defensive screen—our most dangerous most terrible weapon—that could burn him to nothingness if he touched it?"

The commander stared at him.

"But—" said the commander. "The screen was shut off, of course, to let the food carrier out, at the same time the door was opened. I assumed—"

"I checked," said the doctor, his eyes burning on the commander. "They turned it on again before he could get out."

"But he *did* get out! You don't mean . . ." the commander's voice faltered and dropped. The three stood caught in a sudden silence like stone. Slowly, as if drawn by strings controlled by an invisible hand, they turned as one to stare up into the empty sky and space beyond.

"You mean—" the commander's voice tried again, and died.

"Exactly!" whispered the doctor.

Halfway across the galaxy, a child of a sensitive race cried out in its sleep and clutched at its mother.

"I had a bad dream," it whimpered.

"Hush," said its mother. "Hush." But she lay still, staring at the ceiling. She, too, had dreamed.

Somewhere, Eldridge was smiling at the stars.

DOLPHIN'S WAY

Of course, there was no reason why a woman coming to Dolphin's Way—as the late Dr. Edwin Knight had named the island research station—should not be beautiful. But Mal had never expected such a thing to happen.

Castor and Pollux had not come to the station pool this morning. They might have left the station, as other wild dolphins had in the past—and Mal nowadays carried always with him the fear that the Willernie Foundation would seize on some excuse to cut off their funds for further research. Ever since Corwin Brayt had taken over, Mal had known this fear. Though Brayt had said nothing. It was only a feeling Mal got from the presence of the tall, cold man. So it was that Mal was out in front of the station, scanning the ocean when the water-taxi from the mainland brought the visitor.

She stepped out on the dock, as he stared down at her. She waved as if she knew him, and then climbed the stairs from the dock to the terrace in front of the door to the main building of the station.

"Hello," she said, smiling as she stopped in front of him. "You're Corwin Brayt?"

Mal was suddenly sharply conscious of his own lean and ordinary appearance in contrast to her startling beauty. She was brown-haired and tall for a girl—but these things did not describe her. There was a perfection to her—and her smile stirred him strangely.

"No," he said. "I'm Malcolm Sinclair. Corwin's inside."

"I'm Jane Wilson," she said. *"Background Monthly* sent me out to do a story on the dolphins. Do you work with them?"

"Yes," Mal said. "I started with Dr. Knight in the beginning."

"Oh, good," she said. "Then, you can tell me some things. You were here when Dr. Brayt took charge after Dr. Knight's death?"

"Mr. Brayt," he corrected automatically. "Yes." The emotion she moved in him was so deep and strong it seemed she must feel it too. But she gave no sign.

"Mr. Brayt?" she echoed. "Oh. How did the staff take to him?"

"Well," said Mal, wishing she would smile again, "everyone took to him."

"I see," she said. "He's a good research head?"

"A good administrator," said Mal. "He's not involved in the research end."

"He's not?" She stared at him. "But didn't he replace Dr. Knight, after Dr. Knight's death?"

"Why, yes," said Mal. He made an effort to bring his attention back to the conversation. He had never had a woman affect him like this before. "But just as administrator of the station, here. You see—most of our funds for work here come from the Willernie Foundation. They had faith in Dr. Knight, but when he died . . . well, they wanted someone of their own in charge. None of us mind."

"Willernie Foundation," she said. "I don't know it."

"It was set up by a man named Willernie, in St. Louis, Missouri," said Mal. "He made his money manufacturing kitchen utensils. When he died he left a trust and set up the Foundation to encourage basic research." Mal smiled. "Don't ask me how he got from kitchen utensils to that. That's not much information for you, is it?"

"It's more than I had a minute ago," she smiled back. "Did you know Corwin Brayt before he came here?"

"No." Mal shook his head. "I don't know many people outside the biological and zoological fields."

"I imagine you know him pretty well now, though, after the six months he's been in charge."

"Well—" Mal hesitated, "I wouldn't say I know him *well*, at all. You see, he's up here in the office all day long and I'm down with Pollux and Castor—the two wild dolphins we've got coming to the station, now. Corwin and I don't see each other much."

"On this small island?"

"I suppose it seems funny—but we're both pretty busy."

"I guess you would be," she smiled again. "Will you take me to him?"

"Him?" Mal awoke suddenly to the fact they were still standing on the terrace. "Oh, yes—it's Corwin you came to see."

"Not just Corwin," she said. "I came to see the whole place."

"Well, I'll take you in to the office. Come along."

He led her across the terrace and in through the front door into the air-conditioned coolness of the interior. Corwin Brayt ran the air-conditioning constantly, as if his own somewhat icy personality demanded the dry, distant coldness of a mountain atmosphere. Mal led Jane Wilson down a short corridor and through another door into a large wide-windowed office. A tall, slim, broadshouldered man with black hair and a brown, coldly handsome face looked up from a large desk, and got to his feet on seeing Jane.

"Corwin," said Mal. "This is Miss Jane Wilson from *Background Monthly*."

"Yes," said Corwin expressionlessly to Jane, coming around the desk to them. "I got a wire yesterday you were coming." He did not wait for Jane to offer her hand, but offered his own. Their fingers met.

"I've got to be getting down to Castor and Pollux," said Mal, turning away.

"I'll see you later then," Jane said, looking over at him.

"Why, yes. Maybe——" he said. He went out. As he closed the door of Brayt's office behind him, he paused for a moment in the dim, cool hallway, and shut his eyes. *Don't be a fool*, he told himself, *a girl like that can do a lot better than someone like you. And probably has already.*

He opened his eyes and went back down to the pool behind the station and non-human world of the dolphins.

When he got there, he found that Castor and Pollux were back. Their pool was an open one, with egress to the open blue waters of the Caribbean. In the first days of the research at Dolphin's Way, the dolphins had been confined in a closed pool like any captured wild animal. It was only later on, when the work at the station had come up against what Knight had called "the environmental barrier" that the notion was conceived of opening the pool to the sea, so that the dolphins they had been working with could leave or stay, as they wished.

They had left—but they had come back. Eventually, they had left for good. But strangely, wild dolphins had come from time to time to take their place, so that there were always dolphins at the station.

Castor and Pollux were the latest pair. They had showed up some four months ago after a single dolphin frequenting the station had disappeared. Free, indepen-

dent—they had been most co-operative. But the barrier
had not been breached.

Now, they were sliding back and forth past each other
underwater utilizing the full thirty-yard length of the pool,
passing beside, over and under each other, their seven-foot
nearly identical bodies almost, but not quite, rubbing as
they passed. The tape showed them to be talking together
up in the supersonic range, eighty to a hundred and
twenty kilocycles per second. Their pattern of movement
in the water now was something he had never seen before.
It was regular and ritualistic as a dance.

He sat down and put on the earphones connected to the
hydrophones, underwater at each end of the pool. He
spoke into the microphone, asking them about their movements, but they ignored him and kept on with the patterned swimming.

The sound of footsteps behind him made him turn. He
saw Jane Wilson approaching down the concrete steps
from the back door of the station, with the stocky, over-
alled, figure of Pete Adant, the station mechanic.

"Here he is," said Pete, as they came up. "I've got to
get back, now."

"Thank you." She gave Pete the smile that had so
moved Mal earlier. Pete turned and went back up the
steps. She turned to Mal. "Am I interrupting something?"

"No." He took off the earphones. "I wasn't getting any
answers, anyway."

She looked at the two dolphins in their underwater
dance with the liquid surface swirling above them as they
turned now this way, now that, just under it.

"Answers?" she said. He smiled a little ruefully.

"We call them answers," he said. He nodded at the two
smoothly streamlined shapes turning in the pool. "Sometimes we can ask questions and get responses."

"Informative responses?" she asked.

"Sometimes. You wanted to see me about something?"

"About everything," she said. "It seems you're the man
I came to talk to—not Brayt. He sent me down here. I
understand you're the one with the theory."

"Theory?" he said warily, feeling his heart sink inside
him.

"The notion, then," she said. "The idea that, if there is
some sort of interstellar civilization, it might be waiting
for the people of Earth to qualify themselves before making contact. And that test might not be a technological

one like developing a faster-than-light means of travel, but a sociological one—"

"Like learning to communicate with an alien culture—a culture like that of the dolphins," he interrupted harshly. "Corwin told you this?"

"I'd heard about it before I came," she said. "I'd thought it was Brayt's theory, though."

"No," said Mal, "it's mine." He looked at her. "You aren't laughing."

"Should I laugh?" she said. She was attentively watching the dolphins' movements. Suddenly he felt sharp jealously of them for holding her attention; and the emotion pricked him to something he might not otherwise have had the courage to do.

"Fly over to the mainland with me," he said, "and have lunch. I'll tell you all about it."

"All right." She looked up from the dolphins at him at last and he was surprised to see her frowning. "There's a lot I don't understand," she murmured. "I thought it was Brayt I had to learn about. But it's you—and the dolphins."

"Maybe we can clear that up at lunch, too," Mal said, not quite clear what she meant, but not greatly caring, either. "Come on, the helicopters are around the north side of the building."

They flew a copter across to Carúpano, and sat down to lunch looking out at the shipping in the open roadstead of the azure sea before the town, while the polite Spanish of Venezuelan voices sounded from the tables around them.

"Why should I laugh at your theory?" she said again, when they were settled, and eating lunch.

"Most people take it to be a crackpot excuse for our failure at the station," he said.

Her brown arched brows rose. "Failure?" she said. "I thought you were making steady progress."

"Yes. And no," he said. "Even before Dr. Knight died, we ran into something he called the environmental barrier."

"Environmental barrier?"

"Yes." Mal poked with his fork at the shrimp in his seafood cocktail. "This work of ours all grew out of the work done by Dr. John Lilly. You read his book, 'Man and Dolphin'?"

"No," she said. He looked at her, surprised.

"He was the pioneer in this research with dolphins," Mal said. "I'd have thought reading his book would have

been the first thing you would have done before coming
down here."

"The first thing I did," she said, "was try to find out
something about Corwin Brayt. And I was pretty unsuc-
cessful at that. That's why I landed here with the notion
that it was he, not you, who was the real worker with the
dolphins."

"That's why you asked me if I knew much about him?"

"That's right," she answered. "But tell me about this environmental barrier."

"There's not a great deal to tell," he said. "Like most
big problems, it's simple enough to state. At first, in working with the dolphins, it seemed the early researchers were
going great guns, and communication was just around the
corner—a matter of interpreting the sounds they made to
each other, in the humanly audible range, and above it;
and teaching the dolphins human speech."

"It turned out those things couldn't be done?"

"They could. They were done—or as nearly so as
makes no difference. But then we came up against the fact
that communication doesn't mean understanding." He
looked at her. "You and I talk the same language, but do
we really understand perfectly what the other person
means when he speaks to us?"

She looked at him for a moment, and then slowly shook
her head without taking her eyes off his face.

"Well," said Mal, "that's essentially our problem with
the dolphins—only on a much larger scale. Dolphins, like
Castor and Pollux, can talk with me, and I with them, but
we can't understand each other to any great degree."

"You mean intellectually understood, don't you?" Jane
said. "Not just mechanically?"

"That's right," Mal answered. "We agree on denotation
of an auditory or other symbol, but not on connotation. I
can say to Castor—*the Gulf Stream is a strong ocean
current*' and he'll agree exactly. But neither of us really
has the slightest idea of what the other really means. My
mental image of the Gulf Stream is not Castor's image.
My notion of 'powerful' is relative to the fact I'm six feet
tall, weigh a hundred and seventy-five pounds and can lift
my own weight against the force of gravity. Castor's is
relative to the fact that he is seven feet long, can speed up
to forty miles an hour through the water, and as far as he
knows weighs nothing, since his four hundred pounds of
body-weight are balanced out by the equal weight of the

water he displaces. And the concept of lifting something is all but unknown to him. My mental abstraction of 'ocean' is not his, and our ideas of what a current is may coincide, or be literally worlds apart in meaning. And so far we've found no way of bridging the gap between us."

"The dolphins have been trying as well as you?"

"I believe so," said Mal. "But I can't prove it. Any more than I can really prove the dolphin's intelligence to hard-core skeptics until I can come up with something previously outside human knowledge that the dolphins have taught me. Or have them demonstrate that they've learned the use of some human intellectual process. And in these things we've all failed—because, as I believe and Dr. Knight believed, of the connotative gap, which is a result of the environmental barrier."

She sat watching him. He was probably a fool to tell her all this, but he had had no one to talk to like this since Dr. Knight's heart attack, eight months before, and he felt words threatening to pour out of him.

"We've got to learn to think like the dolphins," he said, "or the dolphins have to learn to think like us. For nearly six years now we've been trying and neither side's succeeded." Almost before he thought, he added the one thing he had been determined to keep to himself. "I've been afraid our research funds will be cut off any day now."

"Cut off? By the Willernie Foundation?" she said. "Why would they do that?"

"Because we haven't made any progress for so long," Mal said bitterly. "Or, at least, no provable progress. I'm afraid time's just about run out. And if it runs out, it may never be picked up again. Six years ago, there was a lot of popular interest in the dolphins. Now, they've been discounted and forgotten, shelved as merely bright animals."

"You can't be sure the research won't be picked up again."

"But I feel it," he said. "It's part of my notion about the ability to communicate with an alien race being the test for us humans. I feel we've got this one chance and if we flub it, we'll never have another." He pounded the table softly with his fist. "The worst of it is, I *know* the dolphins are trying just as hard to get through from their side—if I could only recognize what they're doing, how they're trying to make me understand!"

Jane had been sitting watching him.

"You seem pretty sure of that," she said. "What makes you so sure?"

He unclenched his fist and forced himself to sit back in his chair.

"Have you ever looked into the jaws of a dolphin?" he said. "They're this long." He spread his hands apart in the air to illustrate. "And each pair of jaws contains eighty-eight sharp teeth. Moreover, a dolphin like Castor weighs several hundred pounds and can move at water speeds that are almost incredible to a human. He could crush you easily by ramming you against the side of a tank, if he didn't want to tear you apart with his teeth, or break your bones with blows of his flukes." He looked at her grimly. "In spite of all this, in spite of the fact that men have caught and killed dolphins—even we killed them in our early, fumbling researches, and dolphins are quite capable of using their teeth and strength on marine enemies—no dolphin has ever been known to attack a human being. Aristotle, writing in the Fourth Century B.C., speaks of the quote gentle and kindly end quote nature of the dolphin."

He stopped, and looked at Jane sharply.

"You don't believe me," he said.

"Yes," she said. "Yes, I do." He took a deep breath.

"I'm sorry," he said. "I've made the mistake of mentioning all this before to other people and been sorry I did. I told this to one man who gave me his opinion that it indicated that the dolphin instinctively recognized human superiority and the value of human life." Mal grinned at her, harshly. "But it was just an instinct. *'Like dogs,'* he said. *'Dogs instinctively admire and love people—'* and he wanted to tell me about a dachshund he'd had, named Poochie, who could read the morning newspaper and wouldn't bring it in to him if there was a tragedy reported on the front page. He could prove this, and Poochie's intelligence, by the number of times he'd had to get the paper off the front step himself."

Jane laughed. It was a low, happy laugh; and it took the bitterness suddenly out of Mal.

"Anyway," said Mal, "the dolphin's restraint with humans is just one of the indications, like the wild dolphins coming to us here at the station, that've convinced me the dolphins are trying to understand us, too. And have been, maybe, for centuries."

"I don't see why you worry about the research stopping," she said. "With all you know, can't you convince people—"

"There's only one person I've got to convince," said Mal. "And that's Corwin Brayt. And I don't think I'm doing it. It's just a feeling—but I feel as if he's sitting in judgment upon me, and the work. I feel . . ." Mal hesitated, "almost as if he's a hatchet man."

"He isn't," Jane said. "He can't be. I'll find out for you, if you like. There're ways of doing it. I'd have the answer for you right now, if I'd thought of him as an administrator. But I thought of him as a scientist, and I looked him up in the wrong places."

Mal frowned at her, unbelievingly.

"You don't actually mean you can find out that for me?" he asked.

She smiled.

"Wait and see," she replied. "I'd like to know, myself, what his background is."

"It could be important," he said, eagerly. "I know it sounds fantastic—but if I'm right, the research with the dolphins could be important, more important than anything else in the world."

She stood up suddenly from the table.

"I'll go and start checking up right now," she said.

"Why don't you go on back to the island? It'll take me a few hours and I'll take the water-taxi over."

"But you haven't finished lunch yet," he said. "In fact you haven't even started lunch. Let's eat first, then you can go."

"I want to call some people and catch them while they're still at work," she said. "It's the time difference on these long-distance calls. I'm sorry. We'll have dinner together, will that do?"

"It'll have to," he said. She melted his disappointment with one of her amazing smiles, and went.

With her gone, Mal found he was not hungry himself. He got hold of the waiter and managed to cancel the main course of their meals. He sat and had two more drinks— not something usual for him. Then he left and flew the copter back to the island.

Pete Adant encountered him as he was on his way from the copter park to the dolphin pool.

"There you are," said Pete. "Corwin wants to see you in an hour—when he gets back, that is. He's gone over to the mainland himself."

Ordinarily, such a piece of news would have awakened the foreboding about cancellation of the research that rode always like a small, cold, metal weight inside Mal. But the total of three drinks and no lunch had anesthetized him somewhat. He nodded and went on to the pool.

The dolphins were still there, still at their patterned swimming. Or was he just imagining the pattern? Mal sat down on his chair by the poolside before the tape recorder which set down a visual pattern of the sounds made by the dolphins. He put the earphones to the hydrophones on, switching on the mike before him.

Suddenly, it struck him how futile all this was. He had gone through these same motions daily for four years now. And what was the sum total of results he had to show for it? Reel on reel of tape recording a failure to hold any truly productive conversation with the dolphins.

He took the earphones off and laid them aside. He lit a cigarette and sat gazing with half-seeing eyes at the underwater ballet of the dolphins. To call it ballet was almost to libel their actions. The gracefulness, the purposefulness of their movements, buoyed up by the salt water, was beyond that of any human in air or on land. He thought again of what he had told Jane Wilson about the dolphin's refusal to attack their human captors, even when the humans hurt or killed them. He thought of the now-established fact that dolphins will come to the rescue of one of their own who has been hurt or knocked unconscious, and hold him up on top of the water so he would not drown—the dolphin's breathing process requiring conscious control, so that it failed if the dolphin became unconscious.

He thought of their playfulness, their affection, the wide and complex range of their speech. In any of those categories, the average human stacked up beside them looked pretty poor. In the dolphin culture there was no visible impulse to war, to murder, to hatred and unkindness. No wonder, thought Mal, they and we have trouble understanding each other. In a different environment, under different conditions, they're the kind of people we've always struggled to be. We have the technology, the tool-using capability, but with it all in many ways we're more animal than they are.

Who's to judge which of us is better, he thought, looking at their movements through the water with the slight hazy melancholy induced by the three drinks on an empty stomach. I might be happier myself, if I were a dolphin. For a second, the idea seemed deeply attractive. The endless open sea, the freedom, an end to all the complex structure of human culture on land. A few lines of poetry came back to him.

"*Come Children,*" he quoted out loud to himself, "*let us away! Down and away, below . . . !*"

He saw the two dolphins pause in their underwater ballet and saw that the microphone before him was on. Their heads turned toward the microphone underwater at the near end of the pool. He remembered the following lines, and he quoted them aloud to the dolphins.

"*. . . Now my brothers call from the bay,*
"*Now the great winds shoreward blow,*
"*Now the salt tides seaward flow;*
"*Now the wild white horses play,*
"*Champ and chafe and toss in the spray—*"*

He broke off suddenly, feeling self-conscious. He looked down at the dolphins. For a moment they merely hung where they were under the surface, facing the microphone. Then Castor turned and surfaced. His forehead with its blowhole broke out into the air and then his head as he looked up at Mal. His airborne voice from the blowhole's sensitive lips and muscles spoke quacking words at the human.

"*Come, Mal,*" he quacked, "*Let us away! Down and away! Below!*"

The head of Pollux surfaced beside Castor's. Mal stared at them for a long second. Then he jerked his gaze back to the tape of the recorder. There on it, was the rhythmic record of his own voice as it had sounded in the pool, and below it on their separate tracks, the tapes showed parallel, rhythms coming from the dolphins. They had been matching his speech largely in the inaudible range while he was quoting.

Still staring, Mal got to his feet, his mind trembling with a suspicion so great he hesitated to put it into words. Like a man in a daze he walked to the near end of the pool, where three steps led down into the shallower part. Here the water was only three feet deep.

"*Come, Mal!*" quacked Castor, as the two still hung in

* *"The Forsaken Merman,"* by Matthew Arnold, 1849.

the water with their heads out, facing him. *"Let us away! Down and away! Below!"*

Step by step, Mal went down into the pool. He felt the coolness of the water wetting his pants legs, rising to his waist as he stood at last on the pool floor. A few feet in front of him, the two dolphins hung in the water, facing him, waiting. Standing with the water rippling lightly above his belt buckle, Mal looked at them, waiting for some sign, some signal of what they wanted him to do.

They gave him no clue. They only waited. It was up to him to go forward on his own. He sloshed forward into deeper water, put his head down, held his breath and pushed himself off underwater.

In the forefront of his blurred vision, he saw the grainy concrete floor of the pool. He glided slowly over it, rising a little, and suddenly the two dolphins were all about him—gliding over, above, around his own underwater floating body, brushing lightly against him as they passed, making him a part of their underwater dance. He heard the creaking that was one of the underwater sounds they made and knew that they were probably talking in ranges he could not hear. He could not know what they were saying, he could not sense the meaning of their movements about him, but the feeling that they were trying to convey information to him was inescapable.

He began to feel the need to breathe. He held out as long as he could, then let himself rise to the surface. He broke water and gulped air, and the two dolphin heads popped up nearby, watching him. He dove under the surface again. *I am a dolphin*—he told himself almost desperately—*I am not a man, but a dolphin, and to me all this means—what?*

Several times he dove, and each time the persistent and disciplined movements of the dolphins about him underwater convinced him more strongly that he was on the right track. He came up, blowing, at last. He was not carrying the attempt to be like them far enough, he thought. He turned and swam back to the steps at the shallow end of the pool, and began to climb out.

"Come, Mal—let us away!" quacked a dolphin voice behind him, and he turned to see the heads of both Castor and Pollux out of the water, regarding him with mouths open urgently.

"Come Children—down and away!" he repeated, as reassuringly as he could intonate the words.

He hurried up to the big cabinet of the supply locker at the near end of the pool, and opened the door of the section on skin-diving equipment. He needed to make himself more like a dolphin. He considered the air tanks and the mask of the scuba equipment, and rejected them. The dolphins could not breathe underwater any more than he could. He started jerking things out of the cabinet.

A minute or so later he returned to the steps in swimming trunks, wearing a glass mask with a snorkel tube, and swim fins on his feet. In his hand he carried two lengths of soft rope. He sat down on the steps and with the rope tied his knees and ankles together. Then, clumsily, he hopped and splashed into the water.

Lying face down in the pool, staring at the bottom through his glass faceplate, he tried to move his bound legs together like the flukes of a dolphin, to drive himself slantingly down under the surface.

After a moment or two he managed it. In a moment the dolphins were all about him as he tried to swim underwater, dolphinwise. After a little while his air ran short again and he had to surface. But he came up like a dolphin and lay on the surface filling his lungs, before fanning himself down flukefashion with his swim fins. *Think like a dolphin,* he kept repeating to himself over and over. *I am a dolphin. And this is my world. This is the way it is.*

. . . And Castor and Pollux were all about him.

The sun was setting in the far distance of the ocean when at last he dragged himself, exhausted, up the steps of the pool and sat down on the poolside. To his water-soaked body, the twilight breeze felt icy. He unbound his legs, took off his fins and mask and walked wearily to the cabinet. From the nearest compartment he took a towel and dried himself, then put on an old bathrobe he kept hanging there. He sat down in an aluminum deckchair beside the cabinet and sighed with weariness.

He looked out at the red sun dipping its lower edge in the sea, and felt a great warm sensation of achievement inside him. In the darkening pool, the two dolphins still swam back and forth. He watched the sun descending . . .

"Mal!"

The sound of Corwin Brayt's voice brought his head around. When he saw the tall, cold-faced man was coming toward him with the slim figure of Jane alongside, Mal got up quickly from his chair. They came up to him.

"Why didn't you come in to see me as I asked?" Brayt

said. "I left word for you with Pete. I didn't even know you were back from the mainland until the water-taxi brought Miss Wilson out just now, and she told me."

"I'm sorry," said Mal. "I think I've run into something here—"

"Never mind telling me now." Brayt's voice was hurried and sharpened with annoyance. "I had a good deal to speak to you about but there's not time now if I'm to catch the mainland plane to St. Louis. I'm sorry to break it this way—" He checked himself and turned to Jane. "Would you excuse us, Miss Wilson? Private business. If you'll give us a second—"

"Of course," she said. She turned and walked away from them alongside the pool, into the deepening twilight. The dolphins paced her in the water. The sun was just down now, and with the sudden oncoming of tropical night, stars could be seen overhead.

"Just let me tell you," said Mal. "It's about the research."

"I'm sorry," said Brayt. "There's no point in your telling me now. I'll be gone a week and I want you to watch out for this Jane Wilson, here." He lowered his voice slightly. "I talked to *Background Monthly* on the phone this afternoon, and the editor I spoke to there didn't know about the article, or recognize her name—"

"Somebody new," said Mal. "Probably someone who didn't know her."

"At any rate it makes no difference," said Brayt. "As I say, I'm sorry to tell you in such a rushed fashion, but Willernie has decided to end its grant of funds to the station. I'm flying to St. Louis to settle details." He hesitated. "I'm sure you knew something like this was coming, Mal." Mal stared, shocked.

"It was inevitable," said Brayt coldly. "You knew that." He paused. "I'm sorry."

"But the station'll fold without the Willernie support!" said Mal, finding his voice. "You know that. And just today I found out what the answer is! Just this afternoon! Listen to me!" He caught Brayt's arm as the other started to turn away. "The dolphins have been trying to contact us. Oh, not at first, not when we experimented with captured specimens. But since we opened the pool to the sea. The only trouble was we insisted on trying to communicate by sound alone—and that's all but impossible for them."

"Excuse me," said Brayt, trying to disengage his arm.

"Listen, will you!" said Mal, desperately. "Their communication process is an incredibly rich one. It's as if you and I communicated by using all the instruments in a symphony orchestra. They not only use sound from four to a hundred and fifty kilocycles per second, they use movement, and touch—and all of it in reference to the ocean conditions surrounding them at the moment."

"I've got to go."

"Just a minute. Don't you remember what Lilly hypothecated about the dolphin's methods of navigation? He suggested that it was a multivariable method, using temperature, speed, taste of the water, position of the stars, sun and so forth, all fed into their brains simultaneously and instantaneously. Obviously, it's true, and obviously their process of communication is also a multivariable method utilizing sound, touch, position, place and movement. Now that we know this, we can go into the sea with them and try to operate across their whole spectrum of communication. No wonder we weren't able to get across anything but the most primitive exchanges, restricting ourselves to sound. It's been equivalent to restricting human communication to just the nouns in each sentence, while maintaining the sentence structure—"

"I'm very sorry!" said Brayt, firmly. "I tell you, Mal. None of this makes any difference. The decision of the Foundation is based on financial reasons. They've got just so much money available to donate, and this station's allotment has already gone in other directions. There's nothing that can be done, now."

He pulled his arm free.

"I'm sorry," he said again. "I'll be back in a week at the outside. You might be thinking of how to wind up things, here."

He turned with that, and went away, around the building toward the parking spot of the station copters. Mal, stunned, watched the tall, slim, broadshouldered figure move off into darkness.

"It doesn't matter," said the gentle voice of Jane comfortingly at his ear. He jerked about and saw her facing him. "You won't need the Willernie funds any more."

"He told you?" Mal stared at her as she shook her head, smiling in the growing dimness. "You heard? From way over there?"

"Yes," she said. "And you were right about Brayt. I got

your answer for you. He was a hatchet man—sent here by the Willernie people to decide whether the station deserved further funds."

"But we've got to have them!" Mal said. "It won't take much more, but we've got to go into the sea and work out ways to talk to the dolphins in their own mode. We've got to expand to their level of communication, not try to compress them to ours. You see, this afternoon, I had a breakthrough—"

"I know," she said. "I know all about it."

"You know?" He stared at her. "How do you know?"

"You've been under observation all afternoon," she said. "You're right. You did break through the environmental barrier. From now on it's just a matter of working out methods."

"Under observation? How?" Abruptly, that seemed the least important thing at hand. "But I have to have money," he said. "It'll take time and equipment, and that costs money—"

"No." Her voice was infinitely gentle. "You won't need to work out your own methods. Your work is done, Mal. This afternoon the dolphins and you broke the bars to communication between the two races for the first time in the history of either. It was the job you set out to do and you were part of it. You can be happy knowing that."

"Happy?" He almost shouted at her, suddenly. "I don't understand what you're talking about."

"I'm sorry." There was a ghost of a sigh from her. "We'll show you how to talk to the dolphins, Mal, if men need to. As well as some other things—perhaps." Her face lifted to him under the star-marked sky, still a little light in the west. "You see, you were right about something more than dolphins, Mal. Your idea that the ability to communicate with another intelligent race, an alien race, was a test that had to be passed before the superior species of a planet could be contacted by the intelligent races of the galaxy—that was right, too."

He stared at her. She was so close to him, he could feel the living warmth of her body, although they were not touching. He saw her, he felt her, standing before him; and he felt all the strange deep upwelling of emotion that she had released in him the moment he first saw her. The deep emotion he felt for her still. Suddenly understanding came to him.

"You mean you're not from Earth—" his voice was

hoarse and uncertain. It wavered to a stop. "But you're human!" he cried desperately.

She looked back at him a moment before answering. In the dimness he could not tell for sure, but he thought he saw the glisten of tears in her eyes.

"Yes," she said, at last, slowly. "In the way you mean that—you can say I'm human."

A great and almost terrible joy burst suddenly in him. It was the joy of a man who, in the moment when he thinks he has lost everything, finds something of infinitely greater value.

"But how?" he said, excitedly, a little breathlessly. He pointed up at the stars. "If you come from some place—up there? How can you be human?"

She looked down, away from his face.

"I'm sorry," she said. "I can't tell you."

"Can't tell me? Oh," he said with a little laugh, "you mean I wouldn't understand."

"No—" Her voice was almost inaudible, "I mean I'm not allowed to tell you."

"Not allowed—" he felt an unreasoning chill about his heart. "But Jane—" He broke off fumbling for words. "I don't know quite how to say this, but it's important to me to know. From the first moment I saw you there, I . . . I mean, maybe you don't feel anything like this, you don't know what I'm talking about—"

"Yes," she whispered. "I do."

"Then—" he stared at her. "You could at least say something that would set my mind at rest. I mean . . . it's only a matter of time now. We're going to be getting together, your people and I, aren't we?"

She looked up at him out of darkness.

"No," she said, "we aren't, Mal. Ever. And that's why I can't tell you anything."

"We aren't?" he cried. "We aren't? But you came and saw us communicate— Why aren't we?"

She looked up at him for the last time, then, and told him. He, having heard what she had to say, stood still; still as a stone, for there was nothing left to do. And she, turning slowly and finally away from him, went off to the edge of the pool and down the steps into the shallow water, where the dolphins came rushing to meet her, their foamy tearing of the surface making a wake as white as snow.

Then the three of them moved, as if by magic, across the surface of the pool and out the entrance of it to the ocean. And so they continued to move off until they were

lost to sight in darkness and the starlit, glinting surface of
the waves.

It came to Mal then, as he stood there, that the dolphins must have been waiting for her all this time. All the
wild dolphins, who had come to the station after the first
two captives, were set free to leave or stay as they wanted. The dolphins had known, perhaps for centuries, that it
was to them alone on Earth that the long-awaited visitors
from the stars would finally come.

AND THEN THERE WAS PEACE

At nine hundred hours there were explosions off to the right at about seven hundred yards. At eleven hundred hours the slagger came by to pick up the casualties among the gadgets. Charlie saw the melting head at the end of its heavy beam going up and down like the front end of a hardworking chicken only about fifty yards west of his foxhole. Then it worked its way across the battlefield for about half an hour and, loaded down with melted forms of damaged robots, of all shapes and varieties, disappeared behind the low hill to the west, and left, of Charlie. It was a hot August day somewhere in or near Ohio, with a thunderstorm coming on. There was that yellow color in the air.

At twelve hundred hours the chow gadget came ticking over the redoubt behind the foxhole. It crawled into the foxhole, jumped up on the large table and opened itself out to reveal lunch. The menu this day was liver and onions, whole corn, whipped potato and raspberries.

"And no whip cream," said Charlie.

"You haven't been doing your exercises," said the chow gadget in a fine soprano voice.

"I'm a front-line soldier," said Charlie. "I'm an infantryman in a fox-hole overlooking ground zero. I'll be damned if I take exercises."

"In any case, there is no excuse for not shaving."

"I'll be damned if I shave."

"But why *not* shave? Wouldn't it be better than having that itchy, scratchy beard—"

"No," said Charlie. He went around back of the chow gadget and began to take its rear plate off.

"What are you doing to me?" said the chow gadget.

"You've got something stuck to you here," said Charlie. "Hold still." He surreptitiously took a second out to scratch at his four-day beard. "There's a war on, you know."

"I know that," said the chow gadget. "Of course."

"Infantrymen like me are dying daily."

"Alas," said the chow gadget, in pure, simple tones.

"To say nothing," said Charlie, setting the rear plate to one side, "of the expenditure of you technical devices. Not that there's any comparison between human lives and the wastage of machines."

"Of course not."

"So how can any of you, no matter how elaborate your computational systems, understand—" Charlie broke off to poke among the innards of the chow machine.

"Do not damage me," it said.

"Not if I can help it," said Charlie. "—understand what it feels like to a man sitting here day after day, pushing an occasional button, never knowing the results of his button pushing, and living in a sort of glass-case comfort except for the possibility that he may just suddenly be dead—suddenly, like that, before he knows it." He broke off to probe again. "It's no life for a man."

"Terrible, terrible," said the chow gadget. "But there is still hope for improvement."

"Don't hold your breath," said Charlie. "There's—ah!" He interrupted himself, pulling a small piece of paper out of the chow gadget.

"Is there something the matter?" said the chow gadget.

"No," said Charlie. He stepped over to the observation window and glanced out. The slagger was making its return. It was already within about fifty yards of the foxhole. "Not a thing," said Charlie. "As a matter of fact, the war's over."

"How interesting," said the chow gadget.

"That's right," said Charlie. "Just let me read you this little billet-doux I got from Foxhole thirty-four. *Meet you back at the bar, Charlie. It's all over. Your hunch that we could get a message across was the clear quill. Answer came today the same way, through the international weather reports. They want to quit as well as we do. Peace is agreed on, and the gadgets—*" Charlie broke off to look at the chow gadget. "That's you, along with the rest of them."

"Quite right. Of course," said the chow gadget.

"*—have already accepted the information. We'll be out of here by sundown.* And that takes care of the war."

"It does indeed," said the chow gadget. "Hurrah! And farewell."

"Farewell?" said Charlie.

"You will be returning to civilian life," said the chow gadget. "I will be scrapped."

"That's right," said Charlie. "I remember the pre-programing for the big units. This war's to be the last, they were programed. Well—" said Charlie. For a moment he hesitated. "What d'you know? I may end up missing you a little bit, after all."

He glanced out the window. The slagger was almost to the dugout.

"Well, well," he said. "Now that the time's come . . . we did have quite a time together, three times a day. No more string beans, huh?"

"I bet not," said the chow gadget with a little laugh.

"No more caramel pudding."

"I guess so."

Just then the slagger halted outside, broke the thick concrete roof off the dugout and laid it carefully aside.

"Excuse me," it said, its cone-shaped melting head nodding politely some fifteen feet above Charlie. "The war's over."

"I know," said Charlie.

"Now there will be peace. There are orders that all instruments of war are to be slagged and stockpiled for later peaceful uses." It had a fine baritone voice. "Excuse me," it said, "but are you finished with that chow gadget there?"

"You haven't touched a bite," said the chow gadget. "Would you like just a small spoonful of raspberries?"

"I don't think so," said Charlie, slowly. "No, I don't think so."

"Then farewell," said the chow gadget. "I am now expendable."

The melting head of the slagger dipped toward the chow gadget. Charlie opened his mouth suddenly, but before he could speak, there was a sort of invisible flare from the melting head and the chow gadget became a [sort of] puddle of metal which the melting head picked up magnetically and swung back to the hopper behind it.

"Blast it!" said Charlie with feeling. "I could just as well have put in a request to keep the darn thing for a souvenir."

The heavy melting head bobbed apologetically back.

"I'm afraid that wouldn't be possible," it said. "The order allows no exceptions. *All* military instruments are to be slagged and stockpiled."

"Well—" said Charlie. But it was just about then that he noticed the melting head was descending toward him.

THE MAN FROM EARTH

The Director of the crossroads world of Duhnbar had no other name, nor needed any; and his handsomeness and majesty were not necessarily according to the standards of the human race. But then, he had never heard of the human race.

He sat in his equivalent of a throne room day by day, while the representatives of a thousand passing races conducted their business below and before the dais on which his great throne chair sat. He enjoyed the feeling of life around him, so he permitted them to be there. He did not like to be directly involved in that life. Therefore none of them looked or spoke in his direction.

Before him, he saw their numbers spread out through a lofty hall. At the far end of the hall, above the lofty portal, was a balcony pierced through to the outside, so that it overlooked not only the hall but the armed guards on the wide steps that approached the building. On this balcony, more members of different races talked and stood.

Next to the Director's chair, on his left, was a shimmering mirror surface suspended in midair, so that by turning his head only slightly he could see himself reflected at full length. Sometimes he looked and saw himself.

But at this moment, now, he looked outward. In his mind's eye, he looked beyond the throne room and the balcony and the steps without. He saw in his imagination all the planetwide city surrounding, and the five other worlds of this solar system, which were the machine shops and granaries of this crown-world of Duhnbar. This world and system he . . . *ruled* is too mild a word. This world he owned, and wore like a ring on his finger.

All of it, seen in his mind's eye, had the dull tinge of familiarity and sameness.

He moved slightly the index one of his four-jointed fingers, of which he had three, with an opposed thumb on each hand. The male adult of his own race who currently filled a role something like that of chamberlain stepped forward from behind the throne chair. The Director did not look at the Chamberlain, knowing he would be there. The Director's thin lips barely moved in his expressionless pale green face.

"It has been some moments," he said. "Is there still nothing new?"

"Director of All," said the low voice of the Chamberlain at his ear. "Since you last asked, there has been nothing on the six worlds which has not happened before. Only the landing here at the throne city of a single alien of a new race. He has passed into the city now, omitting to sacrifice at a purple shrine but otherwise behaving as all behave on your worlds."

"Is there anything new," said the Director, "about his failure to sacrifice?"

"The failure is a common one," said the Chamberlain. "It has been many generations since anyone seriously worshiped at a purple shrine. The sacrifice is a mere custom of our port. Strangers not knowing of it invariably fail to light incense on the cube before the purple."

The Director said nothing immediately. The Chamberlain stood waiting. If he had been left to wait until he collapsed from fatigue or starvation, another would have taken his place.

"Is there a penalty for this?" said the Director at last.

"The penalty," said the Chamberlain, "by ancient rule is death. But for hundreds of years it has been remitted on payment of a small fine."

The Director turned these words over in his mind.

"There is a value in old customs," he said after a while. "Old customs long fallen into disuse seem almost like something new when they are revived. Let the ancient penalty be reestablished."

"From this transgressor," asked the Chamberlain, "as well as all others after?"

The Director moved his index finger in silent assent and dismissal. The Chamberlain stepped backward and spoke to the under-officers who were always waiting.

The Director, sated with looking out over the hall, turned his gaze slightly to his own seated image in the mirror surface at his left. He saw there an individual a trifle over seven feet in height, seated in a tall, carven chair with ornate armrests. Four-fingered hands lay upon the curved ends of the armrests. The arms, the legs, the body was covered in a slim, simple garment of sky blue. From the neck of the garment emerged a tall and narrow head with lean features, a straight, almost lipless mouth, narrow nose and a greenish, hairless skull. The eyes were golden, enormous and beautiful.

But neither the eyes nor the face showed any expression. The faces of the Chamberlain and the guards and others of the race sometimes showed expressions. But the Director's face, never. He was several hundreds of years old and would live until some rare accident killed him, or he became weary of life.

He had never known what it was to be sick. He had never known cold, hunger or discomfort. He had never known fear, hatred, loneliness or love. He watched himself now in the mirror; for he posed an unending enigma to himself—an enigma that alone relieved the boredom of his existence. He did not attempt to investigate the enigma. He only savored it as a connoisseur might savor fine wine.

The image in the mirror he gazed upon was the image of a being who could find no alternative but to consider himself as a God.

Will Mauston was broken-knuckled and wrinkled about the eyes. The knuckles he had broken on human and alien bones, fighting for what belonged to him. The wrinkles about the eyes had come from the frowning harshness of expression evolved from endless bargains driven. On the infrequent occasions that he got back to Earth to see his wife and two young children, the wrinkles almost disappeared ... for a while. But Earth was overcrowded and the cost of living there was high. He always had to leave again, and the wrinkles always came back. He was twenty-six years old.

He had heard of Duhnbar through a race of interstellar traders called the Kjaka, heavy-bodied, lion-featured and honest. He had assumed there must be such a world, as on Earth in the past there had been ancient cities like Samarkand under Tamerlane, where the great trade routes crossed. He had searched and inquired and the Kjakas had told him. Duhnbar was the Samarkand of the stars. One mighty stream of trade flowed out from the highly developed worlds of the galaxy's center and met here with several peripheral routes among the outlying, scattered stars.

Will had come alone and he was the first from Earth to

reach it. From this one trip, he could well make enough to retire and not have to leave his family on Earth again. The Kjakas were honest and had taught him the customs of the Duhnbar port. They had sent him to Khal Dohn, one of their own people on Duhnbar, who would act as Will's agent there. They had forgotten the small matter of the purple shrine. The custom was all but obsolete, the fine was nominal. They had talked of larger transactions and values.

Passing through the terminal building of the port, Will saw a cube of metal, a purple cloth hanging on the wall above it and small purple slivers that fumed and reeked. He passed at a good distance. Experience had taught him not to involve himself with the religions and customs of peoples he did not know.

Riding across the city in an automated vehicle set for the address of his agent, Will passed a square in which there was what seemed to be a sort of forty-foot high clothespole. What was hung on it, however, were not clothes, but bodies. The bodies were not all of the native race, and he was glad to leave it behind.

He reached the home of the Kjakan agent. It was a pleasant, two story, four-sided structure surrounding an interior courtyard rich with vegetation unknown to Will. He and his host sat on an interior balcony of the second floor overlooking the courtyard, and talked. The agent's name was Khal Dohn. He ate a narcotic candy particular to his own race and saw that Will was supplied with a pure mixture of distilled water and ethyl alcohol—to which Will added a scotch flavor from one of the small vials he carried at his belt. Will had set up a balance of credit on several Kjakan worlds. Khal Dohn would buy for him on Duhnbar against that credit.

They were beginning a discussion of what was available on Duhnbar that would be best for Will to purchase, speaking in the stellar lingua franca, the trading language among the stars. Abruptly, they were interrupted by a voice from one of the walls, speaking in a tongue Will did not understand. Khal Dohn listened, answered and turned his heavy, leonine face on Will.

"We must go downstairs," he said.

He led Will back down to the room which led to the street before his home. Waiting there were two of the native race in black, short robes, belted at the waist with silver belts. A black rod showed in a sort of silver pencil-case attached to the belt of each native.

As Will and Khal came down a curving ramp to them, the golden eyes of both natives fastened on Will with mild curiosity.

"Stranger and alien," said one of them in the trade tongue, "you are informed that you are under arrest."

Will looked at them, and opened his mouth. But Khal Dohn was already speaking in the native tongue; and after a little while the natives bowed shortly and went out. Khal Dohn turned back to Will.

"Did you see in the terminal—" Khal Dohn described the Purple Shrine. Will nodded. "Did you go near it?"

"No," said Will. "I always steer clear of such things, unless I know about them."

Khal Dohn stared at him for a long moment. Below the heavy, rather oriental fold of flesh, his eyes were sad, dark and unreadable to Will.

"I don't understand," he said at last. "But you are my guest, and my duty is to protect you. We'd better go see an acquaintance of mine—one who has more influence here in the throne city than I do."

He led Will out to one of the automated vehicles. On their way to the home of the acquaintance he answered Will's questions by describing the custom of the Purple Shrine.

"—I don't understand," the Kjaka said. "I should have been able to pay your fine to the police and settle it. But they had specific orders to arrest you and take you in."

"Why didn't they, then?" asked Will.

The dark eyes swung and met his own.

"You're my guest," said Khal Dohn. "I've taken on the responsibility of your surrender at the proper time, while they fulfill my request for the verification of the order to arrest you."

Outside the little vehicle, as they turned into the shadow of a taller building, a coolness seemed to gather about them and reach inside to darken and slow Will's spirits.

"Do you think it's something really important?" he said.

"No," answered Khal Dohn. "No. I'm sure it's all a mistake."

They stopped before a building very like the home of Khal Dohn. Khal led Will up a ramp to a room filled with oversize furniture. From one large chair rose a narrow-bodied, long-handed alien with six fingers to a hand. His face was narrow and horselike. He stood better than seven and a half feet, in jacket and trousers of a dark red color. A dagger hung at his belt.

"You are my guest as always, Khal Dohn!" he cried. His voice was strident and high-pitched. He spoke the trade tongue, but he pronounced the Kjakan name of Khal Dohn with a skill Will had not been able to master. "And welcome as the guest of my guest is—" he turned to Will, speaking to Khal—"what is its name—?"

"*His* name," said Khal, "is Will Mau—" his own, Kjakan tongue failed the English *st* sound—"Will Mauzzon."

"Welcome," said the tall alien. "I am Avoa. What is it?"

"Something I don't understand." Khal switched to the native tongue of Duhnbar and Will was left out of the conversation. They talked some little while.

"I will check," cried Avoa, finally, breaking back into the trade tongue. "Come tomorrow early, Khal Dohn. Bring it with you."

"Him," said Khal. "I will bring him."

"Of course. Of course. Come together. I'll have news for you then. It can be nothing serious."

Khal and Will left and came back to the balcony above the courtyard of Khal's home. They sat talking. The sunset of the planet spread across the western skyline of the throne city, its light staining the white ceiling above them with a wash of red.

"You're sure it's nothing to worry about?" Will asked the Kjaka.

"I'm sure." Khal Dohn fingered one of his narcotic candies in thick fingers. "They have a strict but fair legal code here. And if there is any misunderstanding, Avoa can resolve it. He has considerable influence. Shall we return to talk of business?"

So they talked as the interior lights came on. Later they ate their different meals together—Will's from supplies he had brought from his ship—and parted for the night.

It was a comfortable couch in a pleasant, open-balconied room giving on the courtyard below, that Khal assigned Will. But Will found sleep standing off some distance from him. He was a man of action, but here there was no action to be taken. He walked to the balcony and looked down into the courtyard.

Below, the strange plants were dim shapes in the light of a full moon too weak and pale to be the moon of Earth. He wondered how his wife and the two children were. He wondered if, across the light-years of distance, they were thinking of him at this moment, perhaps worrying about him.

He breathed the unfamiliar, tasteless night air and it seemed heavy in his lungs. At his belt was a container of barbiturates, four capsules of seconal. He had never found the need to take one before in all these years between the stars. He took one now, washing it down with the flat, distilled water they had left in this room for him.

He slept soundly after that, without dreams.

When he woke in the morning, he felt better. Khal Dohn seemed to him to be quite sensible and undisturbed. They rode over to the home of Avoa together; and Will took the opportunity he had neglected before to pump Khal about the city as they rode through it.

When they entered the room where they had met Avoa the day before, the tall alien was dressed in clothing of a lighter, harsher red but seemed the same in all other ways.

"Well," said Will to him, smiling, after they had greeted each other in the trade tongue. "What did you find out the situation is?"

Avoa stared back at him for a moment, then turned and began to speak rapidly to Khal in the native tongue. Khal answered. After a moment they both stopped and looked at Will without speaking.

"What's happened?" said Will. "What is it?"

"I'm sorry," said Khal slowly, in the trade tongue. "It seems that nothing can be done."

Will stared at him. The words he had heard made no sense.

"Nothing can be done?" he said. "About what? What do you mean?"

"I'm sorry," said Khal. "I mean, Avoa can do nothing."

"Nothing?" said Will.

Neither of the aliens answered. They continued to watch him. Suddenly, Avoa shifted his weight slightly on his long feet, and half-turned toward the doorway of the room.

"I am sorry!" he cried sharply. "Very sorry. But it is a situation out of my control. I can do nothing."

"Why?" burst out Will. He turned on Khal. "What's wrong? You told me their legal system was fair. I didn't know about the shrine!"

"Yes," said Khal. "But this isn't a matter for their law. Their Director has given an order."

"Director?" The word buzzed as deadly and foolishly as a tropical mosquito in Will's ears. "The one on the throne? What's he got to do with it?"

"It was his command," said Avoa suddenly in his strident voice. "The ancient penalty was to be enforced. After he heard about your omission. From now on, newcomers will be warned. They are fair here."

"Fair!" the word broke from between Will's teeth. "What about me? Doesn't this Director know about me? What is he, anyway?"

Khal and Avoa looked at each other, then back at Will.

"These people here," said Khal slowly, "control trade for light-years in every direction. Not because of any virtue in themselves, but because of the accident of their position here among the stars. They know this—so they need something. A symbol, something to set up, to reassure themselves of their right position."

"In all else, they are reasonable," said Avoa.

"Their symbol," said Khal, "is the Director. They identify with him as being all-powerful, over things in the universe. His slightest whim is obeyed without hesitation. He could order them all to cut their own throats and they would do it, without thinking. But of course he will not. He is not in the least irresponsible. He is sane and of the highest intelligence. But the only law he knows is his own."

Cried Avoa, "He is all but impotent. Ordinarily he does nothing. We interest and amuse him, and he is bored, so he lets us trade here with impunity. But if he does act, there is no appeal. It is a risk we all take. You are not the only one."

"But I've got a wife—" Will broke off suddenly. He had shouted out without thinking in English. They were gazing back at him now without understanding. For a moment a watery film blurred them before his eyes.

The desert-dry wind of a despair blew through him, shriveling his hopes. What did they know of wives and children, or Earth? He saw their faces clearly now, both alien, one heavy and leonine, one patrician and equine. He thought of his wife again, and the children. Without his income they would be forced to emigrate. A remembrance of the bitter, crude and barren livings of the frontier planets came to his mind like strangling smoke.

"Wait," he said, as Avoa turned to go. Will brought his voice down to a reasonable tone. "There must be someone I can appeal to. Khal Dohn." He turned to the Kjaka. "I'm your guest."

"You are my guest," said Khal. "But I can't protect you against this. It's like a natural, physical force—a great wind, an earthquake against which I would be helpless to protect any guest, or even myself."

He looked at Will with his dark, alien eyes, like the eyes of an intelligent beast.

"Pure chance—the chance of the Director hearing about you and the shrine when he did," said Khal, "has selected you. All those who face the risk of trading among the stars know the chance of death. You must have figured the risk, as a good trader should."

"Not like this—" said Will between his teeth, but Avoa interrupted, turning to leave.

"I must go," he said. "I have appointments on the throne room balcony. Khal Dohn, give it anything that will make these last hours comfortable and my house will supply. You must surrender it before midday to the police."

"No!" Will called after the tall alien. "If nobody else can save me, then I want to see him!"

"Him?" said Khal. Avoa suddenly checked, and slowly turned back.

"The Director." Will looked at both of them. "I'll appeal to him."

Khal and Avoa looked at each other. There was a silence.

"No," said Avoa, finally. "It is never done. No one speaks to him." He seemed about to turn again.

"Wait." It was Khal who spoke this time. Avoa looked sharply at him. Khal met the taller alien's eyes. "Will Mauzzon is my guest."

"It is not *my* guest," said Avoa.

"*I* am your guest," said Khal, without emotion.

Avoa stared now at the shorter, heavier-bodied alien. Abruptly he said something sharply in the native tongue.

Khal did not answer. He stood looking at Avoa without moving.

"It is already dead," Avoa said at last slowly, in the trade tongue, glancing at Will, "and being dead can have no further effect upon the rest of us. You waste your credit with me."

Still Khal neither spoke nor moved. Avoa turned and went out.

"My guest," said Khal, sitting down heavily in one of the oversize chairs of the room, "you have little cause for hope."

After that he sat silent. Will paced the room. Occasionally he glanced at the chronometer on his wrist, adjusted to local time. It showed the equivalent of two and three-quarters hours to noon when the wall chimed and spoke in Avoa's voice.

"You have your audience," said Khal, rising. "I would still advise against hope." He looked with his heavy face and dark eyes at Will. "Worlds can't afford to war against worlds to protect their people, and there is no reason for a Director to change his mind."

He took Will in one of the small automated vehicles to the throne room. Inside the portal, at the steps leading up to the balcony, he left Will.

"I'll wait for you above," Khal said. "Good luck, my guest."

Will turned. At the far end of the room he saw the dais and the Director. He went toward it through the crowd, that at first had hardly noticed him but grew silent and parted before him as he proceeded, until he could hear in the great and echoing silence of the hall the sound of his own footsteps as he approached the dais, the seated figure and the throne, behind which stood natives with the silver pencil cases and black rods at their silver belts.

He came at last to the edge of the dais and stopped, looking up. Above him, the high greenish skull, the narrow mouth, the golden eyes leaned forward to look down at him; and he saw them profiled in the mirror surface alongside. The profile was no more remote than the living face it mirrored.

Will opened his mouth to speak, but one of the natives behind the throne, wearing the Chamberlain's silver badge, stepped forward as the finger of the Director gestured.

"Wait," said the Chamberlain in the trade tongue. He turned and spoke behind him. Will waited, and the silence stretched out long in the hall. After a while there was movement and two natives appeared, one with a small chair, one with a tube-shaped container of liquid.

"Sit," said the Chamberlain. "Drink. The Director has said it."

Will found himself seated and with the tube in his hand. An odor of alcohol diluted with water came to his nostrils; and for a moment a burst of wild laughter trembled inside him. Then he controlled it and sipped from the tube.

"What do you say?" said the Chamberlain.

Will lifted his face to the unchanging face of the Director. Like the unreachable stare of an insect's eyes the great golden orbs regarded him.

"I haven't intentionally committed any crime," said Will.

"The Director," said the Chamberlain, "knows this."

His voice was flat, uninflected. But he seemed to wait. The golden eyes of the throned figure seemed to wait, also watching. Irrationally, Will felt the first small flame of a hope flickered to life within him. His trader's instinct stirred. If they would listen, there must always be a chance.

"I came here on business," he said, "the same sort of business that brings so many. Certainly this world and the trading done on it are tied together. Without Duhnbar there could be no trading place here. And without the trading would Duhnbar and its other sister worlds still be the same?"

He paused, looking upward for some reaction.

"The Director," said the Chamberlain, "is aware of this."

"Certainly, then," said Will, "if the traders here respect the laws and customs of Duhnbar, shouldn't Duhnbar respect the lives of those who come to trade?" He stared at the golden eyes hanging above him, but he could read no difference in them, no response. They seemed to wait still. He took a deep breath. "Death is—"

He stopped. The Director had moved on his throne. He leaned slowly forward until his face hung only a few feet above Will's. He spoke in the trade tongue, in a slow, deep, unexpectedly resonant voice.

"Death," he said, "is the final new experience."

He sat slowly back in his chair. The Chamberlain spoke.

"You will go now," he said.

Will sat staring at him, the tube of alcohol and water still in his grasp.

"You will go," repeated the Chamberlain. "You are free until midday and the moment of your arrest."

Will's head jerked up. He snapped to his feet from the chair.

"Are you all insane?" he shouted at the Chamberlain. "You can't do this sort of thing without an excuse! My people take care of their own—"

He broke off at the sight of the Chamberlain's unmoved face. He felt suddenly dizzy and nauseated at the pit of his stomach.

Said the Chamberlain, "It is understandable that you do not want to die. You will go now or I will have you taken away."

Something broke inside Will.

It was like the last effort of a man in a race who feels the running man beside him pulling away and tries, but cannot match the pace. Dazedly, dully, he turned. Blindly he walked the first few steps back toward the distant portal.

"Wait."

The Chamberlain's voice turned him around.

"Come back," said the Chamberlain. "The Director will speak."

Numbly he came back. The Director leaned forward once more, until when Will halted their faces were only a few feet apart.

"You will not die," said the Director.

Will stared up at the alien face without understanding. The words rang and reechoed like strange, incomprehensible sounds in his ears.

"You will live," said the Director. "And when I send for you, from time to time, you will come again and talk to me."

Will continued to stare. He felt the smooth, flexible tube of liquid in his right hand, and he felt it bulge between his fingers as his fingers contracted spasmodically. He opened his lips but no words worked their way past his tight muscles of his throat.

"It is interesting," said the deep and thrilling voice of the Director, as his great, golden eyes looked down at Will, "that you do not understand me. It is interesting to explain myself to you. You give me reasons why you should not die."

"—Reasons?" Between Will's dry lips, the little word slipped huskily out. Miraculously, out of the ashes of his despair, he felt the tiny warmth of a new hope.

"Reasons," said the Director. "You give me reasons. And there are no reasons. There is only me."

The hope flickered and stumbled in its reach for life.

"I will make you understand now," said the deep and measured voice of the Director. "It is I who am responsible for all things that happen here. It is my whim that moves them. There is nothing else."

The golden eyes looked into Will's.

"It was my whim," said the Director, "that the penalty of the shrine's neglect should be imposed once more. Since I had decided so, it was unavoidable that you should die. For when I decide, all things follow inexorably. There is no other way or thing."

Will stared, the muscles of his neck stiff as an iron brace.

"But then," said the deep voice beneath the glorious eyes, "as you were leaving another desire crossed my mind. That you might interest me again on future occasions."

He paused.

"Once more," he said, "all things followed. If you were to interest me in the future, you could not die. And so you are not to." His eyes held Will's. "And now you understand."

A faint thoughtfulness clouded his golden eyes.

"I have done something with you this day," he said almost to himself, "that I have never done before. It is quite new. I have made you know what you are, in respect to what I am. I have taken a creature not even of my own people and made it understand it has no life or death or reasons of its own, except those my desires desire."

He stopped speaking. But Will still stood, rooted.

"Do not be afraid," said the Director. "I killed you. But I have brought another creature who understands to life in your body. One who will walk this world of mine for many years before he dies."

A sudden brilliance like a sheet of summer lightning flared in Will's head, blinding him. He heard his own voice shouting, in a sound that was rage without meaning. He flung his right arm forward and up as his sight cleared, and saw the liquid in the tube he had held splash itself against the downward-gazing, expressionless face above him, and the container bounce harmlessly from the sky-blue robe below the face.

There was a soundless jerk through all the natives behind the throne. A soundless gasp as if the air had changed. Native hands had flown to the black rods. But there they hung.

The Director had not moved. The watered alcohol dripped slowly from his nose and chin. But his features were unchanged, his hands were still, no finger on either hand stirred.

He continued to gaze at Will. After a long second, Will turned. He was not quite sure what he had done, but something sullen and brave burned redly in him.

He began to walk up the long aisle through the crowd, toward the distant portal. In that whole hall he was the only thing moving. The thousand different traders followed him with their eyes, but otherwise none moved, and no one made a sound. From the crowd there was silence. From the balcony overlooking, and the steps beyond the entrance, there was silence.

Step by echoing step he walked the long length of the hall and passed through the towering archway into the bright day outside. He made it as far as halfway down the steps before, inside the hall, the Director's finger lifted, the message of that finger was flashed to the ranked guards outside, and the black rods shot him down with flame in the sunlight.

On the balcony above, overlooking those steps, Avoa stirred at last, turning his eyes from what was left of Will and looking down at Khal Dohn beside him.

"What was . . ." Avoa's voice fumbled and failed. He added, almost humbly. "I am sorry. I do not even know the proper pronoun."

"He," said Khal Dohn, still looking down at the steps.

"He. What did he call himself?" Avoa said. "You told me, but I do not remember. I should have listened, but I did not. What did you say—what was he?"

Khal Dohn lifted his heavy head and looked up at last.

"He was a man," said Khal Dohn.

BLACK CHARLIE

You ask me, what is art? You expect me to have a logical answer at my fingertips, because I have been a buyer for museums and galleries long enough to acquire a plentiful crop of gray hairs. It's not that simple.

Well, what is art? For forty years I've examined, felt, admired and loved many things fashioned as hopeful vessels for that bright spirit we call art—and I'm unable to answer the question directly. The layman answers easily—beauty. But art is not necessarily beautiful. Sometimes it is ugly. Sometimes it is crude. Sometimes it is incomplete.

I have fallen back, as many men have in the business of making like decisions, on *feel*, for the judgment of art. You know this business of *feel*. Let us say that you pick up something. A piece of statuary—or better, a fragment of stone, etched and colored by some ancient man of prehistoric times. You look at it. At first it is nothing, a half-developed reproduction of some wild animal, not even as good as a grade-school child could accomplish today.

But then, holding it, your imagination suddenly reaches through rock and time, back to the man himself, half-squatted before the stone wall of his cave—and you see there, not the dusty thing you hold in your hand—but what the man himself saw in the hour of its creation. You look beyond the physical reproduction to the magnificent accomplishment of his imagination.

This, then, may be called art—no matter what strange guise it appears in—this magic which bridges all gaps between the artist and yourself. To it, no distance, nor any difference is too great. Let me give you an example from my own experience.

Some years back, when I was touring the newer worlds as a buyer for one of our well-known art institutions, I received a communication from a man named Cary Longan, asking me, if possible, to visit a planet named Elman's World and examine some statuary he had for sale.

Messages rarely came directly to me. They were usually referred to me by the institution I was representing at the time. Since, however, the world in question was close, being of the same solar system as the planet I was then visiting, I spacegraphed my answer that I would come. After cleaning up what remained of my business where I was, I took an interworld ship and, within a couple of days, landed on Elman's World.

It appeared to be a very raw, very new planet indeed. The port we landed at was, I learned, one of the only two suitable for deep-space vessels. And the city surrounding it was scarcely more than a village. Mr. Longan did not meet me at the port, so I took a cab directly to the hotel where I had made a reservation.

That evening, in my rooms, the annunciator rang, then spoke, giving me a name. I opened the door to admit a tall, brown-faced man, with uncut, dark hair and troubled, green-brown eyes.

"Mr. Longan?" I asked.

"Mr. Jones?" he countered. He shifted the unvarnished wooden box he was carrying to his left hand and put out his right to shake mine. I closed the door behind him and led him to a chair.

He put the box down, without opening it, on a small coffee table between us. It was then that I noticed his rough, bush-country clothes, breeches and tunic of drab plastic. Also an embarrassed air about him, like that of a man unused to city dealings. An odd sort of person to be offering art for sale.

"Your spacegram," I told him, "was not very explicit. The institution I represent . . ."

"I've got it here," he said, putting his hand on the box.

I looked at it in astonishment. It was no more than half a meter square by twenty centimeters deep.

"There?" I said. I looked back at him, with the beginnings of a suspicion forming in my mind. I suppose I should have been more wary when the message had come direct, instead of through Earth. But you know how it is—something of a feather in your cap when you bring in an unexpected item. "Tell me, Mr. Longan," I said, "where does this statuary come from?"

He looked at me, a little defiantly. "A friend of mine made them," he said.

"A friend?" I repeated—and I must admit I was growing somewhat annoyed. It makes a man feel like a fool to be taken in that way. "May I ask whether this friend of yours has ever sold any of his work before?"

"Well, no . . ." Longan hedged. He was obviously suffering—but so was I, when I thought of my own wasted time.

"I see," I said, getting to my feet. "You've brought me on a very expensive side-trip, merely to show me the work of some amateur. Good-by, Mr. Longan. And please take your box with you when you leave!"

"You've never seen anything like this before!" He was looking up at me with desperation.

"No doubt," I said.

"Look. I'll show you . . ." He fumbled, his fingers nervous on the hasp. "Since you've come all this way, you can at least look."

Because there seemed no way of getting him out of there, short of having the hotel manager eject him forcibly, I sat down with bad grace. "What's your friend's name?" I demanded.

Longan's fingers hesitated on the hasp. "Black Charlie," he replied, not looking up at me.

I stared. "I beg your pardon. Black—Charles Black?"

He looked up quite defiantly, met my eye and shook his head. "Just Black Charlie," he said with sudden calmness. "Just the way it sounds. Black Charlie." He continued unfastening the box.

I watched rather dubiously, as he finally managed to loosen the clumsy, handmade wooden bolt that secured the hasp. He was about to raise the lid, then apparently changed his mind. He turned the box around and pushed it across the coffee table.

The wood was hard and uneven under my fingers. I lifted the lid. There were five small partitions, each containing a rock of fine-grained gray sandstone of different but thoroughly incomprehensible shape.

I stared at them—then looked back at Longan, to see if this weren't some sort of elaborate joke. But the tall man's eyes were severely serious. Slowly, I began to take out the stones and line them up on the table.

I studied them one by one, trying to make some sense out of their forms. But there was nothing there, absolutely nothing. One vaguely resembled a regular-sided pyramid. Another gave a foggy impression of a crouching figure. The best that could be said of the rest was that they bore a somewhat disconcerting resemblance to the kind of stones people pick up for paper-weights. Yet they all had obviously been worked on. There were noticeable chisel marks on each one. And, in addition, they had been polished as well as such soft, grainy rock could be.

I looked up at Longan. His eyes were tense with waiting. I was completely puzzled about his discovery—or what he felt was a discovery. I tried to be fair about his acceptance of this as art. It was obviously nothing more than loyalty to a friend, a friend no doubt as unaware of what constituted art as himself. I made my tone as kind as I could.

"What did your friend expect me to do with these, Mr. Longan?" I asked gently.

"Aren't you buying things for that museum-place on Earth?" he said.

I nodded. I picked up the piece that resembled a crouching animal figure and turned it over in my fingers. It was an awkward situation. "Mr. Longan," I said. "I have been in this business many years . . ."

"I know," he interrupted. "I read about you in the newsfax when you landed on the next world. That's why I wrote you."

"I see," I said. "Well, I've been in it a long time, as I say and, I think, I can safely boast that I know something about art. If there is art in these carvings your friend has made, I should be able to recognize it. And I do not."

He stared at me, shock in his greenish-brown eyes.

"You're . . ." he said, finally. "You don't mean that. You're sore because I brought you out here this way."

"I'm sorry," I said. "I'm *not* sore and I *do* mean it. These things are not merely not good—there is nothing of value in them. Nothing! Someone has deluded your friend into thinking that he has talent. You'll be doing him a favor if you tell him the truth."

He stared at me for a long moment, as if waiting for me to say something to soften the verdict. Then, suddenly, he rose from the chair and crossed the room in three long strides, staring tensely out the window. His calloused hands clenched and unclenched spasmodically.

I gave him a little time to wrestle it out with himself. Then I started putting the pieces of stone back into their sections of the box.

"I'm sorry," I told him.

He wheeled about and came back to me, leaning down from his lanky height to look in my face. "Are you?" he said. "*Are* you?"

"Believe me," I said sincerely, "I am." And I was.

"Then will you do something for me?" The words came in a rush. "Will you come and tell Charlie what you've told me? Will *you* break the news to him?"

"I . . ." I meant to protest, to beg off, but with his tortured eyes six inches from mine, the words would not come. "All right," I said.

The breath he had been holding came out in one long sigh. "Thanks," he said. "We'll go out tomorrow. You don't know what this means. Thanks."

I had ample time to regret my decision, both that night and the following morning, when Longan roused me at an early hour, furnished me with a set of bush clothes like his own, including high, impervious boots, and whisked me off in old air-ground combination flyer that was loaded down with all kinds of bush-dweller's equipment. But a promise is a promise—and I reconciled myself to keeping mine.

We flew south along a high chain of mountains until we came to a coastal area and what appeared to be the swamp delta of some monster river. Here, we began to descend—much to my distaste. I have little affection for hot, muggy climates and could not conceive of anyone wanting to live under such conditions.

We set down lightly in a little open stretch of water— and Longan taxied the flyer across to the nearest bank, a tussocky mass of high brown weeds and soft mud. By myself, I would not have trusted the soggy ground to refrain from drawing me down like quicksand—but Longan stepped out onto the bank confidently enough, and I followed. The mud yielded, little pools of water springing up around my boot soles. A hot rank smell of decaying vegetation came to my nose. Under a thin but uniform blanket of cloud, the sky looked white and sick.

"This way," said Longan, and led off to the right.

I followed him along a little trail and into a small, swampy clearing with dome-shaped huts of woven branches, plastered with mud, scattered about it. And, for the first time, it struck me that Black Charlie might be something other than an expatriate Earthman—might, indeed, be a native of this planet, though I had heard of no other humanlike race on other worlds before. My head spinning,

I followed Longan to the entrance of one of the huts and halted as he whistled.

I don't remember now what I expected to see. Something vaguely humanoid, no doubt. But what came through the entrance in response to Longan's whistle was more like a large otter, with flat, muscular grasping pads on the ends of its four limbs, instead of feet. It was black, with glossy, dampish hair all over it. About four feet in length, I judged, with no visible tail and a long, snaky neck. The creature must have weighed one hundred to, perhaps, one hundred and fifty pounds. The head on its long neck was also long and narrow, like the head of a well-bred collie—covered with the same black hair, with bright, intelligent eyes and a long mouth.

"This is Black Charlie," said Longan.

The creature stared at me and I returned his gaze. Abruptly, I was conscious of the absurdity of the situation. It would have been difficult for any ordinary person to think of this being as a sculptor. To add to this a necessity, an obligation, to convince it that it was *not* a sculptor—mind you, I could not be expected to know a word of its language—was to pile Pelion upon Ossa in a madman's farce. I swung on Longan.

"Look here," I began with quite natural heat, "how do you expect me to tell—"

"He understands you," interrupted Longan.

"Speech?" I said, incredulously, "Real human speech?"

"No," Longan shook his head. "But he understands actions." He turned from me abruptly and plunged into the weeds surrounding the clearing. He returned immediately with two objects that looked like gigantic puffballs, and handed one to me.

"Sit on this," he said, doing so himself. I obeyed.

Black Charlie—I could think of nothing else to call him—came closer, and we sat down together. Charlie was half-squatting on ebony haunches. All this time, I had been carrying the wooden box that contained his sculptures and, now that we were seated, his bright eyes swung inquisitively toward it.

"All right," said Longan, "give it to me."

I passed him the box, and it drew Black Charlie's eyes like a magnet. Longan took it under one arm and pointed toward the lake with the other—to where we had landed the flyer. Then his arm rose in the air in a slow, impres-

sive circle and pointed northward, from the direction we
had come.

Black Charlie whistled suddenly. It was an odd note,
like the cry of a loon—a far, sad sound.

Longan struck himself on the chest, holding the box
with one hand. Then he struck the box and pointed to me.
He looked at Black Charlie, looked back at me—then put
the box into my numb hands.

"Look them over and hand them back," he said, his
voice tight. Against my will, I looked at Charlie.

His eyes met mine. Strange, liquid, black inhuman eyes,
like two tiny pools of pitch. I had to tear my own gaze
away.

Torn between my feeling of foolishness and a real sympathy for the waiting creature, I awkwardly opened the
box and lifted the stones from their compartments. One by
one, I turned them in my hand and put them back. I
closed the box and returned it to Longan, shaking my
head, not knowing if Charlie would understand that.

For a long moment, Longan merely sat facing me,
holding the box. Then, slowly, he turned and set it, still
open, in front of Charlie.

Charlie did not react at first. His head, on its long neck,
drooped over the open compartments as if he was sniffing
them. Then, surprisingly, his lips wrinkled back, revealing
long, chisel-shaped teeth. Daintily, he reached into the box
with these and lifted out the stones, one by one. He held
them in his forepads, turning them this way and that, as if
searching for the defects of each. Finally, he lifted one—it
was the stone that faintly resembled a crouching beast. He
lifted it to his mouth—and, with his gleaming teeth, made
slight alterations in its surface. Then he brought it to me.

Helplessly I took it in my hands and examined it. The
changes he had made in no way altered it toward something recognizable. I was forced to hand it back, with another headshake, and a poignant pause fell between us.

I had been desperately turning over in my mind some
way to explain, through the medium of pantomime, the
reasons for my refusal. Now, something occurred to me. I
turned to Longan.

"Can he get me a piece of unworked stone?" I asked.

Longan turned to Charlie and made motions as if he
were breaking something off and handing it to me. For a
moment, Charlie sat still, as if considering this. Then he

went into his hut, returning a moment later with a chunk of rock the size of my hand.

I had a small pocket knife, and the rock was soft. I held the rock out toward Longan and looked from him to it. Using my pocket knife, I whittled a rough, lumpy caricature of Longan, seated on the puffball. When I was finished, I put the two side by side, the hacked piece of stone insignificant on the ground beside the living man.

Black Charlie looked at it. Then he came up to me—and, peering up into my face, cried softly, once. Moving so abruptly that it startled me, he turned smoothly, picked up in his teeth the piece of stone I had carved. Soon he disappeared back into his hut.

Longan stood up stiffly, like a man who has held one position too long. "That's it," he said. "Let's go."

We made our way to the combination and took off once more, headed back toward the city and the spaceship that would carry me away from this irrational world. As the mountains commenced to rise, far beneath us, I stole a glance at Longan, sitting beside me at the controls of the combination. His face was set in an expression of stolid unhappiness.

The question came from my lips before I had time to debate internally whether it was wise or not to ask it.

"Tell me, Mr. Longan," I said, "has—er—Black Charlie some special claim on your friendship?"

The tall man looked at me with something close to amazement.

"Claim!" he said. Then, after a short pause, during which he seemed to search my features to see if I was joking. "He saved my life."

"Oh," I said. "I see."

"You do, do you?" he countered. "Suppose I told you it was just after I'd finished killing his mate. They mate for life, you know."

"No, I didn't know," I answered feebly.

"I forget people don't know," he said in a subdued voice. I said nothing, hoping that, if I did not disturb him, he would say more. After a while he spoke. "This planet's not much good."

"I noticed," I answered. "I didn't see much in the way of plants and factories. And your sister world—the one I came from—is much more populated and built up."

"There's not much here," he said. "No minerals to speak of. Climate's bad, except on the plateaus. Soil's not much good." He paused. It seemed to take effort to say what came next. "Used to have a novelty trade in furs, though."

"Furs?" I echoed.

"Off Charlie's people," he went on, fiddling with the combination's controls. "Trappers and hunters used to be after them, at first, before they knew. I was one of them."

"You!" I said.

"Me!" His voice was flat. "I was doing fine, too, until I trapped Charlie's mate. Up till then, I'd been getting them out by themselves. They did a lot of traveling in those swamps. But, this time, I was close to the village. I'd just clubbed her on the head when the whole tribe jumped me." His voice trailed off, then strengthened. "They kept me under guard for a couple of months.

"I learned a lot in that time. I learned they were intelligent. I learned it was Black Charlie who kept them from killing me right off. Seems he took the point of view that I was a reasonable being and, if he could just talk things over with me, we could get together and end the war." Longan laughed, a little bitterly. "They called it a war, Charlie's people did." He stopped talking.

I waited. And when he remained quiet, I prompted him. "What happened?" I asked.

"They let me go, finally," he said. "And I went to bat for them. Clear up to the Commissioner sent from Earth. I got them recognized as people instead of animals. I put an end to the hunting and trapping."

He stopped again. We were still flying through the upper air of Elman's World, the sun breaking through the clouds at last, revealing the ground below like a huge green relief map.

"I see," I said, finally.

Longan looked at me stonily.

We flew back to the city.

I left Elman's World the next day, fully believing that I had heard and seen the last of both Longan and Black Charlie. Several years later, at home in New York, I was visited by a member of the government's Foreign Service. He was a slight, dark man, and he didn't beat about the bush.

"You don't know me," he said. I looked at his card— *Antonio Walters*. "I was Deputy Colonial Representative on Elman's World at the time you were there."

I looked up at him, surprised. I had forgotten Elman's World by that time.

"Were you?" I asked, feeling a little foolish, unable to think of anything better to say. I turned his card over several times, staring at it, as a person will do when at a loss. "What can I do for you, Mr. Walters?"

"We've been requested by the local government on Elman's World to locate you, Mr. Jones," he answered. "Cary Longan is dying—"

"Dying!" I said.

"Lung fungus, unfortunately," said Walters. "You catch it in the swamps. He wants to see you before the end—and, since we're very grateful to him out there for the work he's been doing all these years for the natives, a place has been kept for you on a government courier ship leaving for Elman's World right away—if you're willing to go."

"Why, I . . . ." I hesitated. In common decency, I could not refuse. "I'll have to notify my employers."

"Of course," he said.

Luckily, the arrangements I had to make consisted of a few business calls and packing my bags. I was, as a matter of fact, between trips at the time. As an experienced traveler, I could always get under way with a mimimum of fuss. Walters and I drove out to Government Port, in northern New Jersey and, from there on, the authorities took over.

Less than a week later, I stood by Longan's bedside in the hospital of the same city I had visited years before. The man was now nothing more than a barely living skeleton, the hard vitality all but gone from him, hardly able to speak a few words at a time. I bent over to catch the whispered syllables from his wasted lips.

"Black Charlie . . . " he whispered.

"Black Charlie," I repeated. "Yes, what about him?"

"He's done something new," whispered Longan. "That carving of yours started him off, copying things. His tribe don't like it."

"They don't?" I said.

"They," whispered Longan, "don't understand. It's not normal, the way they see it. They're afraid . . ."

"You mean they're superstitious about what he carves?" I asked.

"Something like that. Listen—he's an artist . . ."

I winced internally at the last word, but held my tongue for the sake of the dying man.

". . . an artist. But they'll kill him for it, now that I'm gone. You can save him, though."

"Me?" I said.

"You!" The man's voice was like a wind rustling through dry leaves. "If you go out—take this last thing from him—act pleased . . . then they'll be scared to touch him. But hurry. Every day is that much closer . . ."

His strength failed him. He closed his eyes and his straining throat muscles relaxed to a little hiss of air that puffed between his lips. The nurse hurried me from his room.

The local government helped me. I was surprised, and not a little touched, to see how many people knew Longan. How many of them admired his attempts to pay back the natives by helping them in any way he could. They located Charlie's tribe on a map for me and sent me out with a pilot who knew the country.

We landed on the same patch of slime. I went alone toward the clearing. With the brown weeds still walling it about, the locale showed no natural change, but Black Charlie's hut appeared broken and deserted. I whistled and waited. I called. And, finally, I got down on my hands and knees and crawled inside. But there was nothing there save a pile of loose rock and a mass of dried weeds. Feeling cramped and uncomfortable, for I am not used to such gymnastics, I backed out, to find myself surrounded by a crowd.

It looked as if all the other inhabitants of the village had come out of their huts and congregated before Charlie's. They seemed agitated, milling about, occasionally whistling at each other on that one low, plaintive note which was the only sound I had ever heard Charlie make. Eventually, the excitement seemed to fade, the group fell back and one individual came forward alone. He looked up into my face for a brief moment, then turned and glided swiftly on his pads toward the edge of the clearing.

I followed. There seemed nothing else to do. And, at that time, it did not occur to me to be afraid.

My guide led me deep into the weed patch, then abruptly disappeared. I looked around surprised and undecided, half-inclined to turn about and retrace my steps by the trail of crushed weeds I had left in my floundering advance. Then, a low whistle sounded close by. I went forward and found Charlie.

He lay on his side in a little circular open area of

crushed weeds. He was too weak to do more than raise his head and look at me, for the whole surface of his body was crisscrossed and marked with the slashings of shallow wounds, from which dark blood seeped slowly and stained the reeds in which he lay. In Charlie's mouth, I had seen the long, chisel-teeth of his kind, and I knew what had made those wounds. A gust of rage went through me, and I stooped to pick him up in my arms.

He came up easily, for the bones of his kind are cartilaginous, and their flesh is far lighter than our human flesh. Holding him, I turned and made my way back to the clearing.

The others were waiting for me as we came out into the open. I glared at them—and then the rage inside me went out like a blown candle. For there was nothing there to hate. *They* had not hated Charlie. They had merely feared him—and their only crime was ignorance.

They moved back from me, and I carried Charlie to the door of his own hut. There I laid him down. The chest and arms of my jacket were soaked from his dark body fluid, and I saw that his blood was not clotting as our own does.

Clumsily, I took off my shirt and, tearing it into strips, made a poor attempt to bind up the torn flesh. But the blood came through in spite of my first aid. Charlie, lifting his head, with a great effort, from the ground, picked feebly at the bandages with his teeth, so that I gave up and removed them.

I sat down beside him then, feeling sick and helpless. In spite of Longan's care and dying effort, in spite of all the scientific developments of my own human race, I had come too late. Numbly, I sat and looked down at him and wondered why I could not have come one day earlier.

From this half-stupor of self-accusation, I was roused by Charlie's attempts to crawl back into his hut. My first reaction was to restrain him. But, from somewhere, he seemed to have dredged up a remnant of his waning strength—and he persisted. Seeing this, I changed my mind and, instead of hindering, helped. He dragged himself through the entrance, his strength visibly waning.

I did not expect to see him emerge. I believed some ancient instinct had called him, that he would die then and there. But, a few moments later, I heard a sound as of stones rattling from within—and, in a few seconds, he began to back out. Halfway through the entrance, his strength finally failed him. He lay still for a minute, then whistled weakly.

I went to him and pulled him out the rest of the way. He turned his head toward me, holding in his mouth what I first took to be a ball of dried mud.

I took it from him and began to scrape the mud off with my fingernails. Almost immediately, the grain and surface of the sandstone he used for his carvings began to emerge—and my hands started to shake so hard that, for a moment, I had to put the stone down while I got myself under control. For the first time, the true importance to Charlie, of these things he had chewed and bitten into shape, got home to me.

In that moment, I swore that whatever bizarre form this last and greatest work of his might possess, I would make certain that it was accorded a place in some respectable museum as a true work of art. After all, it had been conceived in honesty and executed in the love that took no count of labor, provided the end was achieved.

And then, the rest of the mud came free in my hands. I saw what it was, and I could have cried and laughed at the same time. For, of all the shapes he could have chosen to work in stone, he had picked the one that no critic would have selected as the choice of an artist of his race. For he had chosen no plant or animal, no structure or natural shape out of his environment, to express the hungry longing of his spirit. None of these had he chosen—instead, with painful clumsiness, he had fashioned an image from the soft and grainy rock; a statue of a standing man.

And I knew what man it was.

Charlie lifted his head from the stained ground and looked toward the lake where my flyer waited. I am not an intuitive man—but, for once, I was able to understand the meaning of a look. He wanted me to leave while he was still alive. He wanted to see me go, carrying the thing he had fashioned. I got to my feet, holding it and stumbled off. At the edge of the clearing, I looked back. He still watched. And the rest of his people still hung back from him. I did not think they would bother him now.

And so I came home.

But there is one thing more to tell. For a long time, after I returned from Elman's World, I did not look at the crude statuette. I did not want to, for I knew that seeing it would only confirm what I had known from the start, that all the longing and desires in the world cannot create art where there is no talent, no true visualization. But at the end of one year I was cleaning up all the little details of my office. And, because I believe in system and order—and also, because I was ashamed of myself for having put it off so long—I took the statuette from a bottom drawer of my desk, unwrapped it and set it on the desk's polished surface.

I was alone in my office at the time, at the end of a day, when the afternoon Sun, striking red through the tall window beside my desk, touched everything between the walls with a clear, amber light. I ran my fingers over the grainy sandstone and held it up to look at it.

And then—for the first time—I saw it, saw through the stone to the image beyond, saw what Black Charlie had seen, with Black Charlie's eyes, when he looked at Longan. I saw men as Black Charlie's kind saw men—and I saw what the worlds of men meant to Black Charlie. And, above all, overriding all, I saw art as Black Charlie saw it, through his bright alien eyes—saw the beauty he had sought at the price of his life, and had half-found.

But, most of all, I saw that this crude statuette was *art*.

One more word. Amid the mud and weeds of the swamp, I had held the carving in my hands and promised myself that this work would one day stand on display. Following that moment of true insight in my office, I did my best to place it with the institution I represented, then with others who knew me as a reputable buyer.

But I could find no takers. No one, although they trusted me individually, was willing to exhibit such a poor-looking piece of work on the strength of a history that I, alone, could vouch for. There are people, close to any institution, who are only too ready to cry, "Hoax!" For several years, I tried without success.

Eventually, I gave up on the true story and sold the statuette, along with a number of other odd pieces, to a dealer of minor reputation, representing it as an object whose history I did not know.

Curiously, the statuette has justified my belief in what is art, by finding a niche for itself. I traced it from the dealer, after a time, and ran it to Earth quite recently. There is a highly respectable art gallery on this planet which has an extensive display of primitive figures of early American Indian origin.

And Black Charlie's statuette is among them. I will not tell which or where it is.

ZEEPSDAY

*TRIAL 47 Court Session 192384726354028475635 of the
Galactic Court of People's Manners, within the Federation
of Planet-Originated Races.*

RECORDER:

*This trial record by Aki, brood-brother of Po, Domsker
from Ju, graduate court reporter. Recorded in accordance
with reportorial precept—"Let it be a full record; let no
least spuggl twung unnoticed and unremarked."*

RECORD BEGINS:

*Two ulbls (four hours, twenty minutes, Human time; 38
Gisnk, Sloonian time) after sunrise on Beldor, Galactic
Court World. A blithe day with the courtroom well filled
with polite audience, of many varieties of goodly life
forms. To the left of the Judge's bench, the compound of
the defendant, one Garth Paulson, a Human from Earth,
surrounded by friends and well-wishers. To the right, the
compound of the plaintiff, Drang Usussis, a Nesbler from
Sloon, similarly surrounded by friends and well-wishers.
Approach of his honor, the presiding judge, Umka, a
Bolver from Bol, is noted.*

COURT BAILIFF: His honor, Judge Umka, now rolling
upon his bench. All those fearing offense to personal and
delicate sensibilities are warned to retire.

JUDGE: Thank you, Bailiff. You may scurry off now.
Where is my scanner—ah, yes, I see here by the legal challenge submitted to me that the plaintiff charges the
defendant with having committed a personal and verbal
impoliteness upon the plaintiff, specifically the defendant's
audible reference to the plaintiff upon one occasion as a

being possessing four tentacles. Ah—um—do these three dozen old eyes deceive me? It seems to the bench from here that the plaintiff in question does indeed seem to be possessed of f—

MYSELF (*interrupting in accordance with legalized tradition and duty of court reporters on such occasions*): Psst, your honor—(*the rest of my words off the record*).

JUDGE: Oh—ah. Thank you, clerk. The bench extends its courtesies to the *three*-tentacled Mr. Usussis and the purchasing press agent—is that correct?—Mr. Paulson.

DEFENDANT: Press agent is correct, your honor. I am the city purchasing press agent for the city hall of the City of Los Angeles in the Metropolis of Los Angeles, Earth.

JUDGE: And Mr. Usussis. Your occupation?

MR. USUSSIS: Your honor, I am a registered dilettante, of the planet of Sloon, long may its purple oceans reek.

JUDGE (*pounding for order*): Order! Order! The court will not permit patriotic outbursts of this sort. The plaintiff is cautioned that the sensibilities of those here present may not be offended. Mr. Usussis, this is a challenge of a minor nature you have brought before this court, but it seems to the bench that your compound is well-peopled by legal talent of the highest order. And is not that the great criminal legalist, Spod Draxel of Nv, I see beside you?

MR. USUSSIS: It is indeed, your honor. However, he and these other gentlebeings are merely present as friends and well-wishers of the plaintiff and in no official capacity. I shall attempt to prosecute my case with my own feeble talents.

JUDGE (*turning to defendant*): And You, Mr. Paulson, seem equally well supplied. Is not that Earth's foremost Corporation Sharpie I see in your compound?

DEFENDANT: It is indeed Sol Blitnik, your honor. However, as is the case with the honorable plaintiff, he and these others are merely chance acquaintances who have prevailed on me for a seat in my compound the better to amuse themselves with witnessing this trial. I, also, will defend myself to the best of my poor ability.

JUDGE: Very well. The bench cautions both plaintiff and defendant against extraneous issues. We will proceed. Will the plaintiff take the stand and submit to questioning?

(*The plaintiff slithers across the floor and mounts the stand.*)

JUDGE: Will the defendant open the action of his response to the challenge of the plaintiff?

(*The defendant consults with the chance acquaintances in his compound.*)

DEFENDANT: We—that is, I think, your honor, that it would save time and trouble if the plaintiff were to commence by stating his cause of offense briefly in his own words, for the court's benefit.

JUDGE: It is so ordered. Go ahead, Mr. Usussis.

PLAINTIFF: The occasion was actually a simple one, your honor. I was transacting a minor piece of business with the defendant at the time. We had just signed a contract for the purchase of certain Sloonian commodities recently become in high demand in the city of Los Angeles, when the defendant suddenly began to scratch himself vigorously. When I inquired politely what was the matter, he replied, "Now I get it. I should have known better than to trust a slippery customer like you, you—" and here, your honor, he made use of that obscene, disgusting, and unmentionable accusation against myself which is the reason for my present action against him in this court.

JUDGE: Allow me to interrupt for a moment. The bench would like to know whether the plaintiff is seeking punitive action in this case, or merely an injunction restraining the defendant from further verbal assault?

PLAINTIFF: Your honor, I want an injunction backed up by a threat of punitive action to the full rigor of the law—a two-year sentence, I believe.

JUDGE (*severely*): The plaintiff is warned against attempting to instruct the bench. A two-year sentence is, indeed, possible for a breach of politeness between races. However, the sentencing and conditions of sentence are up to the court.

PLAINTIFF (*humbly*): I apologize, your honor.

JUDGE: Your apology is accepted. *(turning to defendant)*: It seems that the plaintiff has adequately stated the situation at the time of the alleged insult. What does the defendant wish—by the way, will the defendant explain to the bench why his chance acquaintance Sol Blitnik has adopted a position with his lips almost touching the defendant's ear?

DEFENDANT: I humbly beg the court to excuse my infirmities. The ear in question has a slight itch which is eased by Mr. Blitnik's murmuring into it from time to time.

JUDGE: That's all right, Mr. Paulson. I was merely curious. Proceed.

DEFENDANT: Is the plaintiff aware that the city of Los Angeles is identical with the Metropolis of Los Angeles?

PLAINTIFF: I am, naturally.

DEFENDANT: And that the cities of Cairo, Hong Kong and Capetown are suburbs of the same Metropolis of Los Angeles?

PLAINTIFF: Well—I—uh—

WELL-WISHER *(from the plaintiff's compound)*: Objection!

JUDGE: Order in the court! Spectators will not interrupt court proceedings.

PLAINTIFF: Your honor, I object.

JUDGE: On what grounds?

PLAINTIFF: Er—the question is immaterial and irrelevant.

JUDGE: How about that, Mr. Paulson?

DEFENDANT: Your honor, I am trying to show that the plaintiff was attempting to mislead the court when he referred to the business between us as minor and that that business has a direct bearing on the conversation which culminated in the offense alleged.

JUDGE: Objection overruled. Continue, Mr. Paulson— by the way how does your ear feel now? I notice Mr. Blitnik working on it again.

DEFENDANT: Much better, thanks, your honor. Will your honor direct the witness to answer that last question?

'JUDGE: Answer the question.

PLAINTIFF: Well yes, I do.

DEFENDANT: In short, what you have referred to as minor business was actually concerned with millions of units of manufactured items for the planet Earth as a whole. Right?

PLAINTIFF: Well, yes.

DEFENDANT: Your honor, I would now like to call my secretary, Marge Jolman, to the stand.

JUDGE: Very well—you are dismissed, Mr. Usussis. Subject to later recall, if necessary, of course.
(The plaintiff slithers off the stand and back to his compound. From the compound of the defendant approaches a Human female—young, well-developed and red-haired. Slightly nervous, the witness performs a brief version of the Human hand-clasping ceremony with the defendant as he helps her up on the stand.)

PLAINTIFF *(from his own compound)*: Your honor, objection.

JUDGE: On what grounds, Mr. Usussis?

PLAINTIFF: This witness is known to be contemplating mating ceremonies with the defendant. I ask your honor to consider the possibility that this may cause her to be prejudiced.

JUDGE: For, or against him, you mean?

PLAINTIFF: For, your honor. Human matings are considered to be on grounds of affection.

JUDGE: Prejudice on grounds of affection or animosity are a practical impossibility for this court to take into account. Otherwise you yourself would have to be disqualified from pleading on the grounds of obvious prejudice, Mr. Usussis. Is there any direct connection between the contemplated mating ceremonies and your charge of impoliteness?

PLAINTIFF: No *direct* connection, your honor, but—

JUDGE: Overruled. Proceed, Mr. Paulson.

DEFENDANT: Marge, do you remember being at work in my outer office the day Mr. Usussis first came to see me?

WITNESS: Oh, yes.

DEFENDANT: Will you tell the court what he said to you on that occasion.

WITNESS: Well, I don't remember his exact words—

DEFENDANT: With your honor's permission, I will ask the witness to tell us the substance of what the plaintiff said to her at that time.

JUDGE: Go ahead. Plaintiff can always object after he hears how she puts it.

DEFENDANT: Go ahead, Marge.

WITNESS: Well, he had an appointment to see Garth—I mean Mr. Paulson, but he hadn't said what about. So I asked him. He said it was about Zeepsday.

JUDGE: Zeepsday? I don't—

MYSELF: Your honor, psst—(*the rest of my words off the record*)

JUDGE: Of course. Naturally. Hrmph! Continue.

WITNESS: I asked him what that was; and he said that was what he had come here to explain and could he see Mr. Paulson about it. I called Garth on the intercom and told him, and he said for both of us to come in.

JUDGE: Just a minute. Has plaintiff any objections so far?

PLAINTIFF: Not at this time, your honor.

DEFENDANT: And what took place in my office, Marge? Will you tell the court that?

WITNESS: Well, you wanted me to take notes, you said. So I stayed. Then you asked Mr. Usussis what it was all about. And he said it was a delicate matter and he didn't want to step on the toes of any human taboos he might not know about. But what was the reason no humans made use of Zeepsday?

(The witness pauses and seems flustered.)

JUDGE *(encouragingly)*: Go ahead, Miss Jolman.

WITNESS: Well, Garth said, "What do you mean, Zeepsday?" and then Mr. Usussis explained that he didn't know the human word for it, but it was the day that came between the days we called Wednesday and Thursday.

JUDGE: Just a minute. I think that this is a point that ought to be clarified before we go any further. I think the witness can step down for a moment. Is there a temporal authority in the courtroom? —No, no, I don't want an expert from either the plaintiff's or the defendant's compound, disinterested as those gentlebeings may be. I want one from the courtroom audience. You sir—there in the back—would you consent?
(A Vbuldo from O rises in the back of the courtroom and clanks forward to the stand.)

JUDGE: Will you tell us your name and qualifications, sir?

WITNESS: Gladly. I am Porniarsk Prime Three and have advanced degrees in temporals general.

JUDGE: Will you explain in the simplest possible terms the temporal situation under consideration, here?

WITNESS: With pleasure. The plaintiff, being a Nesbler from Sloon, is native to Stress Two area of the Galaxy. As a result, he is particular to a curvilinear time with a factor of .84736209, approximately. The temporal quantity being radial to space curvature, it results in a greater positive number of temporal divisions to the same temporal area for one from Nesbler than for one from Earth, where an alinear time with a factor of .76453839476, approximately, is in present effect.

JUDGE: And the practical result of this—?

WITNESS: That the plaintiff has a total of eight days in his week for seven of the defendant's. In short, the days Monday, Tuesday, Wednesday, Zeepsday, Thursday, Friday, Saturday and Sunday.

JUDGE: Thank you. You are dismissed.
(The witness bows, descends from the stand and clanks back to his seat in the audience section of the courtroom.)

JUDGE: Recall the previous witness.

(The Human female Marge Jolman reascends the stand.)

JUDGE: Miss Jolman, you have heard the last witness. Was this, in essence, what Mr. Ususis told you and the defendant?

WITNESS: Yes, your honor. He wanted to know what we humans did during the twenty-four hours between midnight Wednesday and the first minute of Thursday morning.

JUDGE: Do you mean to imply that the plaintiff intimated his belief that Humans also had eight days in their week?

WITNESS: That's what it sounded like, your honor.

JUDGE: Hmm—well, go on with your questioning, Mr. Paulson.

DEFENDANT: Thank you, your honor. Now, Marge, what did I say when Mr. Ususis said that?

WITNESS: You didn't believe it. And Mr. Ususis offered to show you.

DEFENDANT: Thank you. That's all.

JUDGE: Cross-examine, Mr. Ususis?

PLAINTIFF: Not at this time, your honor.

JUDGE: You may step down.
(Witness returns to seat in defendant's compound.)

JUDGE: And now, Mr. Paulson?

DEFENDANT: Your honor, I would like to call Gundar Jorgenson, also of Earth, to the stand.

JUDGE: Proceed.

DEFENDANT: Gundar—
(A middle-aged male Human, large for the species, approaches and mounts the stand.)

DEFENDANT: Will you tell the court your name and occupation?

WITNESS: Gundar Jorgenson, from Earth. I am a temporal physicist.

DEFENDANT: Will you tell the court what your connection is with this case?

WITNESS: I will. One sparkling spring morning last May, the defendant requested me to accompany him on a visit to Zeepsday—
(*Consternation in the court. Cries of Objection! Objection! from the plaintiff's compound.*)

JUDGE (*pounding for order*): Order! Order in the court! Another outburst like that and I shall clear the courtroom. Will the defendant approach the bench?

DEFENDANT: Here I am, your honor.

JUDGE: Mr. Paulson, I must admit I had my suspicions earlier that in this trial the action was trending toward matters outside—the jurisdiction of this court. Surely the defendant is aware—and if he is not, I am sure any of his chance acquaintances sharing the compound with him at present can enlighten him—that any case concerning temporal illegalities must be considered by the High Crimes Commission. Both planets involved must be sequestered, their native products embargoed, and a hundred-year decontamination process of both parties put into effect. Does the defendant mean to charge the plaintiff with an actual derangement of the temporal structure around his home world?

DEFENDANT: No such thought entered my mind, your honor. As has already been stated, I am merely an inexperienced private citizen engaged in a small altercation with another citizen over a minor matter. As your honor knows, a conviction for the derangement of temporal structure is practically a legal impossibility; and in fact it is for that reason that the High Crimes Commission has seen fit to make the situation so uncomfortable to both the criminal and his victim that both parties, innocent and guilty, would shrink from becoming involved in such a case. Certainly I would not wish to be responsible for bringing such grief upon my world. Consequently, I would like to clear up any doubt in the court's mind about what actually happened, in a temporal sense. It is my theory that none of the temporal irregularities concerned in this trial actually happened; but that those of us who seemed to be concerned with them were actually only hypnotized into believing they had.

JUDGE: Hypnotized! And does the plaintiff agree to admit that he hypnotized the defendant?

PLAINTIFF (*smirking*): I do, your honor, with the stipulation that the defendant in this case subconsciously wanted to be hypnotized, so that the action cannot be said to have been taken against the defendant's will.

JUDGE: Does the defendant agree to the stipulation?

DEFENDANT: I do, your honor, provisional to the theoretical nature of my contention.

JUDGE: Does the plaintiff agree to the theoretical nature of the defendant's contention?

PLAINTIFF: In theory I agree to the defendant's theory.

JUDGE (*looking somewhat glazed about the lower two dozen of his eyes, mutters something*).

MYSELF: What was that, your honor?

JUDGE: Nothing—nothing. Continue questioning your witness, Mr. Paulson.

DEFENDANT: Mr. Jorgenson, you were associated with me on our theoretical visit to Zeepsday. Will you tell the court what we did and what we discovered there?

WITNESS: I would be more than glad to. As I said, one balmy May night, we left the common, ordinary Earth behind—

JUDGE: Just a minute, Mr. Paulson. Why do you need a technical expert to testify to the facts of something that theoretically did not happen or exist?

DEFENDANT: I assure your honor, these non-existent facts have a vital bearing on the case.

JUDGE: Well ... well—continue.

DEFENDANT: Go ahead, Mr. Jorgenson.

WITNESS: We left in a Sloonian spaceship. Earth fell away behind us. At a distance from the world, where the planet seemed to swim like some great clouded crystal ball in emptiness, we waited until 12:00 midnight, Wednesday. Then, at the witching hour, we activated the temporal distorter on the ship—

DEFENDANT: You mean the illusion of a temporal distorter.

WITNESS: Oh, yes. The temp—this illusion, that is—was the largest I had ever seen. My acquaintance with such heretofore had been confined to tiny laboratory models.

JUDGE: Of illusions, or of temporal distorters, Mr. Jorgenson?

WITNESS: Temporal distorters, your honor. Still, I knew the principle on which it worked. Briefly, it dilated an aperture in the normal temporal structure; and through this aperture one may discover any excess time that may be available in the area.

JUDGE: Just a minute. I would like to ask the former technical witness a question. You needn't come up to the stand, Mr. Porniarsk Prime Three; but is this description essentially correct?

VBULDONIAN VOICE (from the back of the courtroom): Quite correct, your honor.

JUDGE: Continue, Mr. Jorgenson.

WITNESS: Sure enough, when we landed again on Earth at 00:06 A.M. Zeepsday, we found a deserted planet.

JUDGE: Deserted planet?

WITNESS: Deserted indeed, your honor. The cities, highways and homes of Earth were there as they had always been; but they were untenanted by a living soul. We stared, amazed. Here was the broad expanse of lands—

JUDGE: Excuse me a minute. Is the witness by any chance an amateur poet or writer?

WITNESS *(with a mild rush of circulatory fluid to the face)*: As a matter of fact, I am, in a slight way. How did your honor guess? I've actually published a few minor items in *Literary Frontiers*. Not for money, of course. I don't believe in commercializing my art, but—

JUDGE: The bench applauds the witness's altruism; but perhaps, in these sordid legal chambers, it would be better if the witness restrained himself to ordinary prose.

WITNESS: No place is too sordid for the soul of poetry to enter—

JUDGE *(somewhat grimly)*: Perhaps not; but until it is admitted as a witness, it will have to preserve the order of this courtroom by remaining silent. Continue, Mr. Paulson.

DEFENDANT: Go ahead, Mr. Jorgenson.

WITNESS: Well—I mean—anyway, there weren't any people there. I made some tests.

JUDGE: Of this illusion.

WITNESS: Yes, your honor. I had wished to expose a few guinea pigs or hamsters as test subjects first. But it turned out to be unnecessary. As far as my tests could distinguish, this was good, perfectly experienceable time, comparable to Earth's own in every respect.

DEFENDANT: As a result of this experience, what was your conclusion on our return at the end of twenty-four hours to normal Earth Thursday?

WITNESS: It was my conclusion that Earth had an extra day available in every week, of which we humans had been failing to take advantage.

DEFENDANT: Thank you, Mr. Jorgenson. That is all.

JUDGE: Cross-examination, Mr. Usussis?

PLAINTIFF: No cross-examination, your honor. I would like to compliment the witness on his fair testimony to this illusion.

JUDGE: I'm sure the witness is gratified. You may step down, Mr. Jorgenson. Any more witnesses, Mr. Paulson?

DEFENDANT: Your honor, at this point I would like to call myself as a witness—that is, I would like to make a statement for the record and the information of the court.

JUDGE: Is there no other way of bringing this information out, Mr. Paulson? Can't you put someone else on the stand who was present and elicit the information by questioning?

DEFENDANT: Unfortunately not, your honor. I was alone at the time in question.

JUDGE: I am against it. This sort of thing simplifies matters enormously and is against all legal tradition. However, if you must, I suppose you must. Go ahead.

DEFENDANT: On first discovering and experiencing Zeepsday for myself, I must admit I was overjoyed. Here was a boon for Earth, indeed. One extra day in the week—one extra day to get all those things done that people were never having the time to get done. One extra day for resting, for visiting, for reestablishing family ties. What could the human race not accomplish now? You all know our human record for rapid technological development—
(Murmurs of shocked protest from the courtroom audience.)

JUDGE *(sternly)*: No propaganda, Mr. Paulson. I've already had to warn the plaintiff about that. I don't want to have to speak to either of you again in this regard.

DEFENDANT: Sorry, your honor—I got carried away. As I said, I thought of all the benefits Zeepsday could bring my world. I was enthusiastic. I went to bed that Thursday night happy, having arranged with the plaintiff—who by sheer chance happened to have a friend who is factory comptroller general back on Sloon—to sign a contract the

following day for purchase of various useful Sloonian
commodities. Such items as nine-day clocks, four hundred
and seventeen day calendars, and other items, with last,
but not least, the equipment to dilate time sufficiently to
make Zeepsday planetwide on Earth. The next morning,
however, I awoke with some doubt in mind. I thought to
myself, as I was brushing my teeth—

*(Wild screech from the back of the courtroom. General
consternation as a Daffyd from Lyx is carried out, his pe-
tals stiff and rigid in a state of hysterical shock.)*

JUDGE *(pounding)*: Order! Order! This sort of oc-
curance is taking place far too frequently of late. The
bailiff clearly announced at the beginning of this sitting
that those who feared offense to personal and delicate
sensibilities were warned to retire. The gentlebeing from
Lyx saw with perfect clarity that the defendant in this
case is of a dentate species, and should have forseen that
mention of teeth or chewing might very well enter the discussion. A mature entity should be responsible for his own
emotional welfare, and not expect this court to shoulder
that burden for him . . . Continue.

DEFENDANT: As I say, the next morning I found myself,
while not exactly at that time suspicious, somewhat more
sober in my assessment of the good to come from
Zeepsday on Earth. What, I asked myself, about the legal
status of this new day? Should it be a holiday or a work-
day? What would Congress say? How would the labor
unions react? What, in particular, would be the position
taken by the powerful bloc represented by the votes of
school-age children? Would Zeepsday, in short, really
prove to be an unmixed blessing?

JUDGE *(graciously)*: Your reflective caution does you
credit, Mr. Paulson, if—

DEFENDANT *(with equal graciousness)*: I thank your
honor. Those were practically the words with which the
plaintiff sought to reassure me later on that same day
when we met for the signing of the contract.

JUDGE *(sternly)*:—*if*, I was going to say, Mr. Paulson,
before you interrupted me, it can be proved. While I, myself, would be inclined to give you the benefit of the doubt

in this respect, this is after all a court of law; and we are concerned only with the facts. For proper substantiation you should have a witness to your sensible thoughts.

DEFENDANT: As a matter of fact, I have, your honor. Shortly before the plaintiff arrived with his contract, I expressed these same doubts to my secretary. If you will allow me to put Miss Jolman back on the stand—

PLAINTIFF: Objection! The witness in question is in court and has just heard the defendant claim the attitude under scrutiny. How do we know that she will not confuse these recent statements with those the defendant may have made earlier—
(Murmurs of protest from the audience. Cries of Shame! from a Tyrannosauroid Sapiens, who is ejected by the bailiff for disturbing the court.)

JUDGE: The plaintiff has already been answered concerning the admissibility of the question of prejudice in a witness. May the bench add that it feels no doubt about the competence of this witness. Overruled. Miss Jolman, will you take the stand, please?
(The witness ascends the stand.)

JUDGE: Mr. Paulson—

DEFENDANT: Thank you, your honor. Marge—will you tell the court what I said to you?

WITNESS *(tremulously)*: I'll never forget it.

DEFENDANT *(clearing throat noisily)*: Just the facts, Marge.

WITNESS: I remember every word. "Marge, Honey," you said to me, "I wonder if I'm really doing the right thing? You know you have to be tough to be a purchasing press agent, Marge, when billions of interstellar credits of currency depend on your unofficial decision. And I've always been tough. But now I'm starting to wonder. What sort of a world is it going to be for humans here on Earth—for you and me—us, Marge, if this deal goes through? What kind of a world for future generations, with a Zeepsday in it? All of a sudden, that's important to me—" and then you took me in your arms—

DEFENDANT: Please, Marge, just the facts.

WITNESS: "—because of you, Marge," you said, "because I love you." *(Witness is suddenly afflicted by a rush of circulatory fluid to the face similar to that which affected a previous witness.)* And I said, "I love you, too—" and then you asked me to marry you and we talked for a while; and after a while I said, about Zeepsday—you ought to do what you thought was right and then things would be sure to turn out for the best.

DEFENDANT *(mopping brow)*: Thank you, Marge. That's all.

(Spontaneous applause as the witness leaves the stand, quelled by the Judge pounding for order and interrupted by cries of Objection! *from the Plaintiff.)*

JUDGE: Yes, Mr. Usussis?

PLAINTIFF: I demand to know whether the defendant is to be allowed to sway the court by these unfair emotional appeals. I demand—

JUDGE: The bench is *not* swayed. *(adds, sternly)*: And I warn you against imputing such a weakness to the bench under pain of being held in contempt of this court. Now, do you wish to examine the witness?

PLAINTIFF: I have no interest in this witness whatsoever.

JUDGE: Yes—or no?

PLAINTIFF *(more subdued)*: No, your honor.

JUDGE: Very well. Mr. Paulson?

DEFENDANT: It only remains for me to state that my misgivings were well founded. Shortly after signing the contract, I was to discover that the Zeepsday Mr. Jorgenson and I had been taken to visit was not native Earth time at all, but a deliberately contrived intrusion of Sloonian time into our Earth week—

(Pandemonium in the courtroom. Cries of Objection! *from the plaintiff's compound.)*

JUDGE: Order! *Order!* Mr. Usussis, what is it this time?

PLAINTIFF *(excitedly)*: The defendant's statement is unsubstantiated, unfair, and unprovable.

DEFENDANT: But it's the truth.

PLAINTIFF: That is beside the point. We have agreed that everything you experienced was nothing more than an illusion. An illusion does not exist. Therefore whether it is truthful or not is irrelevant.

DEFENDANT (*turning to Judge*): And just there, exactly, is my point, your honor. The plaintiff has admitted that everything up to the signing of the contract was based on something that did not exist—

PLAINTIFF: Which does not render the contract null and void—"A commercial agreement shall be binding without respect to its relation to the real universe." Nuggle *vs.* Jwickx, Galactic Court Decision 1328474639475635. You are legally committed to the purchase of twenty quintillions of galactic monetary units worth of goods from Sloon.

DEFENDANT: That I admit, provided the plaintiff wishes to enforce the contract. My point is otherwise. The contract, being a real thing with a real existence in its own right, even though the basis of it was non-existent, is unchallengeable. However, the insult for which the plaintiff has brought suit against me, having no real existence of its own, merely a *reported* existence, to be real must have a basis in reality. Since the plaintiff denies the real basis of the insult—to wit, the situation and causes out of which it stemmed—and further denies any physical basis for the insult—that is, the plaintiff insists that he possesses only *three* tentacles—then the insult, having no real basis, has no real existence. In other words, not only was the original insult beyond the authority of this court to punish, but repetitions of this insult would likewise be so. I ask dismissal of the plaintiff's suit on the basis of non-existence of cause.

PLAINTIFF (*wildly*): This is barefaced robbery. He knows that I'd never be accepted by polite society on Sloon again if I permitted myself to be freely insulted. Your honor, he's out to make me tear up the contract by forcing myself to deny having ever been associated with him or it. If you permit him to continue to insult me, I'll have no alternative. I—

JUDGE: Order! The plaintiff will restrain himself! (*Plaintiff subsides with twitching tentacles.*) Now, if the plaintiff wishes to rebut the defendant's contentions, he will do so in a legal manner.

PLAINTIFF (*shakily, but with growing strength and confidence*): Pardon me, your honor. I had forgotten that I had a legal answer at my disposal. The defendant forgets that an injunction need not necessarily show real cause to be granted. *Fear* of insult is sufficient reason for an injunction to be granted enjoining restraint upon one or more parties. Then, if insult occurs and witnesses to it can be found, no further proof is needed. Twingo *vs.* ¼Kud, Galactic Court Decision 19483738473645485937. I rest my case.

JUDGE: Any further comment, Mr. Paulson?

DEFENDANT: No, your honor, except to point out that the whole economic system of Earth trembles upon the outcome of this trial—

JUDGE: That has no bearing on this case, which is solely a question of manners and morals between two private parties, irrespective of race or residence. I see no reason to stretch out this hearing, if both parties have concluded their pleadings. It will not be necessary for me to retire to consider my decision, since the law in this case is perfectly clear and allows of only one interpretation and one conclusion. I myself am of course completely impartial and would have nothing but comtempt for anyone who might pretend to see behind this trial a clever con game by an unscrupulous being who has seen an opportunity to take advantage of a particular current legal condition. But even if I were so uncontemptuous of such a point of view as to share it myself, it would remain my duty to render my decision with the same scrupulosity as if I were an outspoken adherent of that being, be he tentacled or be he not tentacled and regardless of the number of tentacles. The defendant has presented an ingenious, and perhaps some of the prejudiced among the spectators might say, a gallant structure of logic to show cause why an injunction should not be issued restraining him from insulting the plaintiff in terms of the number of tentacles the plaintiff possesses. The court is forced to admit that he is perfectly correct in his contention that the original insult under the conditions alleged had no real existence. However, the plaintiff's contention that real cause is not necessary to an injunction is also correct. Consequently: Be it ordered by this court that Garth Paulson, Human presently residing on the planet Earth, be restrained from expressing an opinion about the number of tentacles possessed by Drang Usussis, Nesbler of the planet Sloon, where such expression may be construed to be damaging or injurious to the sensibilities of the said Drang Usussis, Nesbler of the planet Sloon. Further, if the said Garth Paulson shall, in defiance of the order of this court, so express such an opinion, be it ordered that he be visited by the full penalty of the law in such cases: to wit confinement for not less than two years in the place or places determined by a person to be appointed by this court, who shall have him in custody. Full expense of both prisoner and custodian to be borne by the plaintiff in this suit. Unka, a Bolver from Bol, decisioning. . . . Clerk, you will provide all interested parties with copies of his decision.

DEFENDANT (*shouting*): Your honor, don't leave the bench! Let go of me, Marge—I know what I'm doing! To hell with the penalty. Listen, Usussis! I don't care what they do to me. You've got four tentacles and you know it—
(*Bloodcurdling scream from the plaintiff. Uproar in the court.*)

DEFENDANT (*shouting more loudly*):—not three, *four!* Everybody knows it; and if you try to come to Earth and enforce that contract you swindled me out of, there isn't a red-blooded human that won't stand up to you, face to face, and point out that *fourth* tentacle. Listen, folks, do you know why he doesn't want to admit to that fourth tentacle?
(*Plaintiff fights furiously to reach defendant. Is restrained by well-wishers and the court bailiff.*)

DEFENDANT: Do you know what he uses it for? That fourth tentacle is the one he uses to zorrgle his grob! (*Plaintiff shrieks and faints.*) Didn't know I knew you were a grob-zorrgler, did you, Usussis? But I do. I—

JUDGE: Order! Order! Be silent, Mr. Paulson. Order in the court! Before I order it cleared!
(*The noise in the court gradually subsides, except in the compound of the plaintiff, where the plaintiff, now revived and convulsed with shame, is furiously gnashing his teeth and tearing up a contract-sized sheaf of legal papers.*)

JUDGE: Bailiff, apprehend the prisoner and bring him before me.
(*Bailiff does so.*)

JUDGE: Garth Paulson, you have just been witnessed in the flagrant act of violating an injunction issued by this court. Do you plead guilty or not guilty?

PRISONER: Guilty, your honor. And let me say that I would gladly do it again—and *will* do it again, if necessary.

JUDGE: Silence! The law is not to be flouted with impunity, whatever good motives the prisoner may conceive himself to have.

PRISONER: Give me liberty or give me death.

JUDGE: You are forbidden to attempt to instruct the court. I hereby sentence you to two years in terms of the time on your native world, in the custody of a person to be appointed by the court, who will determine the places and conditions of your confinement. And I appoint as custodian of this prisoner, the Human female Marge Jolman, provided that, the better to carry out the duties hereby imposed on her by the court, she submits to the mating ceremony with the prisoner without delay. Expenses of both prisoner and jailer to be borne by the plaintiff in this case for the duration of the sentence. That's all. Court concluded. Clear the room, Bailiff.

PRISONER: Thank you, Judge.

JUDGE (*with twinkles in his top dozen eyes*): Don't thank me, Mr. Paulson. It was a pleasure to put a spoke in the wheel of that sneaky Sloonian's finagling. Where will you children be going on this honeymoon of yours at Ususss' expense? May I recommend the resort areas on Elysia? Nothing but the best, there.

PRISONER: We'll think about it, Judge.

JUDGE: There's just one thing, though. How did you manage to discover that Ususss had actually salted your week with that fake Zeepsday made out of Sloonian time?

I've always understood it was almost impossible for even an expert to distinguish alien from natural time when it's been firmly intruded in the temporal structure.

PRISONER: Well, I know it's supposed to be—

CUSTODIAN OF THE PRISONER: It's just that Garth is so sensitive—

PRISONER: Let me tell him, Marge. You see, Judge, there was nothing you could put your finger on, at first. But the morning I signed the contract I had begun to itch; and shortly after I did sign the contract, I took a look at the wrist I was scratching; and the truth jumped at me.

JUDGE: Ah, yes, I remember something being said about that.

PRISONER: Exactly.

JUDGE: You saw on your wrist . . . ?

PRISONER: Hives. I was allergic to Sloonian time.

JUDGE: Marvelous! Truly virtue triumphs in the most unexpected— Clerk, what are you doing, putting all this down? The court has concluded. Close your record.

RECORD CLOSED.

TRANSCRIPT CONCLUDED.

LULUNGOMEENA

Blame Clay Harbank, if you will, for what happened at Station 563 of the Sirius Sector; or blame Willian Peterborough, whom we called the Kid. I blame no one. But I am a Dorsai man.

The trouble began the day the kid joined the station, with his quick hands and his gambler's mind, and found that Clay, alone of all the men there, would not gamble with him—for all that he claimed to having been a gambling man himself. And so it ran on for four years of service together.

But the beginning of the end was the day they came off shift together.

They had been out on a duty circuit of the frontier station that housed the twenty of us—searching the outer bubble for signs of blows or leaks. It's a slow two-hour tramp, that duty, even outside the station on the surface of the asteroid where there's no gravity to speak of. We, in the recreation room, off duty, could tell by the sound of their voices as the inner port sucked open and the clanging clash of them removing their spacesuits came echoing to us along the metal corridor, that the Kid had been needling Clay through the whole tour.

"Another day," came the Kid's voice, "another fifty credits. And how's the piggy bank coming along, Clay?"

There was a slight pause, and I could see Clay carefully controlling his features and his voice. Then his pleasant baritone, softened by the burr of his Tarsusian accent, came smoothly to us.

"Like a gentleman, Kid," he answered. "He never overeats and so he runs no danger of indigestion."

It was a neat answer, based on the fact that the Kid's own service account was swollen with his winnings from the rest of the crew. But the Kid was too thick-skinned for rapier thrusts. He laughed; and they finished removing their equipment and came on into the recreation room.

They made a striking picture as they entered, for they were enough alike to be brothers—although father and son would have been a more likely relationship, considering the difference in their ages. Both were tall, dark, wide-shouldered men with lean faces, but experience had weathered the softer lines from Clay's face and drawn thin parentheses about the corners of his mouth. There were other differences, too; but you could see in the Kid the youth that Clay had been, and in Clay the man that the Kid would some day be.

"Hi, Clay," I said.

"Hello, Mort," he said, sitting down beside me.

"Hi, Mort," said the Kid.

I ignored him; and for a moment he tensed. I could see the anger flame up in the ebony depths of his black pupils under the heavy eyebrows. He was a big man; but I come from the Dorsai Planets and a Dorsai man fights to the death, if he fights at all. And, in consequence, among ourselves, we of Dorsai are a polite people.

But politeness was wasted on the Kid—as was Clay's delicate irony. With men like the Kid, you have to use a club.

We were in bad shape. The twenty of us at Frontier Station 563, on the periphery of the human area just beyond Sirius, had gone sour, and half the men had applications in for transfer. The trouble between Clay and the Kid was splitting the station wide open.

We were all in the Frontier Service for money; that was the root of the trouble. Fifty credits a day is good pay—but you have to sign up for a ten-year hitch. You can buy yourself out—but that costs a hundred thousand. Figure it out for yourself. Nearly six years if you saved every penny you got. So most go in with the idea of staying the full decade.

That was Clay's idea. He had gambled most of his life away. He had won and lost several fortunes. Now he was getting old and tired and he wanted to go back—to Lulungomeena, on the little planet of Tarsus, which was the place he had come from as a young man.

But he was through with gambling. He said money made that way never stuck, but ran away again like quicksilver. So he drew his pay and banked it.

But the Kid was out for a killing. Four years of play with the rest of the crew had given him more than enough to buy his way out and leave him a nice stake. And perhaps he would have done just that, if it hadn't been that the Service account of Clay's drew him like an El Dorado. He could not go off and leave it. So he stayed with the outfit, riding the older man unmercifully.

He harped continually on two themes. He pretended to disbelieve that Clay had ever been a gambler; and he derided Lulungomeena, Clay's birthplace: the older man's goal and dream, and the one thing he could be drawn into talk about. For, to Clay, Lulungomeena was beautiful, the most wonderful spot in the Universe; and with an old man's sick longing for home, he could not help saying so.

"Mort," said the Kid, ignoring the rebuff and sitting down beside us, "what's a Hixabrod like?"

My club had not worked so well, after all. Perhaps, I, too, was slipping. Next to Clay, I was the oldest man on the crew, which was why we were close friends. I scowled at the Kid.

"Why?" I asked.

"We're having one for a visitor," he said.

Immediately, all talk around the recreation room ceased and all attention was focused on the Kid. All aliens had to clear through a station like ours when they crossed the frontier from one of the other great galactic power groups into human territory. But isolated as Station 563 was, it was seldom an alien came our way, and when one did, it was an occasion.

Even Clay succumbed to the general interest. "I didn't know that," he said. "How'd you find out?"

"The notice came in over the receiver when you were down checking the atmosphere plant," answered the Kid with a careless wave of his hand. "I'd already filed it when you came up. What'll he be like, Mort?"

I had knocked around more than any of them—even Clay. This was my second stretch in the Service. I remembered back about twenty years, to the Denebian Trouble.

"Stiff as a poker," I said. "Proud as Lucifer, honest as sunlight and tight as a camel on his way through the eye of a needle. Sort of a humanoid, but with a face like a collie dog. You know the Hixabrodian reputation, don't you?"

Somebody at the back of the crowd said no, although they may have been doing it just to humor me. Like Clay with his Lulungomeena, old age was making me garrulous.

"They're the first and only mercenary ambassadors in

the known Universe," I said. "A Hixabrod can be hired, but he can't be influenced, bribed or forced to come up with anything but the cold truth—and, brother, it's cold the way a Hixabrod serves it up to you. That's why they're so much in demand. If any kind of political dispute comes up, from planetary to interalien power group levels, both sides have to hire a Hixabrod to represent them in the discussions. That way they know the other side is being honest with them. The opposing Hixabrod is a living guarantee of that."

"He sounds good," said the Kid. "What say we get together and throw him a good dinner during his twenty-four hour stopover?"

"You won't get much in the way of thanks from him," I grunted. "They aren't built that way."

"Let's do it anyway," said the Kid. "Be a little excitement for a change."

A murmur of approval ran through the room. I was outvoted. Even Clay liked the idea.

"Hixabrods eat what we eat, don't they?" asked the Kid, making plans. "Okay, then, soups, salad, meats, champagne and brandy—" he ran on, ticking the items off on his fingers. For a moment, his enthusiasm had us all with him. But then, just as the end, he couldn't resist getting in one more dig at Clay.

"Oh, yes," he finished, "and for entertainment, you can tell him about Lulungomeena, Clay."

Clay winced—not obviously, but we all saw a shadow cross his face. Lulungomeena on Tarsus, his birthplace, held the same sort of obsession for him that his Service account held for the Kid; but he could not help being aware that he was prone to let his tongue run away on the subject of its beauty. For it was where he belonged, in the stomach-twisting, throat-aching way that sometimes only talk can relieve.

I was a Dorsai man and older than the rest. I understood. No one should make fun of the bond tying a man to his home world. It is as real as it is intangible. And to joke about it is cruel.

But the Kid was too young to know that yet. He was fresh from Earth—Earth, where none of the rest of us had been, yet which, hundreds of years before, had been the origin of us all. He was eager and strong and contemptuous of emotion. He saw, as the rest of us recognized also, that Clay's tendency to let his talk wander ever to the wonder of Lulungomeena was the first slight crack in what had once been a man of unflawed steel. It was the first creeping decay of age.

But, unlike the rest of us, who hid our boredom out of sympathy, the Kid saw here a chance to break Clay and his resolution to do no more gambling. So he struck out constantly at this one spot so deeply vital that Clay's self-possession was no defense.

Now, at this last blow, the little fires of anger gathered in the older man's eyes.

"That's enough," he said harshly. "Leave Lulungomeena out of the discussion."

"I'm willing to," said the Kid. "But somehow you keep reminding me of it. That and the story that you once were a gambler. If you won't prove the last one, how can you expect me to believe all you say about the first?"

The veins stood out on Clay's forehead; but he controlled himself.

"I've told you a thousand times," he said between his teeth. "Money made by gambling doesn't stick. You'll find that out for yourself one of these days."

"Words," said the Kid airily. "Only words."

For a second, Clay stood staring whitely at him, not even breathing. I don't know if the Kid realized his danger or cared, but I didn't breathe, either, until Clay's chest expanded and he turned abruptly and walked out of the recreation room. We heard his bootsteps die away down the corridor toward his room in the dormitory section.

Later, I braced the Kid about it. It was his second shift time, when most of the men in the recreation room had to go on duty. I ran the Kid to the ground in the galley where he was fixing himself a sandwich. He looked up, a little startled, more than a little on the defensive, as I came in.

"Oh, hi, Mort," he said with a pretty good imitation of casualness. "What's up?"

"You," I told him. "Are you looking for a fight with Clay?"

"No," he drawled with his mouth full. "I wouldn't exactly say that."

"Well, that's what you're liable to get."

"Look, Mort," he said, and then paused until he had swallowed. "Don't you think Clay's old enough to look after himself?"

I felt a slight and not unpleasant shiver run down between my shoulder-blades and my eyes began to grow hot. It was my Dorsai blood again. It must have showed on my face, for the Kid, who had been sitting negligently on one edge of the galley table, got up in a hurry.

"Hold on, Mort," he said. "nothing personal."

I fought the old feeling down and said as calmly as I could, "I just dropped by to tell you something. Clay has been around a lot longer than you have. I'd advise you to lay off him."

"Afraid he'll get hurt?"

"No," I answered. "I'm afraid you will."

The Kid snorted with sudden laughter, half choking on his sandwich. "Now I get it. You think I'm too young to take care of myself."

"Something like that, but not the way you think. I want to tell you something about yourself and you don't have to say whether I'm right or wrong—you'll let me know without words."

"Hold it," he said, turning red. "I didn't come out here to get psyched."

"You'll get it just the same. And it's not for you only— it's for all of us, because men thrown together as closely as we are choose up sides whenever there's conflict, and that's as dangerous for the rest of us as it is for you."

"Then the rest of you can stay out of it."

"We can't," I said. "What affects one of us affects us all. Now I'll tell you what you're doing. You came out here expecting to find glamor and excitement. You found monotony and boredom instead, not realizing that that's what space is like almost all the time."

He picked up his coffee container. "And now you'll say I'm trying to create my own excitement at Clay's expense. Isn't that the standard line?"

"I wouldn't know; I'm not going to use it, because that's not how I see what you're doing. Clay is adult enough to stand the monotony and boredom if they'll get him what he wants. He's also learned how to live with others and with himself. He doesn't have to prove himself by beating down somebody either half or twice his age."

He took a drink and set the container down on the table. "And I do?"

"All youngsters do. It's their way of experimenting with their potentialities and relationships with other people. When they find that out, they can give it up—they're mature then—although some never do. I think you will, eventually. The sooner you stop doing it here, though, the better it'll be for you and us."

"And if I don't?" he challenged.

"This isn't college back on Earth or some other nice, safe home planet, where hazing can be a nuisance, but where it's possible to escape it by going somewhere else. There isn't any 'somewhere else' here. Unless the one doing the hazing sees how reckless and dangerous it is, the one getting hazed takes it as long as he can—and then something happens."

"So it's Clay you're really worried about, after all."

"Look, get it through your skull. Clay's a man and he's been through worse than this before. You haven't. If anybody's going to get hurt, it'll be you."

He laughed and headed for the corridor door. He was still laughing as it slammed behind him. I let him go. There's no use pushing a bluff after it's failed to work.

The next day, the Hixabrod came. His name was Dor Lassos. He was typical of his race, taller than the tallest of us by half a head, with a light green skin and that impassive Hixabrodian canine face.

I missed his actual arrival, being up in the observation tower checking meteor paths. The station itself was well protected, but some of the ships coming in from time to time could have gotten in trouble with a few of the larger ones that slipped by us at intervals in that particular sector. When I did get free, Dor Lassos had already been assigned to his quarters and the time of official welcoming was over.

I went down to see him anyhow on the off-chance that we had mutual acquaintants either among his race or mine. Both of our peoples are few enough in number, God knows, so the possibility wasn't too far-fetched. And, like Clay, I yearned for anything connected with my home.

"*Wer velt d'hatchen, Hixabrod*—" I began, walking into his apartment—and stopped short.

The Kid was there. He looked at me with an odd expression on his face.

"Do you speak Hixabrodian?" he asked incredulously.

I nodded. I had learned it on extended duty during the Denebian Trouble. Then I remembered my manners and turned back to the Hixabrod; but he was already started on his answer.

"*En gles Ter, I tu, Dorsaiven,*" returned the collie face, expressionlessly. "*Da Tr'amgen lang. Met zurres nebent?*"

"Em getluc. Me mi Dorsai fene. Nono ne—ves luc Les Lassos?"

He shook his head.

Well, it had been a shot in the dark anyway. There was only the faintest chance that he had known our old interpreter at the time of the Denebian Trouble. The Hixabrods have no family system of nomenclature. They take their names from the names of older Hixabrods they admire or like. I bowed politely to him and left.

It was not until later that it occurred to me to wonder what in the Universe the Kid could find to talk about with a Hixabrod.

I actually was worried about Clay. Since my bluff with the Kid had failed, I thought I might perhaps try with Clay himself. At first I waited for an opportune moment to turn up; but following the last argument with the Kid, he'd been sticking to his quarters. I finally scrapped the casual approach and went to see him.

I found him in his quarters, reading. It was a little shocking to find that tall, still athletic figure in a dressing gown like an old man, eyes shaded by the lean fingers of one long hand, poring over the little glow of a scanner with the lines unreeling before his eyes. But he looked up as I came in, and the smile on his face was the smile I had grown familiar with over four years of close living together.

"What's that?" I asked, nodding at the book scanner.

He set it down and the little light went out, the lines stopped unreeling.

"A bad novel," he said, smiling, "by a poor author. But they're both Tarsusian."

I took the chair he had indicated. "Mind if I speak straight out, Clay?"

"Go ahead," he invited.

"The Kid," I said bluntly. "And you. The two of you can't go on this way."

"Well, old fire-eater," answered Clay lightly. "what've you got to suggest?"

"Two things. And I want you to think both of them over carefully before answering. First, we see if we can't get up a nine-tenths majority here in the station and petition him out as incompatible."

Clay slowly shook his head. "We can't do that, Mort."

"I think I can get the signatures if I ask it," I said. "Everybody's pretty tired of him . . . They'd come across."

"It's not that and you know it," said Clay. "Transfer by petition isn't supposed to be prejudicial, but you and I know it is. He'd be switched to some hard-case station, get in worse trouble there, and end up in a penal post generally shot to hell. He'd know who to blame for it, and he'd hate us for the rest of his life."

"What of it? Let him hate us."

"I'm a Tarsusian. It'd bother me and I couldn't do it."

"All right," I said. "Dropping that, then, you've got nearly seven years in, total, and half the funds you need to buy out. I've got nearly enough saved, in spite of myself, to make up the rest. In addition, for your retirement, I'll sign over to you my pay for the three years I've got left. Take that and get out of the Service. It isn't what you figured on having, but half a loaf . . ."

"And how about your home-going?" he asked.

"Look at me."

He looked; and I knew what he was seeing—the broken nose, the scars, the lined face—the Dorsai face.

"I'll never go home," I said.

He sat looking at me for a long moment more, and I fancied I saw a little light burn deep in back of his eyes. But then the light went out and I knew that I'd lost with him, too.

"Maybe not," he said quietly. "But I'm not going to be the one that keeps you from it."

I left him to his book.

Shifts are supposed to run continuously, with someone on duty all the time. However, for special occasions, like this dinner we had arranged for the Hixabrod, it was possible, by getting work done ahead of time and picking the one four-hour stretch during the twenty-four when there were no messages or ships due in, to assemble everybody in the station on an off-duty basis.

So we were all there that evening, in the recreation room, which had been cleared and set up with a long table for the dinner. We finished our cocktails, sat down at the table and the meal began.

As it will, the talk during the various courses turned to things outside the narrow limits of our present lives. Remembrances of places visited, memories of an earlier life, and the comparison of experiences, some of them pretty weird, were the materials of which our table talk was built.

Unconsciously, all of us were trying to draw the Hixabrod out. But he sat in his place at the head of the table between Clay and myself, with the Kid a little farther down, preserving a frosty silence until the dessert had been disposed of and the subject of Media unexpectedly came up.

"—Media," said the Kid. "I've heard of Media. It's a little planet, but it's supposed to have everything from soup to nuts on it in the way of life. There's one little life-form there that's claimed to contain something of value to every metabolism. It's called—let me see now—it's called—"

"It is called *nygti*," supplied Dor Lassos, suddenly, in a metallic voice. "A small quadruped with a highly complex nervous system and a good deal of fatty tissue. I visited the planet over eighty years ago, before it was actually opened up to general travel. The food stores spoiled and we had the opportunity of testing out the theory that it will provide sustenance for almost any kind of known intelligent being."

He stopped.

"Well?" demanded the Kid. "Since you're here to tell the story, I assume the animal kept you alive."

"I and the humans aboard the ship found the *nygti* quite nourishing," said Dor Lassos. "Unfortunately, we had several Micrushni from Polaris also aboard."

"And those?" asked someone.

"A highly developed but inelastic life-form," said Dor Lassos, sipping from his brandy glass. "They went into convulsions and died."

I had had some experience with Hixabrodian ways and I knew that it was not sadism, but a complete detachment that had prompted this little anecdote. But I could see a wave of distaste ripple down the room. No life-form is so universally well liked as the Micrushni, a delicate iridescent jellyfish race with a bent toward poetry and philosophy.

The men at the table drew away almost visibly from Dor Lassos. But that affected him no more than if they had applauded loudly. Only in very limited ways are the Hixabrod capable of empathy where other races are concerned.

"That's too bad," said Clay slowly. "I have always liked the Micrushni." He had been drinking somewhat heavily and the seemingly innocuous statement came out like a half-challenge.

Dor Lassos' cold brown eyes turned and rested on him. Whatever he saw, whatever conclusions he came to, however, were hidden behind his emotionless face.

"In general," he said flatly, "a truthful race."

That was the closest a Hixabrod could come to praise, and I expected the matter to drop there. But the Kid spoke up again.

"Not like us humans," he said. "Eh, Dor Lassos?"

I glared at him from behind Dor Lassos' head. But he went recklessly on.

"I said, 'Not like us humans, eh?'" he repeated loudly. The Kid had also apparently been drinking freely, and his voice grated on the sudden silence of the room.

"The human race varies," stated the Hixabrod emotionlessly. "You have some individuals who approach truth. Otherwise, the human race is not notably truthful."

It was a typical, deadly accurate Hixabrodian response. Dor Lassos would have answered in the same words if his throat was to have been cut for them the minute they left his mouth. Again, it should have shut the Kid up, and again it apparently failed.

"Ah, yes," said the Kid. "Some approach truth, but in general we are untruthful. But you see, Dor Lassos, a certain amount of human humor is associated with lies. Some of tell lies just for fun."

Dor Lassos drank from his brandy glass and said nothing.

"Of course," the Kid went on, "sometimes a human thinks he's being funny with his lies when he isn't. Some lies are just boring, particularly when you're forced to hear them over and over again. But on the other hand, there are some champion liars who are so good that even you would find their untruths humorous."

Clay sat upright suddenly, and the sudden start of his movement sent the brandy slopping out over the rim of his glass and onto the white tablecloth. He stared at the Kid.

I looked at them all—at Clay, at the Kid and at Dor Lassos; and an ugly premonition began to form in my brain.

"I do not believe I should," said Dor Lassos.

"Ah, but you should listen to a real expert," said the Kid feverishly, "when he has a good subject to work on.

Now, for example, take the matter of home worlds. What is your home world, Hixa, like?"

I had heard enough and more than enough to confirm the suspicion forming within me. Without drawing any undue attention to myself, I rose and left the room.

The alien made a dry sound in his throat and his voice followed me as I went swiftly down the empty corridor.

"It is very beautiful," he said in his adding machine tones. "Hixa has a diameter of thirty-eight thousand universal meters. It possesses twenty-three great mountain ranges and seventeen large bodies of salt water . . ."

The sound of his voice died away and I left it behind me.

I went directly through the empty corridors and up the ladder to the communications shack. I went in the door without pausing, without—in neglect of all duty rules—glancing at the automatic printer to see if any fresh message out of routine had arrived, without bothering to check the transmitter to see that it was keyed into the automatic location signal for approaching spacecraft.

All this I ignored and went directly to the file where the incoming messages are kept.

I flicked the tab and went back to the file of two days previous, skimming through the thick sheaf of transcripts under that dateline. And there, beneath the heading "Notices of Arrivals," I found it, the message announcing the coming of Dor Lassos. I ran my finger down past the statistics on our guest to the line of type that told me where the Hixabrod's last stop had been.

Tarsus.

Clay was my friend. And there is a limit to what a man can take without breaking. On a wall of the communications shack was a roster of the men at our station. I drew the Dorsai sign against the name of William Peterborough, and checked my gun out of the arms locker.

I examined the magazine. It was loaded. I replaced the magazine, put the gun inside my jacket, and went back to the dinner.

Dor Lassos was still talking.

". . . The flora and the fauna are maintained in such excellent natural balance that no local surplus has exceeded one per cent of the normal population for any species in the last sixty thousand years. Life on Hixa is regular and predictable. The weather is controlled within the greatest limits of feasibility."

As I took my seat, the machine voice of the Hixabrod hesitated for just a moment, then gathered itself, and went on: "One day I shall turn there."

"A pretty picture," said the Kid. He was leaning forward over the table now, his eyes bright, his teeth bared in a smile. "A very attractive home world. But I regret to inform you, Dor Lassos, that I've been given to understand that it pales into insignificance when compared to one other spot in the Galaxy."

The Hixabrod are warriors, too. Dor Lassos' features remained expressionless, but his voice deepened and rang through the room.

"Your planet?"

"I wish it were," returned the Kid with the same wolfish smile. "I wish I could lay claim to it. But this place is so wonderful that I doubt if I would be allowed there. In fact," the Kid went on, "I have never seen it. But I have been hearing about it for some years now. And either it is the most wonderful place in the Universe, or else the man who has been telling me about it—"

I pushed my chair back and started to rise, but Clay's hand clamped on my arm and held me down.

"You were saying—" he said to the Kid, who had been interrupted by my movement.

"—The man who has been telling me about it," said the Kid, deliberately, "is one of those champion liars I was telling Dor Lassos about."

Once more I tried to get to my feet, but Clay was there before me. Tall and stiff, he stood at the end of the table.

"My right—" he said out of the corner of his mouth to me.

Slowly and with meaning, he picked up his brandy glass and threw the glass straight into the Kid's face. It bounced on the table in front of him and sent brandy flying over the front of the Kid's immaculate dress uniform.

"Get your gun!" ordered Clay.

Now the Kid was on his feet. In spite of the fact that I knew he had planned this, emotion had gotten the better of him at the end. His face was white with rage. He leaned on the edge of the table and fought with himself to carry it through as he had originally intended.

"Why guns?" he said. His voice was thick with restraint, as he struggled to control himself.

"You called me a liar."

"Will guns tell me if you are?" The Kid straightened up,

breathing more easily; and his laugh was harsh in the room. "Why use guns when it's possible to prove the thing one way or another with complete certainty?" His gaze swept the room and came back to Clay.

"For years now you've been telling me all sorts of things," he said. "But two things you've told me more than all the rest. One was that you used to be a gambler. The other was that Lulungomeena—your precious Lulungomeena on Tarsus—was the most wonderful place in the Universe. Is either one of those the truth?"

Clay's breath came thick and slow.

"They're both the truth," he said, fighting to keep his voice steady.

"Will you back that up?"

"With my life!"

"Ah," said the Kid mockingly, holding up his forefinger, "but I'm not asking you to back those statements up with your life—but with that neat little hoard you've been accumulating these past years. You claimed you're a gambler. Will you bet that those statements are true?"

Now, for the first time, Clay seemed to see the trap.

"Bet with me," invited the Kid, almost lightly. "That will prove the first statement."

"And what about the second?" demanded Clay.

"Why—" the Kid gestured with his hand toward Dor Lassos—"what further judge do we need? We have here at our table a Hixabrod." Half-turning to the alien, the Kid made him a little bow. "Let him say whether your second statement is true or not."

Once more I tried to rise from my seat and again Clay's hand shoved me down. He turned to Dor Lassos.

"Do you think you could judge such a point, sir?" he asked.

The brown inhuman eyes met his and held for a long moment.

"I have just come from Tarsus," said the Hixabrod. "I was there as a member of the Galactic Survey Team, mapping the planet. It was my duty to certify to the truth of the map."

The choice was no choice. Clay stood staring at the Hixabrod as the room waited for his answer. Rage burning within me, I looked down the table for a sign in the faces of the others that this thing might be stopped. But where I expected to see sympathy, there was nothing. Instead, there was blankness, or cynicism, or even the wet-lipped interest of men who like their excitement written in blood or tears.

And I realized with a sudden sinking of hopes that I stood alone, after all, as Clay's friend. In my own approaching age and garrulity I had not minded his talk of Lulungomeena, hour on repetitive hour. But these others had grown weary of it. Where I saw tragedy, they saw only retribution coming to a lying bore.

And what Clay saw was what I saw. His eyes went dark and cold.

"How much will you bet?" he asked.

"All I've got," responded the Kid, leaning forward eagerly "Enough and more than enough to match that bank roll of yours. The equivalent of eight years' pay."

Stiffly, without a word, Clay produced his savings book and a voucher pad. He wrote out a voucher for the whole amount and laid book and voucher on the table before Dor Lassos. The Kid, who had obviously come prepared, did the same, adding a thick pile of cash from his gambling of recent weeks.

"That's all of it?" asked Clay.

"All of it," said the Kid.

Clay nodded and stepped back.

"Go ahead," he said.

The Kid turned toward the alien.

"Dor Lassos," he said. "We appreciate your cooperation in this matter."

"I am glad to hear it," responded the Hixabrod, "since my cooperation will cost the winner of the bet a thousand credits."

The abrupt injection of this commercial note threw the Kid momentarily off stride. I, alone in the room, who knew the Hixabrod people, had expected it. But the rest had not, and it struck a sour note, which reflected back on the Kid. Up until now, the bet had seemed to most of the others like a cruel but at least honest game, concerning ourselves only. Suddenly it had become a little like hiring a paid bully to beat up a stationmate.

But it was too late now to stop; the bet had been made. Nevertheless, there were murmurs from different parts of the room.

The Kid hurried on, fearful of an interruption. Clay's savings were on his mind.

"You were a member of the mapping survey team?" he asked Dor Lassos.

"I was," said the Hixabrod.

"Then you know the planet?"

"I do."

"You know its geography?" insisted the Kid.

"I do not repeat myself." The eyes of the Hixabrod were chill and withdrawn, almost a little baleful, as they met those of the Kid.

"What kind of a planet is it?" The Kid licked his lips. He was beginning to recover his usual self-assurance. "Is it a large planet?"

"No."

"Is Tarsus a rich planet?"

"No."

"Is it a pretty planet?"

"I did not find it so."

"*Get to the point!*" snapped Clay with strained harshness.

The Kid glanced at him, savoring this moment. He turned back to the Hixabrod.

"Very well, Dor Lassos," he said, "we get to the meat of the matter. Have you ever heard of Lulungomeena?"

"Yes."

"Have you ever been to Lulungomeena?"

"I have."

"And do you truthfully—" for the first time, a fierce and burning anger flashed momentarily in the eyes of the Hixabrod; the insult the Kid had just unthinkingly given Dor Lassos was a deadly one—"*truthfully* say that in your considered opinion Lulungomeena is the most wonderful place in the Universe?"

Dor Lassos turned his gaze away from him and let it wander over the rest of the room. Now, at last, his contempt for all there was plain to be read on his face.

"*Yes, it is,*" said Dor Lassos.

He rose to his feet at the head of the stunned group around the table. From the pile of cash he extracted a thousand credits, then passed the remainder, along with the two account books and the vouchers, to Clay. Then he took one step toward the Kid.

He halted before him and offered his hands to the man—palms up, the tips of his fingers a scant couple of inches short of the Kid's face.

"My hands are clean," he said.

His fingers arced; and, suddenly, as we watched, stubby,

gleaming claws shot smoothly from those fingertips to tremble lightly against the skin of the Kid's face.

"Do you doubt the truthfulness of a Hixabrod?" his robot voice asked.

The Kid's face was white and his cheeks hollowed in fear. The needle points of the claws were very close to his eyes. He swallowed once.

"No—" he whispered.

The claws retracted. The hands returned to their owner's sides. Once more completely withdrawn and impersonal, Dor Lassos turned and bowed to us all.

"My appreciation of your courtesy," he said, the metallic tones of his voice loud in the silence.

Then he turned and, marching like a metronome, disappeared through the doorway of the recreation room and off in the direction of his quarters.

"And so we part," said Clay Harbank as we shook hands. "I hope you find the Dorsai Planets as welcome as I intend to find Lulungomeena."

I grumbled a little. "That was plain damn foolishness. You didn't have to buy me out as well."

"There were more than enough credits for the both of us," said Clay.

It was a month after the bet and the two of us were standing in the Deneb One spaceport. For miles in every direction, the great echoing building of this central terminal stretched around us. In ten minutes I was due to board my ship for the Dorsai Planets. Clay himself still had several days to wait before one of the infrequent ships to Tarsus would be ready to leave.

"The bet itself was damn foolishness," I went on, determined to find something to complain about. We Dorsai do not enjoy these moments of emotion. But a Dorsai is a Dorsai. I am not apologizing.

"No foolishness," said Clay. For a moment a shadow crossed his face. "You forget that a real gambler bets only on a sure thing. When I looked into the Hixabrod's eyes, I was sure."

"How can you say 'a sure thing?' "

"The Hixabrod loved his home," Clay said.

I stared at him, astounded. "But you weren't betting on Hixa. Of course he would prefer Hixa to any other place in the Universe. But you were betting on Tarsus—on Lulungomeena—remember?"

The shadow was back for a moment on Clay's face.

"The bet was certain. I feel a little guilty about the Kid, but I warned him that gambling money never stuck. Besides, he's young and I'm getting old. I couldn't afford to lose."

"Will you come down out of the clouds," I demanded, "and explain this thing? Why was the bet certain? What was the trick, if there was one?"

"The trick?" repeated Clay. He smiled at me. "The trick was that the Hixabrod could not be otherwise than truthful. It was all in the name of my birthplace—Lulungomeena."

He looked at my puzzled face and put a hand on my shoulder.

"You see, Mort," he said quietly, "it was the name that fooled everybody. Lulungomeena stands for something in my language. But not for any city or town or village. Everybody on Tarsus has his own Lulungomeena. Everybody in the Universe has."

"How do you figure that, Clay?"

"It's a word," he explained. "A word in the Tarsusian language. It means 'home.'"

AN HONORABLE DEATH

From the arboretum at the far end of the patio to the landing stage of the transporter itself, the whole household was at sixes and sevens over the business of preparing the party for the celebration. As usual, Carter was having to oversee everything himself, otherwise it would not have gone right; and this was all the harder in that, of late, his enthusiasms seemed to have run down somewhat. He was conscious of a vague distaste for life as he found it, and all its parts. He would be forty-seven this fall. Could it be the imminent approach of middle age, seeking him out even in the quiet backwater of this small, suburban planet? Whatever it was, things were moving even more slowly than usual this year. He had not even had time to get into his costume of a full dress suit (19th-20th cent.) with tails, which he had chosen as not too dramatic, and yet kinder than most dress-ups to his tall, rather awkward figure—when the chime sounded, announcing the first arrival.

Dropping the suit on his bed, he went out, cutting across the patio toward the gathering room, where the landing stage of the transporter was—and almost ran headlong into one of the original native inhabitants of the planet, standing like a lean and bluish post with absolute rigidity in the center of the pretty little flagstone path.

"What are *you* doing here?" cried Carter.

The narrow, indigo, horselike face leaned confidentially down toward Carter's own. And then Carter recognized the great mass of apple blossoms, like a swarming of creamy-winged moths, held to the inky chest.

"Oh—" began Carter, on a note of fury. Then he threw up his hands and took the mass of branches. Peering around the immovable alien and wincing, he got a glimpse of his imported apple tree. But it was not as badly violated as he had feared. "Thank you. Thank you," he said, and waved the native out of the way.

But the native remained. Carter stared—then saw that in addition to the apple blossoms the thin and hairless creature, though no more dressed than his kind ever were, had in this instance contrived belts, garlands, and bracelets of native flowers for himself. The colors and patterns would be arranged to convey some special meaning—they always did. But right at the moment Carter was too annoyed and entirely too rushed to figure them out, though he did think it a little unusual the native should be holding a slim shaft of dark wood with a fire-hardened point. Hunting was most expressly forbidden to the natives.

"Now what?" said Carter. The native (a local chief, Carter suddenly recognized) lifted the spear and unexpectedly made several slow, stately hops, with his long legs flicking up and down above the scrubbed white of the flagstones—like an Earthly crane at its mating. "Oh, now, don't tell me you want to dance!"

The native chief ceased his movements and went back to being a post again, staring out over Carter's head as if at some horizon, lost and invisible beyond the iridescences of Carter's dwelling walls. Carter groaned, pondered, and glanced anxiously ahead toward the gathering room, from which he could now hear the voice of Ona, already greeting the first guest with female twitters.

"All right," he told the chief. "All right—this once. But only because it's Escape Day Anniversary. And you'll have to wait until after dinner."

The native stepped aside and became rigid again. Carter hurried past into the gathering room, clutching the apple blossoms. His wife was talking to a short, brown-bearded man with an ivory-tinted guitar hanging by a broad, tan band over one red-and-white, checked-shirted shoulder.

"Ramy!" called Carter, hurrying up to them. The landing stage of the transporter, standing in the middle of the room, chimed again. "Oh, take these will you, dear?" He thrust the apple blossoms into Ona's plump, bare arms. "The chief. In honor of the day. You know how they are—and I had to promise he could dance after dinner." She stared, her soft, pale face upturned to him. "I couldn't help it."

He turned and hurried to the landing stage, from the small round platform of which were now stepping down a short, academic, elderly man with wispy gray hair and a rather fat, button-nosed woman of the same age, both wearing the ancient Ionian chiton as their costume. Carter had warned Ona against wearing a chiton, for the very reason that these two might show up in the same dress. He allowed himself a small twinge of satisfaction at the thought of her ballroom gown as he went hastily now to greet them.

"Doctor!" he said. "Lidi! Here you are!" He shook hands with the doctor. "Happy Escape Day to both of you."

"I was sure we'd be late," said Lidi, holding firmly to the folds of her chiton with both hands. "The public terminal on Arcturus Five was so crowded. And the doctor won't hurry no matter what I say—" She looked over at her husband, but he, busy greeting Ona, ignored her.

The chime sounded again and two women, quite obviously sisters in spite of the fact that they were wearing dissimilar costumes, appeared on the platform. One was dressed in a perfectly ordinary everyday kilt and tunic—no costume at all. The other wore a close, unidentifiable sort of suit of some gray material and made straight for Carter.

"Cart!" she cried, taking one of his hands in both of her own and pumping it heartily. "Happy Escape Day." She beamed at him from a somewhat plain, strong-featured face, sharply made up. "Ani and I—" She looked around for her sister and saw the kilt and tunic already drifting in rather dreamlike and unconscious fashion toward the perambulating bar at the far end of the room. "I," she corrected herself hastily, "couldn't wait to get here. Who else is coming?"

"Just what you see, Totsa," said Carter, indicating those present with a wide-flung hand. "We thought a small party this year—a little, quiet gathering—"

"So nice! And what do you think of my costume?" She revolved slowly for his appraisal.

"Why—good, very good."

"Now!" Totsa came back to face him. "You can't guess what it is at all."

"Of course I can," said Carter heartily.

"Well, then, what is it?"

"Oh, well, perhaps I won't tell you, then," said Carter.

A small head with wispy gray hair intruded into the circle of their conversation. "An artistic rendering of the space suitings worn by those two intrepid pioneers who this day, four hundred and twenty years ago, burst free in their tiny ship from the iron grip of Earth's prisoning gravitation?"

Totsa shouted in triumph. "I knew you'd know, Doctor! Trust a philosophical researcher to catch on. Carter hadn't the slightest notion. Not an inkling!"

"A host is a host is a host," said Carter. "Excuse me, I've got to get into my own costume."

He went out again and back across the patio. The outer air felt pleasantly cool on his warm face. He hoped that the implications of his last remark—that he had merely been being polite in pretending to be baffled by the significance of her costume—had got across to Totsa, but probably it had not. She would interpret it as an attempt to cover up his failure to recognize her costume by being cryptic. The rapier was wasted on the thick hide of such a woman. And to think he once . . . you had to use a club. And the worst of it was, he *had* grasped the meaning of her costume immediately. He had merely been being playful in refusing to admit it . . .

The native chief was still standing unmoved where Carter had left him, still waiting for his moment.

"Get out of the way, can't you?" said Carter irritably, as he shouldered by.

The chief retreated one long ostrichlike step until he stood half-obscured in the shadow of a trellis of roses. Carter went on into the bedroom.

His suit was laid out for him and he climbed into the clumsy garments, his mind busy on the schedule of the evening ahead. The local star that served as this planet's sun (one of the Pleiades, Asterope) would be down in an hour and a half, but the luminosity of the interstellar space in this galactic region made the sky bright for hours after a setting, and the fireworks could not possibly go on until that died down.

Carter had designed the set piece of the finale himself—a vintage space rocket curving up from a representation of the Earth, into a firmament of stars, and changing into a star itself as it dwindled. It would be unthinkable to waste this against a broad band of glowing rarefied matter just above the western horizon.

Accordingly, there was really no choice about the schedule. At least five hours before the thought of fireworks could be entertained. Carter, hooking his tie into place around his neck before a section of his bedroom wall set on reflection, computed in his head The cocktail session now starting would be good for two and a half, possibly three hours He dared not stretch it out any longer than that or Ani would be sure to get drunk. As it was, it would be bad enough with a full cocktail session and wine with the dinner. But perhaps Totsa could keep her under control. At any rate—three, and an hour and a half for dinner. No matter how it was figured, there would be half an hour or more to fill in there.

Well—Carter worked his way into his dress coat—he could make his usual small speech in honor of the occasion. And—oh, yes, or course—there was the chief. The native dances were actually meaningless, boring things, though Carter had been quite interested in them at first, but then his was the inquiring type of mind. Still, the others might find it funny enough, or interesting for a single performance.

Buttoning up his coat, he went back out across the patio, feeling more kindly toward the native than he had since the moment of his first appearance. Passing him this time, Carter thought to stop and ask, "Would you like something to eat?"

Remote, shiny, mottled by the shadow of the rose leaves, the native neither moved nor answered, and Carter hurried on with a distinct feeling of relief. He had always made it a point to keep some native food on hand for just such an emergency as this—after all, they got hungry, too. But it was a definite godsend not to have to stop now, when he was so busy, and see the stuff properly prepared and provided for this uninvited and unexpected guest.

The humans had all moved out of the gathering room by the time he reached it and into the main lounge with its more complete bar and mobile chairs. On entering, he saw that they had already split up into three different and, in a way, inevitable groups. His wife and the doctor's were at gossip in a corner; Ramy was playing his guitar and singing in a low, not unpleasant, though hoarse voice to Ani, who sat drink in hand, gazing past him with a half-smile into the changing colors of the wall behind him. Totsa and the doctor were in a discussion at the bar. Carter joined them.

"—and I'm quite prepared to believe it," the doctor was saying in his gentle, precise tones as Carter came up. "Well, very good, Cart." He nodded at Carter's costume.

"You think so?" said Carter, feeling his face warm pleasantly. "Awkward get-up, but—I don't know, it just struck me this year." He punched for a lime brandy and watched with pleasure as the bar disgorged the brimming glass by his waiting hand.

"You look armored in it, Cart," Totsa said.

"Thrice-armed is he—" Carter acknowledged the compliment and sipped on his glass. He glanced at the doctor to see if the quotation had registered, but the doctor was already leaning over to receive a refill in his own glass.

"Have you any idea what this man's been telling me?" demanded Totsa, swiveling toward Carter. "He insists we're doomed. Literally doomed!"

"I've no doubt we are—" began Carter. But before he could expand on this agreement with the explanation that he meant it in the larger sense, she was foaming over him in a tidal wave of conversation.

"Well, I don't pretend to be unobjective about it. After all, who are we to survive? But really—how ridiculous! And you back him up just like that, *blindly*, without the slightest notion of what he's been talking about!"

"A theory only, Totsa," said the doctor, quite unruffled.

"I wouldn't honor it by even calling it a theory!"

"Perhaps," said Carter, sipping on his lime brandy, "if I knew a little more about what you two were—"

"The point," said the doctor, turning a little, politely, toward Carter, "has to do with the question of why, on all these worlds we've taken over, we've found no other race comparable to our own. We may," he smiled, "of course be unique in the universe. But this theory supposes that any contact between races of differing intelligences must inevitably result in the death of the inferior race. Consequently, if we met our superiors—" He gave a graceful wave of his hand.

"I imagine it could," said Carter.

"Ridiculous!" said Totsa. "As if we couldn't just avoid contact altogether if we wanted to!"

"That's a point," said Carter. "I imagine negotiations—"

"We," said Totsa, "who burst the bonds of our Earthly home, who have spread out among the stars in a scant four hundred years, are hardly the type to turn up our toes and just die!"

"It's all based on an assumption, Cart"—the doctor put his glass down on the bar and clasped his small hands before him—"that the racial will to live is dependent upon what might be called a certain amount of emotional self-respect. A race of lesser intelligence or scientific ability could hardly be a threat to us. But a greater race, the theory goes, must inevitably generate a sort of death-wish in all of us. We're too used to being top dog. We must conquer or—"

"Absolutely nonsense!" said Totsa.

"Well, now, you can't just condemn the idea offhand like that," Carter said. "Naturally, I can't imagine a human like myself ever giving up, either. We're too hard, too wolfish, too much the last-ditch fighters. But I imagine a theory like this might well hold true for other, lesser races." He cleared his throat. "For example, I've had quite a bit of contact since we came here with the natives which were the dominant life-form on this world in its natural state—"

"Oh, natives!" snapped Totsa scornfully.

"You might be surprised, Totsa!" said Carter, heating up a little. An inspiration took hold of him. "And, in fact, I've arranged for you to do just that. I've invited the local native chief to dance for us after dinner. You might just find it very illuminating."

"Illuminating? How?" pounced Totsa.

"That," said Carter, putting his glass down on the bar with a very slight flourish, "I'll leave you to find out for yourself. And now, if you don't mind, I'm going to have to make my hostly rounds of the other guests."

He walked away, glowing with a different kind of inner warmth. He was smiling as he came up to Ramy, who was still singing ballads and playing his guitar for Totsa's sister.

"Excellent," Carter said, clapping his hands briefly and sitting down with them as the song ended. "What was that?"

"Richard the Lion-heart wrote it," said Ramy hoarsely. He turned to the woman. "Another drink, Ani?"

Carter tried to signal the balladeer with his eyes, but Ramy had already pressed the buttons on the table beside their chairs, and a little moto unit from the bar was already on its way to them with the drinks emerging from its interior. Carter sighed inaudibly and leaned back in his chair. He could warn Totsa to keep an eye on Ani a little later.

He accepted another drink himself. The sound of voices in the room was rising as more alcohol was consumed. The only quiet one was Ani. She sat, engaged in the single-minded business of imbibing, and listened to the conversation between Ramy and himself, as if she was— thought Carter suddenly—perhaps one step removed, beyond some glasslike wall, where the real sound and movement of life came muted, if at all. The poetry of this flash of insight—for Carter could think of no other way to describe it—operated so strongly upon his emotions that he completely lost the thread of what Ramy was saying and was reduced to noncommittal noises by way of comment.

I should take up my writing again, he thought to himself.

As soon as a convenient opportunity presented itself, he excused himself and got up. He went over to the corner where the women were talking.

"—Earth," Lidi was saying, "the doctor and I will never forget it. Oh, Cart—" She twisted around to him as he sat down in a chair opposite. "You must take this girl to Earth sometime. Really."

"Do you think she's the back-to-nature type?" said Carter, with a smile.

"No, stop it!" Lidi turned back to Ona. "Make him take you!"

"I've mentioned it to him. Several times," said Ona, putting down the glass in her hand with a helpless gesture on the end-table beside her.

"Well, you know what they say," smiled Carter. "Everyone talks about Earth but nobody ever goes there any more."

"The doctor and I went. And it was memorable. It's not what you see, of course, but the insight you bring to it. I'm only five generations removed from people living right there on the North American continent. And the doctor had cousins in Turkey when he was a boy. Say what you like, the true stock thins out as generation succeeds generation away from the home world."

"And it's not the expense any more," put in Ona. "Everyone's rich nowadays."

"Rich! What an uncomfortable word!" said Lidi. "You should say *capable*, dear. Remember, our riches are merely the product of our science, which is the fruit of our own capabilities."

"Oh, you know what I mean!" said Ona. "The point is, Cart won't go. He just won't."

"I'm a simple man," Carter said. "I have my writing, my music, my horticulture, right here. I feel no urge to roam—" he stood up—"except to the kitchen right now, to check on the caterers. If you'll excuse me—"

"But you haven't given your wife an answer about taking her to Earth one of these days!" cried Lidi.

"Oh, we'll go, we'll go," said Carter, walking off with a good-humored wave of his hand.

As he walked through the west sunroom to the dining area and the kitchen (homey word!) beyond, his cheerfulness dwindled somewhat. It was always a ticklish job handling the caterers, now that they were all artists doing the work for the love of it and not to be controlled by the price they were paid. Carter would have liked to wash his hands of that end of the party altogether and just leave them to operate on their own. But what if he failed to check and then something went wrong? It was his own artistic conscience operating, he thought, that would not give him any rest.

The dining room was already set up in classic style with long table and individual chairs. He passed the gleam of its tableware and went on through the light-screen into the kitchen area. The master caterer was just in the process of directing his two apprentices to set up the heating tray on which the whole roast boar, papered and gilded, would be kept warm in the centerpiece position on the table during the meal. He did not see Carter enter; and Carter himself stopped to admire, with a sigh of relief, the boar itself. It was a master-work of the carver's art and had been built up so skillfully from its component chunks of meat that no one could have suspected it was not the actual animal itself.

Looking up at this moment, the caterer caught sight of him and came over to see what he wanted. Carter advanced a few small, tentative suggestions, but the response was so artificially polite that after a short while Carter was glad to leave him to his work.

Carter wandered back through the house without returning directly to the lounge. With the change of the mood that the encounter with the caterer had engendered, his earlier feelings of distaste with life—a sort of melancholy—had come over him. He thought of the people he had invited almost with disgust. Twenty years ago, he would not have thought himself capable of belonging to such a crowd. Where were the great friends, the true friends, that as a youngster he had intended to acquire? Not that it was the fault of those in the lounge. They could not help being what they were. It was the fault of the times, which made life too easy for everybody; and—yes, he would be honest—his own fault, too.

His wanderings had brought him back to the patio. He remembered the chief and peered through the light dusk at the trellis under the light arch of which the native stood.

Beyond, the house was between the semi-enclosed patio and the fading band of brilliance in the west. Deep shadow lay upon the trellis itself and the native under it. He was almost obscured by it, but a darkly pale, vertical line of reflection from his upright spear showed that he had made no move. A gush of emotion burst within Carter. He took a single step toward the chief, with the abrupt, spontaneous urge to thank him for coming and offering to dance. But at that moment, through the open doorway of his bedroom, sounded the small metallic chimes of his bedside clock, announcing the twenty-first hour, and he turned hastily and crossed through the gathering room, into the lounge.

"Hors-d'oeuvres! Hors-d'oeuvres!" he called cheerfully, flinging the lounge door wide. "Hors-d'oeuvres, everybody! Time to come and get it!"

Dinner could not go off otherwise than well. Everyone was half-tight and hungry. Everyone was talkative. Even Ani had thrown off her habitual introversion and was smiling and nodding, quite soberly, anyone would swear. She was listening to Ona and Lidi talking about Lidi's grown-up son when he had been a baby. The doctor was in high spirits, and Ramy, having gotten his guitar-playing out of his system earlier with Ani, was ready to be companionable. By the time they had finished the rum-and-butter pie, everyone was in a good mood, and even the caterer, peering through a momentary transparency of the kitchen wall, exchanged a beam with Carter.

Carter glanced at his watch. Only twenty minutes more! The time had happily flown, and, far from having to fill it in, he would have to cut his own speech a little short. If it were not for the fact that he had already announced it, he would have eliminated the chief's dance—no, that would not have done, either. He had always made a point of getting along with the natives of this world. "It's their home, too, after all," he had always said.

He tinkled on a wine glass with a spoon and rose to his feet.

Faces turned toward him and conversation came to a

reluctant halt around the table. He smiled at his assembled guests.

"As you know," said Carter, "it has always been my custom at these little gatherings—and old customs are the best—to say a few—" he held up a disarming hand—"a very few words. Tonight I will be even briefer than usual." He stopped and took a sip of water from the glass before him.

"On this present occasion, the quadricentennial of our great race's Escape into the limitless bounds of the universe, I am reminded of the far road we have come; and the far road—undoubtedly—we have yet to go. I am thinking at the moment," he smiled, to indicate that what he was about to say was merely said in good-fellowship, "of a new theory expressed by our good doctor here tonight. This theory postulates that when a lesser race meets a greater, the lesser must inevitably go to the wall. And that, since it is pretty generally accepted that the laws of chance ensure our race eventually meeting *its* superior, *we* must inevitably and eventually go to the wall."

He paused and warmed them again with the tolerance of his smile.

"May I say *nonsense!*"

"Now, let no one retort that I am merely taking refuge in the blind attitude that reacts with the cry, 'It can't happen to us.' Let me say I believe it *could* happen to us, but it won't. And why not? I will answer that with one word. Civilization.

"These overmen—if indeed they ever show up—must, even as we, be civilized. *Civilized*. Think of what that word means! Look at the seven of us here. Are we not educated, kindly, sympathetic people? And how do we treat the races inferior to us that we have run across?

"I'm going to let you answer these questions for yourselves, because I now invite you to the patio for cognac and coffee—and to see one of the natives of this planet, who has expressed a desire to dance for you. Look at him as he dances, observe him, consider what human gentleness and consideration are involved in the gesture that included him in this great festival of ours." Carter paused. "And consider one other great statement that has echoed down the corridors of time—*As ye have done to others, so shall ye be done by!*"

Carter sat down, flushed and glowing, to applause, then rose immediately to precede his guests, who were getting up to stream toward the patio. Walking rapidly, he outdistanced them as they passed the gathering room.

For a second, as he burst out through the patio doorway, his eyes were befuddled by the sudden darkness. Then his vision cleared as the others came through the doorway behind him and he was able to make out the inky shadow of the chief, still barely visible under the trellis.

Leaving Ona to superintend the seating arrangements in the central courtyard of the patio, he hurried toward the trellis. The native was there waiting for him.

"Now," said Carter, a little breathlessly, "it must be a short dance, a very short dance."

The chief lowered his long, narrow head, looking down at Carter with what seemed to be an aloofness, a sad dignity, and suddenly Carter felt uncomfortable.

"Um—well," he muttered, "you don't have to cut it *too* short."

Carter turned and went back to the guests. Under Ona's direction, they had seated themselves in a small semicircle of chairs, with snifter glasses and coffee cups. A chair had been left for Carter in the middle. He took it and accepted a glass of cognac from his wife.

"Now?" asked Totsa, leaning toward him.

"Yes—yes, here he comes," said Carter, and directed their attention toward the trellis.

The lights had been turned up around the edge of the courtyard, and as the chief advanced unto them from the darkness, he seemed to step all at once out of a wall of night.

"My," said Lidi, a little behind and to the left of Carter, "isn't he big!"

"*Tall,* rather," said the doctor, and coughed dryly at her side.

The chief came on into the center of the lighted courtyard. He carried his spear upright in one hand before him, the arm half-bent at the elbow and half-extended, advancing with exaggeratedly long steps and on tiptoe—in a manner unfortunately almost exactly reminiscent of the classical husband sneaking home late at night. There was a sudden titter from Totsa, behind Carter. Carter flushed.

Arrived in the center of the patio before them, the chief halted, probed at the empty air with his spear in several directions, and began to shuffle about with his head bent toward the ground.

Behind Carter, Ramy said something in a low voice.

There was a strangled chuckle and the strings of the guitar plinked quietly on several idle notes.

"Please," said Carter, without turning his head.

There was a pause, some more indistinguishable murmuring from Ramy, followed again by his low, hoarse, and smothered chuckle.

"Perhaps—" said Carter, raising his voice slightly, "perhaps I ought to translate the dance as he does it. All these dances are stories acted out. This one is apparently called 'An Honorable Death.' "

He paused to clear his throat. No one said anything. Out in the center of the patio, the chief was standing crouched, peering to right and left, his neck craned like a chicken's.

"You see him now on the trail," Carter went on. "The silver-colored flowers on his right arm denote the fact that it *is* a story of death that he is dancing. The fact that they are below the elbow indicates it is an honorable, rather than dishonorable, death. But the fact that he wears nothings at all on the other arm below the elbow tells us this is the full and only story of the dance."

Carter found himself forced to clear his throat again. He took a sip from his snifter glass.

"As I say," he continued, "we see him now on the trail, alone." The chief had now begun to take several cautious steps forward, and then alternate ones in retreat, with some evidence of tension and excitement. "He is happy at the moment because he is on the track of a large herd of local game. Watch the slope of his spear as he holds it in his hand. The more it approaches the vertical, the happier he is feeling—"

Ramy murmured again and his coarse chuckle rasped on Carter's ears. It was echoed by a giggle from Totsa and even a small, dry bark of a laugh from the doctor.

"—the happier he is feeling," repeated Carter loudly. "Except that, paradoxically, the line of the absolute vertical represents the deepest tragedy and sorrow. In a little paper I did on the symbolism behind these dance movements, I advanced the theory that when a native strikes up with his spear from the absolute vertical position, it is because some carnivore too large for him to handle has already downed him. He's a dead man."

The chief had gone into a flurry of movement.

"Ah," said Carter, on a note of satisfaction. The others were quiet now. He let his voice roll out a little. "He has made his kill. He hastens home with it. He is very happy. Why shouldn't he be? He is successful, young, strong. His mate, his progeny, his home await him. Even now it comes into sight."

The chief froze. His spear point dropped.

"But what is this?" cried Carter, straightening up dramatically in his chair. "What has happened? He sees a stranger in the doorway. It is the Man of Seven Spears who—this is a superstition, of course—" Carter interrupted himself—"who has, in addition to his own spear, six other magic spears which will fly from him on command and kill anything that stands in his way. What is this unconquerable being doing inside the entrance of the chief's home without being invited?"

The wooden spear point dropped abruptly, almost to the ground.

"The Man of Seven Spears tells him," said Carter. "He, the Man of Seven Spears, has chosen to desire the flowers about our chief's house. Therefore he has taken the house, killing all within it—the mate and the little ones—that their touch may be cleansed from flowers that are his. Everything is now his."

The soft, tumbling sound of liquid being poured filled in the second of Carter's pause.

"Not too much—" whispered someone.

"What can our chief do?" said Carter sharply. The chief was standing rigid with his head bent forward and his forehead pressed against the perfectly vertical shaft of his spear, now held upright before him. "He is sick—we would say he is weeping, in human terms. All that meant anything to him is now gone. He cannot even revenge himself on the Man of Seven Spears, whose magic weapons make him invincible." Carter, moved by the pathos in his own voice, felt his throat tighten on the last words.

"Ona, dear, do you have an antacid tablet?" the doctor's wife whispered behind him.

"He stands where he has stopped!" cried Carter fiercely. "He has no place else to go. The Man of Seven Spears ignores him, playing with the flowers. For eventually, without moving, without food or drink, he will collapse and die, as all of the Man of Seven Spears' enemies have died. For one, two, three days he stands there in his sorrow; and late on the third day the plan for revenge he has longed for comes to him. He cannot conquer his enemy—

but he can eternally shame him, so that the Man of Seven
Spears, in his turn, will be forced to die.

"He goes into the house." The chief was moving again.
"The Man of Seven Spears sees him enter, but pays no attention to him, for he is beneath notice. And it's a good
thing for our chief this is so—or else the Man of Seven
Spears would call upon all his magic weapons and kill him
on the spot. But he is playing with his new flowers and
pays no attention.

"Carrying his single spear," went on Carter, "the chief
goes in to the heart of his house. Each house has a heart,
which is the most important place in it. For if the heart is
destroyed, the house dies, and all within it. Having come
to the heart of the house, which is before its hearth fire,
the chief places his spear butt down on the ground and
holds it upright in the position of greatest grief. He stands
there pridefully. We can imagine the Man of Seven
Spears, suddenly realizing the shame to be put upon him,
rushing wildly to interfere. But he and all of his seven
spears are too slow. The chief leaps into the air—"

Carter checked himself. The chief was still standing
with his forehead pressed against the spear shaft.

"He leaps into the air," repeated Carter, a little louder.

And at that moment the native *did* bound upward, his
long legs flailing, to an astonishing height. For a second he
seemed to float above the tip of his spear still grasping
it—and then he descended like some great, dark, stricken
bird, heavily upon the patio. The thin shaft trembled and
shook, upright, above his fallen figure.

Multiple screams exploded and the whole company was
on their feet. But the chief, slowly rising, gravely removed
the spear from between the arm and side in which he had
cleverly caught it while falling; and, taking it in his other
hand, he stalked off into the shadows toward the house.

A babble of talk burst out behind Carter. Over all the
other voices, Lidi's rose like a half-choked fountain.

"—absolutely! Heart failure! I never was so upset in my
life—"

"Cart!" said Ona bitterly.

"Well, Cart," spoke Totsa triumphantly in his ear.
"What's the application of all this to what you told me earlier?"

Carter, who had been sitting stunned, exploded roughly
out of his chair.

"Oh, don't be such a *fool!*" He jerked himself away from them into the tree-bound shadows beyond the patio.

Behind him—after some few minutes—the voices lowered to a less excited level, and then he heard a woman's footsteps approaching him in the dark.

"Cart?" said his wife's voice hesitantly.

"What?" asked Carter, not moving.

"Aren't you coming back?"

"In a while."

There was a pause.

"Cart?"

"What?"

"Don't you think—"

"No, I don't think!" snarled Carter. "She can go to bloody hell!"

"But you can't just call her a fool—"

"She *is* a fool! They're all fools—every one of them! I'm a fool, too, but I'm not a stupid damn bloody fool like all of them!"

"Just because of some silly native dance!" said Ona, almost crying.

"Silly?" said Carter. "At least it's something. He's got a dance to do. That's more than the rest of them in there have. And it just so happens that dance is pretty important to him. You'd think they might like to learn something about that, instead of sitting back making their stupid jokes!"

His little explosion went off into the darkness and fell unanswered.

"Please come back, Cart," Ona said, after a long moment.

"At least he has something," said Carter. "At least there's that for him."

"I just can't face them if you don't come back."

"All right, goddammit," said Carter. "I'll go back."

They returned in grim fashion to the patio. The chair tables had been cleared and rearranged in a small circle. Ramy was singing a song and they were all listening politely.

"Well, Cart, sit down here!" invited the doctor heartily as Carter and Ona came up, indicating the chair between himself and Totsa. Carter dropped into it.

"This is one of those old sea ballads, Cart," said Totsa.

"Oh?" asked Carter, clearing his throat. "Is it?"

He sat back, punched for a drink and listened to the

song. It echoed out heartily over the patio with its refrain of *"Haul away, Joe!"* but he could not bring himself to like it.

Ramy ended and began another song. Lidi, her old self again, excused herself a moment and trotted back into the house.

"Are you really thinking of taking a trip Earthside—" the doctor began, leaning confidentially toward Carter— and was cut short by an ear-splitting scream from within the house.

Ramy broke off his singing. The screams continued and all of them scrambled to their feet and went crowding toward the house.

They saw Lidi—just outside the dark entrance to the gathering room—small, fat and stiffly standing, and screaming again and again, with her head thrown back. Almost at her feet lay the chief, with the slim shaft of the spear sticking up from his body. Only, this time, it was actually through him.

The rest flooded around Lidi and she was led away, still screaming, by the doctor. Everyone else gathered in horrified fascination about the native corpse. The head was twisted on one side and Carter could just see one dead eye staring up, it seemed, at him alone, with a gleam of sly and savage triumph.

"Horrible!" breathed Totsa, her lips parted. "Horrible!"

But Carter was still staring at that dead eye. Possibly, the thought came to him, the horrendous happenings of the day had sandpapered his perceptions to an unusually suspicious awareness. But just possibly . . .

Quietly, and without attracting undue attention from the others, he slipped past the group and into the dimness of the gathering room, where the lights had been turned off. Easing quietly along the wall until he came to the windows overlooking the patio, he peered out through them.

A considerable number of the inky natives were emerging from the greenery of the garden and the orchard beyond and approaching the house. A long, slim, fire-hardened spear gleamed in the hand of each. It occurred to Carter like a blow that they had probably moved into position surrounding the house while the humans' attention was all focused on the dancing of their chief.

His mind clicking at a rate that surprised even him, Carter withdrew noiselessly from the window and turned about. Behind him was the transporter, bulky in the dimness. As silently as the natives outside, he stole across the floor and mounted onto its platform. The transporter could move him to anywhere in the civilized area of the Galaxy at a second's notice. And one of the possible destinations was the emergency room of Police Headquarters on Earth itself. Return, with armed men, could be equally instantaneous. Much better this way, thought Carter with a clarity he had never in his life experienced before; much better than giving the alarm to the people within, who would undoubtedly panic and cause a confusion that could get them all killed.

Quietly, operating by feel in the darkness, Carter set the controls for Police Headquarters. He pressed the Send button.

Nothing happened.

He stared at the machine in the impalpable darkness. A darker spot upon the thin lacquered panel that covered its front and matched it to the room's decor caught his eye. He bent down to investigate.

It was a hole. Something like a ritual thrust of a fire-hardened wooden spear appeared to have gone through the panel and into the vitals of the transporter. The machine's delicate mechanism was shattered and broken and pierced.

FLAT TIGER

I am proud and happy to announce that contact with intelligent beings other than ourselves has finally been achieved and that, as a result of that meeting, peace has come at last, with the peoples of all nations firmly united behind a shining new doctrine.

The true story of this final contact has been delayed for several months, for security reasons, which necessitated that any publication of the facts be cleared first with the Secret Service, the FBI, the Treasury Department, the ICC, the Immigration Service and Senator Bang—who, while he had no direct official connection with the matter, would have caused everybody else a lot of trouble if he hadn't been checked with first.

Also, it was necessary to clear with the opposite numbers of the above individuals and organizations in some one hundred and twenty-seven other nations, who either had representatives at the final contact aforementioned, or learned about it afterward in one way or another, and were understandably miffed at not being invited to the conference, as they called it.

The story actually begins some few months back when a spaceship landed on the lawn of the White House one morning about eight A.M. and the President, looking out the window of his bedroom, perceived it.

"A spaceship!" he ejaculated.

"That is correct, sir," replied a voice inside his head. *"The ship you see is the racing spaceabout* Sunbeam *and I am Captain Bligh. Over."*

"Captain Bligh!" echoed the astounded President.

"Why, yes—" The voice broke off suddenly and the President received the impression of a chuckle of amusement. *"Oh, I see the coincidence that startles you, I read you loud and clear. Strange, isn't it, how words will sometimes duplicate themselves in a totally alien language? If*

135

*you will go down to your office, you will meet me and we
can talk there. Over."*

"I'll be right down," said the President, hurriedly grab-
bing for his pants.

"Right. See you then. Over and out."

"Over and out," replied the President mechanically.

He rushed down to his office and locked the door. A
curtain by the window stirred and there stepped into view
a creature slightly shorter than himself, but much heavier,
equipped with tentacles and fangs. The President, however, was pleasantly surprised to note that it—or rather
he, for it later turned out that Captain Bligh was, indeed a
male—did not in the least repel him with his alienness,
this being the first human to discover that no totally unfamiliar form can arouse an emotional response.

"Captain Bligh, I presume," he said politely.

"The same," replied the captain in passable English. "I
have been profiting by the interval since we last spoke to
learn your language and succeeded to some degree. Two-
way mental radio is a marvelous device, you know.
Over."

"Roger—I mean you do very nicely," said the President, passing a hand over his damp brow. "But you know,
my dear sir, that ship of yours will attract all sorts of attention."

"Not at all," answered Bligh. "The spaceabout's light-
reflecting properties have been heterodyned to your personal retinal pattern only. Be assured that you are the
only man on this world that can see it at the present moment."

"That's a relief. You have no idea how the papers
would jump on something like this." He gestured to a
chair. "Won't you sit down?"

"Thanks, but I'd rather stand. No leg joints, you see.
you're probably wondering how I happen to be here."

"Well, I don't think I should commit myself by giving
you a definite answer immediately on that," said the President cautiously.

"No matter," said Bligh. "I will explain anyway. I happen to be in a round-the-Galaxy race at the moment—the
Sunbeam is a stripped-down hot-warp. Unfortunately, as I
was passing your solar system, I got a flat tiger and had to
pull in for repairs."

"I beg your pardon?" queried the President. "Did you
say a flat tiger?"

"Excuse me," said Bligh. "I should have explained. The tiger—*Felis Tigris Longipilis* or what you know as the Siberian tiger—is a discarded mutant variform of a race which was formerly distributed everywhere throughout the Galaxy, but which has since ended its physical existence and passed on—" Captain Bligh's voice took on a reverent hush and he removed the top of his head, considerably startling the President until he realized that it was actually a cap of some sort—"to that great macro-universe up yonder to which we must all go one day."

The President cleared his throat embarrassedly. Captain Bligh put his cap back on and continued his explanation.

"Tigers are, therefore, to be found on every world and familiar to every intelligent race. Since they still possess many of the potentials of their departed master-strain, they have been bred and conditioned to a variety of uses. One of the most widespread of these is as neural governors on the feeders that meter out fuel to the warp engines. The fuel feed must be controlled with such delicacy that no mechanical process can be devised fine enough. I have four warp engines on my *Sunbeam* and therefore, naturally, four tigers; one petty tiger and three tigers second class."

"Ah—yes," the President replied. "But you said that this tiger was flat."

"Exactly. My tigers and others like them have been bred and trained for their work. It is a very exacting job, as you can imagine, since a tiger's attention must not waver for one milli-second while the ship is in operation. To aid them in their concentration, the tigers' lungs are filled with a drug in gaseous form under high pressure, which, being slowly absorbed into the bloodstream, keeps them in a state of hyper-concentration."

"Oh?" said the President. "But why a gaseous drug? I should think an injection—"

"Not at all. A gaseous drug has the great advantage that when the trip is over, or at any moment when the situation may require it, the tiger may exhale and within a few seconds be rid of the effects of the drug. No tiger of your planet, of course, could do it—but our tigers are quite capable of holding their breaths for weeks."

"Then how did this accident occur?"

"My Number One Port Tiger somehow omitted a basal metabolism test at his last physical checkup," said the Captain sadly. "I am sorry to say that he was eighteen points over normal and used up his gas ahead of schedule. There is no room on the ship to set up the gas-manufacturing apparatus and, of course, yours was the only habitable planet for us to land on in this system. I did not know it was—er—civilized."

"And when you saw it was?" prompted the President.

"I looked you up immediately," replied the Captain. "I am in no sense an official, but I could hardly wait to offer you the tentacle of friendship on behalf of the Galactic Confraternity of Intelligences."

Coughing explosively to gain a little time, the President dabbed at his mouth with his handkerchief and put it away again.

"I am only, you must understand, executive head of this one nation."

"Oh? I see—" said Captain Bligh, telepathing the equivalent of a bothered frown. "That makes it troublesome. Time is, of course, relative; but there's this little matter of my possibly losing the race if I have to spend too much time here. I can, of course, notify Exploration when I reach the finish point on Capra IV, but that will mean centuries of red tape. It would short-cut things enormously if I could carry word directly to Confraternity Headquarters that you already consider yourselves a member world."

"Oh, I see," said the President. "Tell me, just how much time can you afford to spend?"

"Well, let me see— To set up the apparatus, one of your days— To gas Number One Port Tiger, two days— To dismantle, half a day. Say, three days from this coming sunset."

"Hum," said the President thoughtfully, "I'll see what I can do."

They went outside to the spaceabout together.

"Be with you in a minute," said the Captain and dived in through the airlock of his vessel, to return a moment later, carrying—he was obviously of inhuman strength—a rather thin, helpless-looking tiger.

"Mr. President," said the Captain. "May I present my Number One Port Tiger, second class."

The Tiger extended a paw.

"This is indeed an honor," it telepathed feebly.

"Not at all, not at all," said the President gingerly shaking the animal's paw.

"The poor fella's worn out," said the Captain in an

aside to the President as he laid the Number One Port Tiger on the White House lawn. "The last of his gas went while we were still a number of light-years short of your system and we went the last stretch on nerve alone. Pretty well took it out of him."

Looking at Number One Port lie on the grass, looking more like a cardboard cut-out of a tiger than the real item, the President was inclined to agree.

"You're going to set up your apparatus here?" he asked, somewhat nervously.

Bligh instantly comprehended the cause of his agitation. "Don't worry," he reassured. "I guarantee complete invisiblity."

"Well, if you think so—" replied the President, rather doubtfully. "I'll leave you to that and see what I can do in this other matter."

The President returned to his office and sat down at his desk, pressing a button as he did so. A few seconds later, his Special Secretary, Morion Stanchly, put in an appearance.

"Yes, Mr. President?" he said.

"Sit down, Morion," said the President. "I have something to discuss with you." And he waved his Special Secretary to a chair.

Morion Stanchly was a little administrative secret. He had been around the White House for forty years, inheriting the office from his father who had had it in turn from his father, and so on back to Preserved Stanchly, who had first been named to the post by General Washington, before the General became President. It was, of course, an unofficial post. Special Secretaries were always carried on the payroll under a different title and usually under a different name. Morion was, at the moment, down on the official books as a White House chauffeur named Joe Smith.

He would remain Joe Smith until some contingency required him to adopt another cover name and occupation. But he would not leave the White House; and the secret of his existence would be passed on by word of mouth as a strictly administrative secret from one President to the next. His duty was to do the impossible.

He was a tall, dark-browed capable-looking man in his early sixties and he nodded agreeably as he took his chair.

"Morion," said the President. "We have been contacted from outer-space."

A true Stanchly, Morion merely raised one eyebrow quizzically. "Yes, sir?" he said. "And—"

The President told him the whole story. Morion got up and looked out the window onto the White House lawn. But, of course, he saw nothing.

"What would you like me to do, sir?" he said, returning to his seat.

"Three days," said the President. "I know it sounds ridiculous—but would there be any possible chance of arranging a meeting of the Four of us inside of three days?" Hardly were the words out of his mouth when he realized how incongruous they sounded. "No, no, of course not," he said. "I'm thrown a little off balance by this thing, Morion. Maybe—"

"Well, now, Mr. President," said Morion judiciously. "*All Four*. Well, now—"

The President looked at him with hope beginning to revive in his eyes.

"Morion!" he said. "You don't mean—"

"There is a certain possibility," said the Special Secretary. "Considering the gravity and urgency of the situation. Mark you—just a possibility. I'll have to swear you to secrecy, of course."

"Anything, Morion, anything!"

"Very well, then," said the Special Secretary.

He rose from his chair and went to one wall of the room. He pushed aside a picture of a former President that was hanging there and revealed the front of a wall safe. His fingers spun the dial, the safe opened and he removed an old-fashioned wall-phone with a handcrank, from which a long cord led back into the depths of the safe. He carried the phone to the desk and set it down.

"Would you lock the door, Mr. President?" he asked courteously.

The President went to do so, hearing behind his back the shirring ring of the phone as Morion turned the bell crank for one long ring and three shorts. There was a slight pause; and then the Special Secretary spoke into the antiquated mouthpiece.

"Hello? Boris? This is Morion ... why, yes. A trifle chilly here. Yes, a head cold. No! You don't say. No! Is that a fact? Not really. No—" He paused, covered the mouthpiece with his hand and turned apologetically to the President.

"If you don't mind, Mr. President," he said. "Perhaps you'd better wait outside, after all."

Bowing his head, the President unlocked the office door and went out, closing it behind him. Outside, he lit a cigarette and paced up and down nervously.

After a short while, he returned to the office door and opened it a crack. The voice of Morion came to his ear, in conversation now with a man apparently named Cecil. The President went back to his pacing for another fifteen minutes and then ventured to open the door again. Morion waved him to come back inside.

"—that's right, Raoul," he was saying into the mouthpiece. "Here tomorrow at three o'clock local time, in the afternoon. Yes . . . Yes. You may bring your man in by the north underground entrance. Yes . . . Yes, indeed. The same to you and Félice. Good-by."

He hung up, returned the phone to the safe, closed the safe and replaced the picture.

"They'll be here tomorrow, sir," he told the President.

"Morion!" said the President, delightedly. "This is miraculous."

"Part of my duties, sir," replied Morion, immovably.

"It is a miracle!" said the President. "What would I do without you? Tell me, Morion—those other men you were talking to. They wouldn't by any chance be the Special Secretaries of—"

"*Mr. President!*" interrupted Morion, deeply shocked.

"Oh, sorry," said the President. "I didn't mean to pry."

"Such information is *absolutely* restricted."

"Sorry."

"Well, now," said Morion, the stern lines of his face relaxing. "No damage was done, fortunately. You understand, though, that the strictest security is necessary in my work."

"Oh, of course," said the President. "Where shall I meet the other—the visitors, Morion?"

"I would suggest right here in your office, Mr. President," said Morion. "Leave the details to me."

"Gladly," said the President. "And now," he added a trifle nervously, "perhaps I'd better go back outside and let Captain Bligh know."

"I would advise that, sir," said Morion Stanchly, nodding soberly.

"I will be honored to attend your meeting," said Captain Bligh, waving a cheerful tentacle as he busily connected pieces of equipment together.

At three o'clock the following day, Captain Bligh and the President were ensconced in the President's office, for the meeting that would start as soon as those others due to be present had arrived. They were talking golf. Or rather the President was talking golf, and the Captain, as befitted a being strongly sportsconscious, was listening.

"The fourteenth on that particular course is a dog-leg," the President was saying. "Three hundred and forty-five yards from tee to pin. I decided to take a chance—"

There was a discreet knock on the door and Morion appeared, ushering in, in that order, the Prime Minister of England, the President of France and the Secretary of a Certain Party in Russia.

The President of the United States rose to his feet.

"Gentlemen," he said warmly. "May I present Captain Bligh of the Galactic Confraternity of Intelligences—" and there was the usual bustle of hand and tentacle shaking and personal introductions, which ended with all four of the humans seated around the President's desk and Bligh standing facing them all.

"To start the ball rolling," said our President, "may I say that there is nothing official about this meeting. Just a little—er—get together."

"Of course," said Great Britain.

"But certainly," said France.

"Maybe," said the Secretary of the Certain Party, looking suspiciously at Bligh.

"Well, at any rate," said the President, hurrying along, "since the meeting's to be informal, I suggest we get right down to business. I assume that you have all been informed of the reasons for Captain Bligh's presence on Earth and his willingness to carry to the Confraternity Earth's wish to join the rest of the Galaxy in that great organization to which he belongs. The question in my mind, and I'm sure in yours, is why it would or would not be feasible for us to do so. Captain Bligh has offered to cast some light on this question for us by explaining something of what life is like as a member of the Confraternity and afterward answering any questions we may wish to put him. Captain Bligh?"

He sat down, leaving the floor to the Captain, who waved a tentacle modestly.

"Well, now," he said. "I'll see what I can do to satisfy you people about the Galaxy. As you know, there's nothing official about my visit or myself and there are many octillions of beings who could describe the situation much better than I—you'll meet some of them if you decide to join the Confraternity. But I'll do my best as an amateur and a sports-being to pinch hit for them.

"I don't happen to know the figures on how many races and inhabited worlds there are in the Confraternity. Let's just say that there are enough of both to make their exact counting a thing of merely academic interest. As for why you haven't been visited before—a question my host here asked me on the first day of my arrival—you know how it is. Most of the Galaxy has been explored; and, without any offense, you are in kind of an out-of-the-way corner here. I'd say it was inevitable that someone should come along sooner or later and find you; but not so surprising that it hasn't happened before this, though for all I know, you may have been noted down in some ship's logbook a few thousand years ago—"

"Look here," interrupted the Prime Minister, "if something like that happened, wouldn't the Confraternity have taken some measures to acquaint us with their existence? Now *wouldn't* they?"

"Well—I suppose they might have," said Bligh, a trifle embarrassed. "But a few thousand years ago, I don't imagine you would have been too much interested in interstellar travel. Plenty to keep you occupied here, then, you know. Not too much point in making a big-to-do about establishing contact. Of course, I don't *know* if that's what might have happened, it's only a reasonable guess."

"Grumpf!" said the Prime Minister.

"How about these flying saucers?" demanded the President of France.

"Pardon me?" asked Bligh.

The President of France explained.

"Oh," said Bligh. "Chlorophyll-sniffers. Perfectly harmless, but a slight menace to low-flying aircraft. Every planet has them flitting in occasionally. A few billion tons of soap bubbles released in your upper atmosphere will scare them off."

The President of France looked uncertain, but made a note of Bligh's answer.

"You're supposed to be telepathic," said the Prime Minister, returning to the attack. "Aren't there some telepaths in this Confraternity that would have received our—er—thought whatchamacallits? *Wouldn't* there?"

"Well, yes," said Bligh. "Bound to be, I suppose. There's some races that can hear an electron scratch its nose in the next spiral nebula. Still, maybe they didn't think it important to mention it. Different people, different ways, you know. It takes all kinds to make a universe."

"Well, dammit!" said the Prime Minister. "Isn't there any organization with the job of finding new cultures?"

"Oh, yes—Exploration," replied Bligh. "But they're mostly a bunch of hobbyists in actual fact, you understand. I mean—no great purpose in finding another new culture when there's so many around to begin with. They might be poking around here; and then they might decide to poke around there. Lots of places, you know, where a new race might pop up."

This announcement seemed to throw the meeting temporarily into silence. Then the Secretary of the Certain Party leaned over and whispered in the ear of the President of the United States, who drew the other two into a huddle, which ended with them all resuming their places and the President facing Bligh again.

"I ask for all of us," said the President, "whether you are truly representative of the intelligence and culture of the normal member of the Confraternity?"

"Not at all, not at all," Bligh hurried to assure him. "There's every conceivable kind of intelligence and culture in the Confraternity. All kinds of life-forms. All kinds and types of intelligences."

There was a moment's silence.

"Then what—" demanded the Secretary, speaking up unexpectedly and gutturally on his own, "do they have in common between them?"

"Love," replied Bligh blissfully. "Their mutual love and affection."

There was another short silence.

"Love each other, eh?" grunted the Prime Minister.

"Yes," said Bligh, "just as they will love you humans if you become a part of the Confraternity."

All four national representatives withdrew into another conference. Little telepathic snatches of conversation reached the mind of Captain Bligh—"The U.N., of course—but the circumstances—decadent capitalistic emotion—now, my dear fellow, be reasonable—" but he very politely ignored them.

The President broke from the huddle and once more approached Bligh.

"Naturally," he said, "none of us here disparage love as a desirable acquisition, where one people are concerned with others. But—er—there is the practical side to any alliance—a question of tangibles—"

"Tangibles? Why, of course!" cried Bligh. "It's with tangibles that the United Peoples of the Confraternity will wish to express their love toward you. Grants-in-aid and rehabilitation funds from the Galactic Treasury—donations of up-to-date equipment and supplies. Technical assistance, of course."

"Of course?" said four voices at once.

"For little things. Merely to raise your standard of living to average Confraternity level," said Captain Bligh. "Electronic power plants—am I correct in assuming you have not yet cracked the electron?—force shields, weather control units, drugs to conquer all your diseases and reverse the process of aging—all these little home comforts will be donated to you as a matter of course."

The four humans looked at each other.

"And—" continued Bligh, "you will want to hook on to the absolutely free Galaxy-wide transportation system. A terminal will be set up on your Moon immediately. You will find," said Captain Bligh with a roguish telepathic twinkle, "many pleasant vacation spots in the Galaxy with all conveniences furnished free of charge by the local lifeform."

He stopped speaking. For a moment, nobody said anything. Then the President cleared his throat and spoke.

"And what kind of tangibles," he said, "would the Confraternity expect us to express our love with?"

"Tangibles? From you? My dear human!" cried Bligh. "What are material things compared to the pure emotion of love? Tangibles can't buy happiness. After all, it's love that makes the Universe go around." He telepathed a quick shake of the head. "No. No. You people will give in return only the rare quality of your affection."

The four men looked doubtful.

"Believe me," went on Captain Bligh, earnestly, "out in the Universe, material things are nothing and less than nothing. With so many differing races, how could a material standard be set up common to all? Useless and less than useless. That is why, among the stars, the common currency is love and people are rated on the quantity and quality of their capability for affection." He beamed at them. "Permit me to say that you people strike me as having great capabilities along that line. I've only had a chance to glance at things here, but judging from your movies, your books and magazines—"

"Ahem!" said the President, clearing his throat abruptly. "Well, now, I must admit you paint an attractive picture, Captain. If you'll excuse us again for a minute—"

Captain Bligh waved a gracefully assenting tentacle, and the four humans withdrew into another huddle. After a few moments of animated conversation, they returned to Bligh.

"I have been deputed to say, for all of us," said the President of the United States, "that while, as I have mentioned before, there is nothing official about this little meeting or ourselves, certainly there seems to be no conceivable reason why we humans should not respond with affection to affection freely given by others."

"My dear sir!" cried Bligh, delighted. "How well you put it. I was sure you would agree." His gaze took in them all. "It was inevitable. While I'm not a particularly perceptive being, as beings go, it seemed to me that I could see Love and Affection hovering around you all like an aura. How right I was. Gentlemen, the Universe is yours, just as soon as you make your adjustment."

"Adjustment?" said the Prime Minister.

"Of course. But a mere bagatelle. A nothing," said Captain Bligh. "A mere matter of love extended logically to include all living creatures. A moment's adjustment by a metabolic ordinator, completely painless. Click-snap and it's over and you are all energy eaters."

"Eaters of what?" said the President of France.

"Energy. My dear sirs," said Captain Bligh. "You surely would not wish to continue with your present diets. How could you eat something you love? And love, like charity, begins at home. Moreover—" he went on—"how could you expect the rest of the Universe to accept you otherwise? Consider the similarity of shapes. For example, what a Red-eyed Inchos would think on arriving to set up a modern weather control system for your planet, if he should see one of you sitting down to—" the Captain shuddered—"a roast turkey, except for a slight difference in size, the exact image of himself. Similarly with a Lullar and a barbecued pig, or a Brvandig and a baked sturgeon."

After a moment, the President of the United States cleared his throat.

"Perhaps—" he suggested, "a strictly vegetarian—"

"Mr. President," said Bligh, interrupting with dignity, "I am myself only one of uncounted myriads, but some of my best friends are plants." He fixed the President with a stern eye. "I hate to think what a Snurlop would say if he happened to see a loaf of your bread and imagined a child of his own being harvested, threshed, ground and even *baked!*"

"But now——" interposed the President of France hastily, "certainly liquids such as wine——"

"Please!" choked Bligh, turning green. He staggered and leaned against the desk beside him. Hastily the President of the United States fanned the Captain's face with a major-general's appointment that happened to be lying close at hand. Slowly, the color returned to Bligh's gums.

"Please," he repeated feebly, "amputation, crushing, fermentation—horrible." He shook his head. "No—no liquids."

"Water," said the Prime Minister.

Bligh looked at him. "Think," he said, "just think of the minute organisms that must die, either through being boiled alive, poisoned with chlorine, or digested living, to provide you with ordinary drinking water. Why, the Fellibriks of——"

"Yes, yes," interrupted the President hastily, "I'm sure your little friends would be shocked. If you will excuse us just once more——"

"Certainly," replied Bligh, faintly, sagging against the desk.

Stout sports-being as he was, the images just conjured up by the recent conversation had turned him pale inside (he was incapable of turning pale outside). As he breathed heavily and tried to recover, little bits of conversation reached him.

"Borscht—civet de lapin—rare steak—roast beef and Yorkshire pudding—sacrifice—solidarity——"

Slowly, but with the look of men who have been through the fire and emerged triumphant, the four representatives of humanity turned back to the representative of the Galactic Confederation of Races.

So that is how peace has come to the world. We are united at last as we have never before been in history, united as one people behind what has come to be known as the UnBligh Doctrine, and which is now emblazoned in letters of gold over the front doors of the U. N. Building.

No government or individual or collection of individuals

shall have the power at any time to come between any other individual and the due and lawful exercise of his appetite.

Let the Galactic Confederation of Races beware!

JAMES

"James gave the huffle *of a snail in danger...."*

(from "Four Friends," a poem by A. A. Milne)

James huffled.

He paused, his horns searching the air. Something was coming toward him along the brick he himself was traversing. For a moment he tensed, then his trained perception recognised that the one approaching was another snail. James glowed with pleasure and hurried to meet him.

"I'm James," he said, joyfully touching horns. "And you?"

"Egbert," replied the other. "Honored to make your acquaintance, James."

"Honored to make yours," replied James; and then, avidly, as all snails do, he asked, "What's new?"

"The word," said the other. "The word is being passed."

"No!" said James.

"Absolutely," confirmed Egbert. "It's Homo Sapiens, of course; you might have expected it." He sighed.

"H. Sapiens?" asked James. "Why, I wouldn't have thought it of them. They seemed like such large harmless creatures, for all their rushing around. I've just been observing one—"

"They may look harmless," interrupted Egbert, sternly, "but the mischief's in them. And we can't tolerate it, of course. After coming halfway across the Galaxy to try and get away from *Them,* you know."

"True," agreed James. He added, a trifle wistfully, "Sometimes I think we should have crushed *Them* the last time they overran the planet we were on. If not the previous time. Or the time before that."

"But what a labor it would have been," protested Egbert. "Of course all they had were primitive material weapons: space warps, disintegrators and the like. But

149

there were so many of *Them*—thousands of planetary systems all populated up to the plimsoll mark. What a weary task to zzitz hard enough to exterminate them all. And how easy, comparatively, to zzitz just enough to protect ourselves."

"Ah, yes," sighed James. "Of course we are by nature sensible and wary of overexertion. Well, I suppose we're better off here after all, even with Homo Sapiens dashing back and forth as if his shell was on fire. Who would ever have thought a life form could become so active? And what is it, by the way, that they've finally done?"

"Well," said Egbert darkly, "brace yourself. It's almost unbelievable, but since it comes through the grapevine, it must be true. The official word just filtered up from the valley of the Euphrates, or the Nile, or someplace around there. One of them—" he spaced the words slowly and impressively "—one—of—them has actually just invented a wheel!"

"No!" cried James, stunned.

"That's the word," insisted Egbert. "I don't blame you for being surprised. I had trouble believing it myself when it was told to me just the month before last."

"That explains it!" cried James. "I thought I'd been seeing things with wheels around; but naturally I couldn't believe my senses on the basis of purely empirical evidence. An old friend of mine was crushed by one the other day. His name was Charlie. You didn't know him, by any chance?"

"No," replied Egbert. "I never knew a Charlie." They brooded in silence for a second.

"He was a Good Snail," said James, at last, bestowing the words of highest tribute upon his deceased friend. His mind swung back to the implications of the news he had just heard. "But this—" he stammered, "—this is terrible!"

"Of course it is," brooded Egbert, darkly. "You know what's bound to happen now, don't you? They'll be settling down, making pottery. First thing you know they'll build pyramids, discover gunpowder. Why, before we can turn around they'll be splitting the atom, and you know what happens then!"

"Spaceflight . . ." breathed James, horrified.

"Exactly!" replied Egbert grimly. "And the minute they get a ship outside the atmosphere, it'll register on *Their* separation-index. And you know what *They'll* do when *They* find out."

"Poor H. Sapiens!" quavered James.

"Yes," said Egbert. "And poor us. The minute a ship gets outside the Earth's atmosphere, it won't be more than three days, local time, before *They* notice it and have a fleet here englobing the planet. Which means we have only the limited time remaining between now and the launching of the first space rocket to take defensive measures. And that time gets shorter by the century. Why, for all we know —at the mad pace these humans move—one of them may be experimenting with a potter's wheel even now."

"Indeed," said James, anxiously, "I could almost swear I've noticed signs of pottery culture among our local H. Sapiens. Of course—" he added hastily "—I have no confirmation of the fact in the way of comparative reports from other Snails."

"True. I too ..." Egbert lowered his voice. "Let us speak off the record, James. Unscientific as it must be for only two observers to compare notes—tell me: You haven't seen any evidence of pyramid building here in North America?"

"N-no ..." answered James cautiously. "I *have* seen some rather odd structures—but no true pyramid."

"Thank heaven for that," said Egbert, with a sigh of relief. "Nor have I. Not that our two unofficial observations mean anything, but they represent a straw in the wind, a hope, James, that what you and I have seen mirrors the Big Picture, and that H. Sapiens is still, essentially, a happy herdsman."

"Still," said James doubtfully, "if I were to venture a guess on my own—"

"James!" reproved Egbert, shocked. "This is unsnaillike. Put such thoughts from your mind. No, no, rest assured that we have some few thousands of years still in which to contact H. Sapiens if the race is to be taught how to zzitz and so protect itself and its planet from *Them*. Reassure yourself that it is merely a matter of contacting the right individual, one who will believe us and who in turn will be believed by his fellows."

For a moment silence hung heavy between the two snails.

"Some people," said James finally, in an apologetic voice, "might call us slow."

"Oh, no!" cried Egbert, profoundly shocked. "Surely not!"

"And perhaps," continued James, his voice strengthening, "who knows but what we actually may be a bit slow? I want to be fair about this. I *will* be fair about this!

Think, Egbert: it has been at least twenty planets, one after the other, which we have seen blown from beneath us, and their native life destroyed by *Them* in spite of all our good intentions about teaching that native life to protect itself by zzitzing."

"But—"

"But me no buts, Egbert! Twenty chances we have had to protect the weak and defenseless. Twenty times—in a row—we have been just a little bit late in giving aid. And I say to you, Egbert, here and now, that if by following our traditional cautious methods we again slip up and see the human race destroyed, then, by all that's holy, we *are* a trifle slow!"

"James," breathed Egbert, shrinking back in awe. "Such energy! Such fire! You are a Snail Transformed!"

And, indeed, James was. Quivering with righteous indignation, he had reared up a full three-quarters of an inch above the surface of the brick and both sets of his horns stuck out rigidly, as if challenging the universe.

"Egbert," he said fiercely, "the tradition of eons is about to be broken. You have spoken of several thousand years in which to contact H. Sapiens. Know, Egbert, that the far end of this brick touches the sill of a window, that that sill overhangs a desk, and that at that desk sits a man high in the councils of the Five Indian Nations, or the United Nations, or some such important organization. This man I have been observing and I have discovered in him the capability to understand and believe the threat *They* will pose to his race, if that self-same race continues this mad plunge of progress which has just recently brought forth the invention of the wheel."

"James!" gasped Egbert. "You mean ... ? You wouldn't ... ? Not without first submitting a report for the consideration of other snails, the formation of an investigative forum, the collection of an adequate number of blanketing reports, a general referendum—"

"Cease, Egbert!" interrupted James sternly. "I would, and I will. What you and other snails have always refused to recognise is the impermanence of the individual H. Sapiens. They are here today, and—if I may coin a phrase—gone tomorrow." The tone of his voice changed. A note almost of pleading crept into it. "Can't you understand, Egbert, that this is a crisis! We can't afford to waste a thousand years here and a thousand years there just to make the matter official."

"But scientific method—" began Egbert.

"Scientific method, bosh!" retorted James, crudely. Egbert gasped. "What good was scientific method to the life forms of the last twenty planets we've inhabited?"

Egbert was struck dumb. It was a good twenty minutes before he managed to answer.

"Why—" he said at last. "I never thought of that. That's true, it didn't help them much, did it?" He stared at James with wonder and admiration dawning in the little eye at the tip of each of his two major horns. "But James—" he said. "To flout tradition in this fashion—to throw off at one fell swoop the age-welded bonds of ancient custom and established means. Why, James—" he went on, falling, as all Snails do when deeply moved, into iambic pentameter "—this step will sound throughout the halls of time; and through the echoing vault of universe; be duplicated in infinity. So that all future ages, hearing it, and looking back, will wonder how you could. And tell me James, how is it that you can?"

James bowed his horns in graceful acknowledgment of the question.

"I am," he replied simply, "what you might possibly characterize as a humanitarian."

"Ah," said Egbert softly, "so that's it."

"Yes," answered James. "And now—my duty calls. Farewell, Egbert."

"Farewell!" choked Egbert, almost too overcome to speak. They broke contact; and James began to turn around. "Farewell, oh *brave* and *gallant* spirit."

Resolutely, James completed his turn and began his march. Inside the window, at the desk, a heavy balding man with tired eyes straightened his glasses and began to read a report stamped TOP SECRET and headed PARTICULARS OF FORTHCOMING FLIGHT OF UN SPACE ROCKET X-1. He read steadily into the report as the sun crept across the sky.

After a while he stopped temporarily to rub his eyes. As he did, he caught sight of a snail which had just crawled across the sill from outside the window. It stood balanced on the edge. It was James, of course, and for a long second they looked at each other. Then the man turned back to the report.

James paused to catch his breath. The trip had been all of eleven inches and he had come at top speed.

Finally he collected himself and turned toward the man. The H. Sapiens' head was bent over a sheaf of paper; but whatever engrossed him there would be small potatoes to what James was about to hit him with. James took a deep breath.

"Huffle," he said. "Huffle. *Huffle! Huffle, huffle, huffle, huffle . . .*"

"James gave the huffle of a snail in danger— And nobody heard him at all."

A. A. Milne

THE QUARRY

"He went in under here," said the older of the two boys. "I saw him."

"He couldn't get under a rock like that, Jix," the other said. "He's too big."

"But he's awful skinny," said Jix. "Raby, you go around the other side and I'll call him. If he comes out your way, you hold him until I get there." Raby went off, and Jim bent down the opening. "Mr. Johnson!" he called. "Come on out, Mr. Johnson! It's only us."

Under the rock William Johnson twitched convulsively and squirmed deeper into the mold-smelling earth. He pressed his mouth to it, its grittiness against his teeth, to hide the sound of his breathing. Hollowed and drawn out between earth and rock, Jix's voice reached down to him again.

"Mr. Johnson, you come out now. If you don't come out, I'll have to come in and get you."

William did not move. Then, after a long, breath-held moment, he heard the rattle and scrape of a body crawling toward him under the rock. He made a high, squeaking sound in his throat and suddenly threw himself away from the approaching sound, scrabbling back and up through the loose earth to the far underside of the rock. The light of day broke suddenly in on him, and he saw the far overhanging edge of the rock. Then he was out from under it, into the grass and the sun. He jerked to his feet, ready to run, and then two slim arms caught and held him.

"Jix!" cried the voice of Raby, triumphant. "I got him! I got him here!"

There was the sound from under the rock behind him and a second later Jix came around to stand before Johnson. Dirt had refused to cling to Jix's shimmering shorts and tunic. He stood in front of William, his head about

155

shoulder-high on the man, his face as beautiful as a profile on a cameo, sad and concerned.

"Mr. Johnson," he said, "why do you run off like that? Don't you know how easy it is for you to get hurt? We've told you and *told* you, Mr. Johnson."

William did not answer. He whimpered and struggled ineffectually in Raby's grasp.

"What'll we do, Jix?" asked Raby. "He's all excited, and he's going to hurt himself if he doesn't stop fighting."

"I think he wants to get back under the rock," said Jix. "Let's take him away to where there's nothing for him to crawl under. Then maybe he'll relax."

He led off. Raby followed, holding William's arms and pushing him along. As they went, William's resistance slowly melted. He ceased to fight against Raby's urging and the tension went out of his arms. After a little while the younger boy let him go and he trudged along with them with his head bowed, his gray hair falling forward over his gaunt, youngish-looking face and his arms in their iridescent sleeves—he was dressed in the same fashion as Jix and Raby—swinging limply on either side.

They had been on the side of a stone-tumbled hill, just below its peak. This peak they went up and over now, and down the far side onto a smooth falling-away of land, so carpeted with fine grass that it seemed almost parklike. In the nearer distance was a great, abrupt hole several acres in area, with a glimpse of vertical sides of white rock. Beyond this were the hazy blue shoulders of the foothills to the mountains, and here and there amongst them a flash or hint of bright color that gave no clue to its shape or purpose in being.

They went on until they reached the smooth lawn-level grass beside the quarry; and there the two boys sat down, pulling William down with them. They sat cross-legged like Indians in a rough circle.

William's eyes, for all that his body was loose again, were still abstract and wild. They stared away at the foothills; and slowly two tears formed in them, welled up and began to streak their way down his hollow cheeks.

"Home—" he said suddenly, brokenly, "home—"

Jix reached over and rhythmically, slowly, soothingly, rubbed William's near shoulder.

"Now, Mr. Johnson," he said, "you know you can't go home. You can only go forward in time, not back. We told you and told you," he almost chanted the words, matching the rhythm of his moving hand, "and *told* you you can't go back."

William put his head down and sobbed.

"Now, Mr. Johnson," said Jix, "it's really no use getting all unhappy. If you'll just look up and around you, you'll see all sorts of things to feel good about. See how the foothills seem to go right up into the air like towers—look, Mr. Johnson." Slowly, as if unwillingly, the man raised his head and turned it toward the foothills. "That darker blue behind them, that haze, that's really the mountains, only the humidity's up and we've got a temperature inversion back a ways. Isn't that something to see, Mr. Johnson?"

William swallowed, looking off in the direction indicated.

"And look at this," broke in Raby, plucking a single blade of grass and holding it up before his face, "look at this, Mr. Johnson. See how fine and sharp the lines are. So beautiful. And all complete and whole in one little piece. Doesn't that make you happy?"

Suddenly, William knocked the hand holding the blade of grass aside.

"No!" he cried. "No!"

"Please, Mr. Johnson," said Jix, now rubbing his hand soothingly up and down the sharp adult spine. "Try just a little bit to like things. You'll feel a lot better if you do. It's nice here, but you won't let yourself like it."

"It's not!" William snapped his head back and forth, glaring first in one young face and then in the other. "Not like home!"

"But you can't *go* home," said Raby. "And it really wasn't very nice back then, Mr. Johnson, you know that as well as we do, but you won't admit it. It was dirty, and people were sick all the time, now wasn't it?"

"No!" exploded William. "It was fine, and plain and natural—" He sobbed again, suddenly. "There were people you could talk to. Plain people, who liked ordinary things and lived in real houses. They ate real food—real, cooked food."

"You can have anything you want to eat, Mr. Johnson," said Jix. "We'll get it right now for you."

"I don't want your food!" cried William, desperately. "It isn't real! It isn't honest."

"Why, yes it is," said Jix. "Now, you know that, too, Mr. Johnson. It's just as real as the food you used to get by killing animals and cooking up plants. It's just made out of the essential raw materials, that's all."

"I say it's fake!" William jerked about on the grass between them as if he would get up and run, but did not do so. "It's not right." He whimpered, dropping his voice and head. "It's not right," he whispered to the grass between his spread legs. He lifted his head. "All right," he said defiantly. "Make me eat it."

Mr. Johnson," said Raby, "we couldn't do a thing like that. Could we, Jix?"

"Not unless Mr. Johnson really wants us to," said Jix, firmly. "And we know he doesn't."

William brought his face around slowly to sneer in the face of the older boy.

"Oh, you're sure about that, are you?" he said, softly. "You're so sure." Jix did not pull his face back or alter his expression as the man's hot breath fanned his eyelashes. "You're so sure you know what I really want, and you try so hard to give it to me, don't you? And why? Why?"

"We feel sorry for you, Mr. Johnson," said Jix.

"I'll bet you do. I'll—just—bet—you—do." William pushed himself suddenly forward and onto his knees, so that he kneeled before Jix looming over him. "Do you know what I am?" he said softly. "I'm a physicist, a research physicist. I've got four degrees, do you know that? *Four college degrees!* I've got a million-dollar appropriation to do whatever I want—and I did something with it nobody ever did before, something nobody was ever intelligent enough and skillful enough, and trained enough to do before. I traveled into the future, into the far future. That's the kind of man I am."

"We know, Mr. Johnson," said Raby, from behind him. "You told us, you know, lots of times."

"Then what're we sitting here for?" cried William, sitting back on his knees and looking from one to the other. "Where are the men who ought to be talking to me? Where are the scientists? Where are the historians? Where are the institutes?"

"There aren't any, Mr. Johnson," said Jix. "Everybody told you that. Not the way you think. Everybody knows all about those things you know, but they're too busy to bother with them."

"Busy? Busy at what?" cried William.

"We told you and told you, Mr. Johsnon," said Raby, patiently, "that it's no use your trying to make us tell you, because there isn't any language for explaining what people do. You've just got to *understand*."

"Try me. Make me understand."

"But you can't," said Raby. "You weren't bred to *understand*. It took generations and generations of gene selection and crossing to evolve people who could *understand*. That's why the grownups don't have anything to talk to you about."

"Then why do you two talk to me?" William clenched his fists. "Why you?"

"But we're just children, Mr. Johnson."

"Children!" William's voice broke on a fresh sob. "Call yourselves children! Oh, no. Children are little and not strong. You show them things. Children believe you. You? Children?"

"But we are," said Jix, calmly.

"No, you're not." William straightened up, staring at them. "Children? You're monsters. Monsters stronger than I am. Monsters who know everything, who can do anything, who haven't a shred of natural feeling. Children? Children laugh. Children cry. You don't laugh or cry, either one of you. You don't hate. You don't love."

"Mr. Johnson!" said Raby. "You know better than that. We love everybody. We love you, too."

"Love? Me? When you torture me like this, day after day? When you follow me around, making a fool of me, always hounding me, showing me up—"

"We'll go away if you want," said Jix. "But every time we go away, you come looking for us."

"Not you! Not you!" William shook his clenched fists above his head. "I want real people, adult people to talk to."

"But nobody has time to talk to you but us," said Jix. "We told you that. Besides, we want to look after you. You're liable to get hurt if we don't watch you. You're always doing something that's going to get you hurt when we leave you alone, then we have to catch you before you do." He gestured at the wide hole a few yards off. "You nearly fell into the quarry, day before yesterday."

"The quarry!" groaned William. "Oh, God! And why did you make a quarry there in the first place? Did you just want one? Or did you want to play King Arthur with a real stone castle?"

"Our father wanted it," said Raby. "We *told* you that."

"He?" William gave a shout of high-pitched laughter. "The great man? The mysterious head of the household, who doesn't even exist part of the time? You mean he needed real stone? Plain stone?" William's voice rose on waves of hysterical laughing. "Plain, ordinary limestone? What for?"

The two boys looked at each other helplessly.

"It's one of those things I have to *understand*, isn't it?" shouted William, leaping to his feet. "Liars! Fake!" he began to dance before them, stamping his feet and bobbing his shoulders like a savage. "Mumbo jumbo! Witch doctor! Witch doctor! Spirits of the mumbo . . . jumbo . . . mumbo—" Abruptly he stopped chanting and dancing and stared at them, his face falling into a look of agony. He fell to his knees and stretched out his skinny arms to them. Dragging himself forward on his knees, he approached them.

"Please," he said, "please . . . oh please! You can do anything. I know you can do anything. Put me out of my misery. Make me happy here. Make me not know any different. Make me forget.. Fix me . . . fix me—"

The two boys looked at him with sad and solemn eyes.

"Poor Mr. Johnson," said Jix. "We can't do that. If you understood, you'd know it wasn't right for us to do it. If we changed you, it would spoil you, and we would be spoiled by doing such a thing. It isn't right for people to be changed, Mr. Johnson, except by themselves."

"But I'm not people," he clawed at their glittering tunics, "I'm an animal. I'm a pet. Have pity . . . oh, have pity—"

"No, Mr. Johnson," said Jix. "Even you know that. You're not an animal or a pet at all. You're a human man with a soul who has to find his own way, like everybody."

"But I can't . . . you all say I can't!"

"Poor Mr. Johnson," said Raby softly. "If only you'd understand."

"Make me understand," William pleaded.

"Nobody can make you understand, Mr. Johnson."

William screamed suddenly and rose to his feet. Extending his shaking hands to the air, he screamed at the sky. And then, whirling, before even the quick reflexes of the boys could stop him, he turned and ran toward the open edge of the quarry. He ran forward and out. For a fraction of a second he continued forward, seeming to run in empty air, and then he dropped from sight.

The boys leaped and ran to the edge of the quarry. Before they reached it, the sound of an impact came up from the depths. They stopped at the edge; and, looking over, saw the broken body of William lying on the pale wet rock, far below.

They looked at each other. Then they started to climb down into the quarry.

Their mother was in the garden of their house, that was like no house William had ever known, as they came up a little later carrying the crushed and ruined body. She turned to face them, a tall woman with pale skin and dark hair and as beautiful as they. Her eyes took in what was left of William and her exchange of glances with the boys seemed to gather the whole story.

"He suddenly jumped, Mother," said Raby. He looked up at the tall woman with eyes that were still the eyes of a child. "Is he all spoiled?"

"No, Raby," she answered. "Nothing is ever all spoiled. Give him to me." She took the dead man from Jix's arms easily up into her own. "I'll give him to your father when he gets back. Your father will fix him, and he'll be as good as ever in the morning."

CALL HIM LORD

There are many characteristics desirable in an Emperor that can be done without if necessary. But there is one that any true ruler absolutely must possess.

> *"He called and commanded me*
> *—Therefore, I knew him;*
> *But later on, failed me; and*
> *—Therefore, I slew him!"*

"Song of the Shield Bearer"

The sun could not fail in rising over the Kentucky hills, nor could Kyle Arnam in waking. There would be eleven hours and forty minutes of daylight. Kyle rose, dressed, and went out to saddle the gray gelding and the white stallion. He rode the stallion until the first fury was out of the arched and snowy neck; and then led both horses around to tether them outside the kitchen door. Then he went in to breakfast.

The message that had come a week before was beside his plate of bacon and eggs. Teena, his wife, was standing at the breadboard with her back to him. He sat down and began eating, rereading the letter as he ate.

"... The Prince will be traveling incognito under one of his family titles, as Count Sirii North; and should not be addressed as 'Majesty'. *You will call him 'Lord'* ..."

"Why does it have to be you?" Teena asked.

He looked up and saw how she stood with her back to him.

"Teena—" he said, sadly.

"Why?"

"My ancestors were bodyguards to his—back in the wars of conquest against the aliens. I've told you that," he said. "My forefathers saved the lives of his, many times when there was no warning—a Rak spaceship would sud-

162

denly appear out of nowhere to lock on, even to flagship.
And even an Emperor found himself fighting for his life,
hand to hand."

"The aliens are all dead now, and the Emperor's got a
hundred other worlds! Why can't his son take his Grand
Tour on them? Why does he have to come here to
Earth—and you?"

"There's only one Earth."

"And only one you, I suppose?"

He sighed internally and gave up. He had been raised
by his father and his uncle after his mother died, and in
an argument with Teena he always felt helpless. He got up
from the table and went to her, putting his hands on her
and gently trying to turn her about. But she resisted.

He sighed inside himself again and turned away to the
weapons cabinet. He took out a loaded slug pistol, fitted it
into the stubby holster it matched, and clipped the holster
to his belt at the left of the buckle, where the hang of his
leather jacket would hide it. Then he selected a dark-han-
dled knife with a six-inch blade and bent over to slip it
into the sheath inside his boot top. He dropped the cuff of
his trouser leg back over the boot top and stood up.

"He's got no right to be here," said Teena fiercely to
the breadboard. "Tourists are supposed to be kept to the
museum areas and the tourist lodges."

"He's not a tourist. You know that," answered Kyle, patiently. "He's the Emperor's oldest son and his great-
grandmother was from Earth. His wife will be, too. Every
fourth generation the Imperial line has to marry back into
Earth stock. That's the law—still." He put on his leather
jacket, sealing it closed only at the bottom to hide the
slug-gun holster, half turned to the door—then paused.

"Teena?" he asked.

She did not answer.

"Teena!" he repeated. He stepped to her, put his hands
on her shoulders and tried to turn her to face him. Again,
she resisted, but this time he was having none of it.

He was not a big man, being of middle height, round-
faced, with sloping and unremarkable-looking, if thick,
shoulders. But his strength was not ordinary. He could
bring the white stallion to its knees with one fist wound in
its mane—and no other man had ever been able to do that.
He turned her easily to look at him.

"Now, listen to me—" he began. But, before he could
finish, all the stiffness went out of her and she clung to
him, trembling.

"He'll get you into trouble—I know he will!" she choked, muffledly into his chest. "Kyle, don't go! There's no law making you go!"

He stroked the soft hair of her head, his throat stiff and dry. There was nothing he could say to her. What she was asking was impossible. Ever since the sun had first risen on men and women together, wives had clung to their husbands at times like this, begging for what could not be. And always the men had held them, as Kyle was holding her now—as if understanding could somehow be pressed from one body into the other—and saying nothing, because there was nothing that could be said.

So, Kyle held her for a few moments longer, and then reached behind him to unlock her intertwined fingers at his back, and loosen her arms around him. Then, he went. Looking back through the kitchen window as he rode off on the stallion, leading the gray horse, he saw her standing just where he had left her. Not even crying, but standing with her arms hanging down, her head down, not moving.

He rode away through the forest of the Kentucky hillside. It took him more than two hours to reach the lodge. As he rode down the valleyside toward it, he saw a tall, bearded man, wearing the robes they wore on some of the Younger Worlds, standing at the gateway to the interior courtyard of the rustic, wooded lodge.

When he got close, he saw that the beard was graying and the man was biting his lips. Above a straight, thin nose, the eyes were bloodshot and circled beneath as if from worry or lack of sleep.

"He's in the courtyard," said the gray-bearded man as Kyle rode up. "I'm Montlaven, his tutor. He's ready to go." The darkened eyes looked almost pleadingly up at Kyle.

"Stand clear of the stallion's head," said Kyle. "And take me in to him."

"Not that horse, for him—" said Montlaven, looking distrustfully at the stallion, as he backed away.

"No," said Kyle. "He'll ride the gelding."

"He'll want the white."

"He can't ride the white," said Kyle. "Even if I let him, he couldn't ride this stallion. I'm the only one who can ride him. Take me in."

The tutor turned and led the way into the grassy courtyard, surrounding a swimming pool and looked down upon, on three sides, by the windows of the lodge. In a lounging chair by the pool sat a tall young man in his late teens, with a mane of blond hair, a pair of stuffed saddlebags on the grass beside him. He stood up as Kyle and the tutor came toward him.

"Majesty," said the tutor, as they stopped, "this is Kyle Arnam, your bodyguard for the three days here."

"Good morning, Bodyguard ... Kyle, I mean." The Prince smiled mischievously. "Light, then. And I'll mount."

"You ride the gelding, Lord," said Kyle.

The Prince stared at him, tilted back his handsome head, and laughed.

"I can ride, man!" he said. "I ride well."

"Not this horse, Lord," said Kyle, dispassionately. "No one rides this horse, but me."

The eyes flashed wide, the laugh faded—then returned.

"What can I do?" The wide shoulders shrugged. "I give in—always I give in. Well, almost always." He grinned up at Kyle, his lips thinned, but frank. "All right."

He turned to the gelding—and with a sudden leap was in the saddle. The gelding snorted and plunged at the shock; then steadied as the young man's long fingers tightened expertly on the reins and the fingers of the other hand patted a gray neck. The Prince raised his eyebrows, looking over at Kyle, but Kyle sat stolidly.

"I take it you're armed good Kyle?" the Prince said slyly. "You'll protect me against the natives if they run wild?"

"Your life is in my hands, Lord," said Kyle. He unsealed the leather jacket at the bottom and let it fall open to show the slug pistol in its holster for a moment. Then he resealed the jacket again at the bottom.

"Will—" The tutor put his hand on the young man's knee. "Don't be reckless, boy. This is Earth and the people here don't have rank and custom like we do. Think before you—"

"Oh, cut it out, Monty!" snapped the Prince. "I'll be just as incognito, just as humble, as archaic and independent as the rest of them. You think I've no memory! Anyway, it's only for three days or so until my Imperial father joins me. Now, let me go!"

He jerked away, turned to lean forward in the saddle, and abruptly put the gelding into a bolt for the gate. He disappeared through it, and Kyle drew hard on the stallion's reins as the big white horse danced and tried to follow.

"Give me his saddlebags," said Kyle.

The tutor bent and passed them up. Kyle made them fast on top of his own, across the stallion's withers. Looking down, he saw there were tears in the bearded man's eyes.

"He's a fine boy. You'll see. You'll know he is!" Montlaven's face, upturned, was mutely pleading.

"I know he comes from a fine family," said Kyle, slowly. "I'll do my best for him." And he rode off out of the gateway after the gelding.

When he came out of the gate, the Prince was nowhere in sight. But it was simple enough for Kyle to follow, by dinted brown earth and crushed grass, the marks of the gelding's path. This brought him at last through some pines to a grassy open slope where the Prince sat looking skyward through a single-lens box.

When Kyle came up, the Prince lowered the instrument and without a word, passed it over. Kyle put it to his eye and looked skyward. There was the whir of the tracking unit and one of Earth's three orbiting power stations swam into the field of vision of the lens.

"Give it back," said the Prince.

"I couldn't get a look at it earlier," went on the young man as Kyle handed the lens to him. "And I wanted to. It's a rather expensive present, you know—it and the other two like it—from our Imperial treasury. Just to keep your planet from drifting into another ice age. And what do we get for it?"

"Earth, Lord," answered Kyle. "As it was before men went out to the stars."

"Oh, the museum areas could be maintained with one station and a half-million caretakers," said the Prince. "It's the other two stations and you billion or so free-loaders I'm talking about. I'll have to look into it when I'm Emperor. Shall we ride?"

"If you wish, Lord." Kyle picked up the reins of the stallion and the two horses with their riders moved off across the slope.

". . . And one more thing," said the Prince, as they entered the farther belt of pine trees. "I don't want you to be misled—I'm really very fond of old Monty, back there. It's just that I wasn't really planning to come here at all— *Look at me, Bodyguard!*"

Kyle turned to see the blue eyes that ran in the Imperial

family blazing at him. Then, unexpectedly, they softened.
The Prince laughed.

"You don't scare easily, do you, Bodyguard . . . Kyle,
I mean?" he said. "I think I like you after all. But look at
me when I talk."

"Yes, Lord."

"That's my good Kyle. Now, I was explaining to you
that I'd never actually planned to come here on my Grand
Tour at all. I didn't see any point in visiting this dusty old
museum world of yours with people still trying to live like
they lived in the Dark Ages. But—my Imperial father
talked me into it"

"Your father, Lord?" asked Kyle.

"Yes, he bribed me, you might say," said the Prince
thoughtfully. "He was supposed to meet me here for these
three days. Now, he's messaged there's been a slight delay
—but that doesn't matter. The point is, he belongs to the
school of old men who still think your Earth is something
precious and vital. Now, I happen to like and admire my
father, Kyle. You approve of that?"

"Yes, Lord."

"I thought you would. Yes, he's the one man in the
human race I look up to. And to please him, I'm making
this Earth trip. And to please him—only to please *him*,
Kyle—I'm going to be an easy Prince for you to conduct
around to your natural wonders and watering spots and
whatever. Now, you understand me—and how this trip is
going to go. Don't you?" He stared at Kyle.

"I understand," said Kyle.

"That's fine," said the Prince, smiling once more. "So
now you can start telling me all about these trees and birds
and animals so that I can memorize their names and please
my father when he shows up. What are those little birds
I've been seeing under the trees—brown on top and whitish
underneath? Like that one—there!"

"That's a Veery, Lord," said Kyle. "A bird of the deep
woods and silent places. Listen—" He reached out a hand
to the gelding's bridle and brought both horses to a halt.
In the sudden silence, off to their right they could hear a
silver bird-voice, rising and falling, in a descending series
of crescendos and diminuendos, that softened at last into
silence. For a moment after the song was ended the Prince
sat staring at Kyle, then seemed to shake himself back to
life.

"Interesting," he said. He lifted the reins Kyle had let go and the horses moved forward again. "Tell me more."

For more than three hours, as the sun rose toward noon, they rode through the wooded hills, with Kyle identifying bird and animal, insect, tree and rock. And for three hours the Prince listened—his attention flashing and momentary, but intense. But when the sun was overhead that intensity flagged.

"That's enough," he said. "Aren't we going to stop for lunch? Kyle, aren't there any towns around here?"

"Yes, Lord," said Kyle. "We've passed several."

"Several?" The Prince stared at him. "Why haven't we come into one before now? Where are you taking me?"

"Nowhere, Lord," said Kyle. "You lead the way, I only follow."

"I?" said the Prince. For the first time he seemed to become aware that he had been keeping the gelding's head always in advance of the stallion. "Of course. But now it's time to eat."

"Yes, Lord," said Kyle. "This way."

He turned the stallion's head down the slope of the hill they were crossing and the Prince turned the gelding after him.

"And now listen," said the Prince, as he caught up. "Tell me I've got it all right." And to Kyle's astonishment, he began to repeat, almost word for word, everything that Kyle had said. "Is it all there? Everything you told me?"

"Perfectly, Lord," said Kyle. The Prince looked slyly at him.

"Could you do that, Kyle?"

"Yes," said Kyle. "But these are things I've known all my life."

"You see?" The Prince smiled. "That's the difference between us, good Kyle. You spend your life learning something—I spend a few hours and I know as much about it as you do."

"Not as much, Lord," said Kyle, slowly.

The Prince blinked at him, then jerked his hand dismissingly, and half-angrily, as if he were throwing something aside.

"What little else there is probably doesn't count," he said.

They rode down the slope and through a winding valley and came out at a small village. As they rode clear of the surrounding trees a sound of music came to their ears.

"What's that?" The Prince stood up in his stirrups. "Why there's dancing going on, over there."

"A beer garden, Lord. And it's Saturday—a holiday here."

"Good. We'll go there to eat."

They rode around to the beer garden and found tables back away from the dance floor. A pretty, young waitress came and they ordered, the Prince smiling sunnily at her until she smiled back—then hurried off as if in mild confusion. The Prince ate hungrily when the food came and drank a stein and a half of brown beer, while Kyle ate more lightly and drank coffee.

"That's better," said the Prince, sitting back at last. "I had an appetite ... Look there, Kyle! Look, there are five, six ... seven drifter platforms parked over there. Then you don't all ride horses?"

"No," said Kyle. "It's as each man wishes."

"But if you have drifter platforms, why not other civilized things?"

"Some things fit, some don't, Lord," answered Kyle. The Prince laughed.

"You mean you try to make civilization fit this old-fashioned life of yours, here?" he said. "Isn't that the wrong way around—" He broke off. "What's that they're playing now? I like that. I'll bet I could do that dance." He stood up. "In fact, I think I will."

He paused, looking down at Kyle.

"Aren't you going to warn me against it?" he asked.

"No, Lord," said Kyle. "What you do is your own affair."

The young man turned away abruptly. The waitress who had served them was passing, only a few tables away. The Prince went after her and caught up with her by the dance floor railing. Kyle could see the girl protesting—but the Prince hung over her, looking down from his tall height, smiling. Shortly, she had taken off her apron and was out on the dance floor with him, showing him the steps of the dance. It was a polka.

The Prince learned with fantastic quickness. Soon, he was swinging the waitress around with the rest of the dancers, his foot stamping on the turns, his white teeth gleaming. Finally the number ended and the members of the band put down their instruments and began to leave the stand.

The Prince, with the girl trying to hold him back,

walked over to the band leader. Kyle got up quickly from his table and started toward the floor.

The band leader was shaking his head. He turned abruptly and slowly walked away. The Prince started after him, but the girl took hold of his arm, saying something urgent to him.

He brushed her aside and she stumbled a little. A busboy among the tables on the far side of the dance floor, not much older than the Prince and nearly as tall, put down his tray and vaulted the railing onto the polished hardwood. He came up behind the Prince and took hold of his arm, swinging him around.

". . . Can't do that here." Kyle heard him say, as Kyle came up. The Prince struck out like a panther—like a trained boxer—with three quick lefts in succession into the face of the busboy, the Prince's shoulder bobbing, the weight of his body in behind each blow.

The busboy went down. Kyle, reaching the Prince, herded him away through a side gap in the railing. The young man's face was white with rage. People were swarming onto the dance floor.

"Who was that? What's his name?" demanded the Prince, between his teeth. "He put his hand on me! Did you see that? *He put his hand on me!*"

"You knocked him out," said Kyle. "What more do you want?"

"He manhandled me—*me!*" snapped the Prince. "I want to find out who he is!" He caught hold of the bar to which the horses were tied, refusing to be pushed farther. "He'll learn to lay hands on a future Emperor!"

"No one will tell you his name," said Kyle. And the cold note in his voice finally seemed to reach through to the Prince and sober him. He stared at Kyle.

"Including you?" he demanded at last.

"Including me, Lord," said Kyle.

The Prince stared a moment longer, then swung away. He turned, jerked loose the reins of the gelding and swung into the saddle. He rode off. Kyle mounted and followed.

They rode in silence into the forest. After a while, the Prince spoke without turning his head.

"And you call yourself a bodyguard," he said, finally.

"Your life is in my hands, Lord," said Kyle. The Prince turned a grim face to look at him.

"Only my life?" said the Prince. "As long as they don't kill me, they can do what they want? Is that what you mean?"

Kyle met his gaze steadily.

"Pretty much so, Lord," he said.

The Prince spoke with an ugly note in his voice.

"I don't think I like you, after all, Kyle," he said. "I don't think I like you at all."

"I'm not here with you to be liked, Lord," said Kyle.

"Perhaps not," said the Prince, thickly. "But I know *your* name!"

They rode on in continued silence for perhaps another half hour. But then gradually the angry hunch went out of the young man's shoulders and the tightness out of his jaw. After a while he began to sing to himself, a song in a language Kyle did not know; and as he sang, his cheerfulness seemed to return. Shortly, he spoke to Kyle, as if there had never been anything but pleasant moments between them.

Mammoth Cave was close and the Prince asked to visit it. They went there and spent some time going through the cave. After that they rode their horses up along the left bank of the Green River. The Prince seemed to have forgotten all about the incident at the beer garden and be out to charm everyone they met. As the sun was at last westering toward the dinner hour, they came finally to a small hamlet back from the river, with a roadside inn mirrored in an artificial lake beside it, and guarded by oak and pine trees behind.

"This looks good," said the Prince. "We'll stay overnight here, Kyle."

"If you wish, Lord," said Kyle.

They halted, and Kyle took the horses around to the stable, then entered the inn to find the Prince already in the small bar off the dining room, drinking beer and charming the waitress. This waitress was younger than the one at the beer garden had been; a little girl with soft, loose hair and round brown eyes that showed their delight in the attention of the tall, good-looking, young man.

"Yes," said the Prince to Kyle, looking out of corners of the Imperial blue eyes at him, after the waitress had gone to get Kyle his coffee. "This is the very place."

"The very place?" said Kyle.

"For me to get to know the people better—what did you think, good Kyle?" said the Prince and laughed at him. "I'll observe the people here and you can explain them—won't that be good?"

Kyle gazed at him, thoughtfully.

"I'll tell you whatever I can, Lord," he said.

They drank—the Prince his beer, and Kyle his coffee—and went in a little later to the dining room for dinner. The Prince, as he had promised at the bar, was full of questions about what he saw—and what he did not see.

". . . But why go on living in the past, all of you here?" he asked Kyle. "A museum world is one thing. But a museum people—" he broke off to smile and speak to the little, soft-haired waitress, who had somehow been diverted from the bar to wait upon their dining-room table.

"Not a museum people, Lord," said Kyle. "A living people. The only way to keep a race and a culture preserved is to keep it alive. So we go on in our own way, here on Earth, as a living example for the Younger Worlds to check themselves against."

"Fascinating . . ." murmured the Prince; but his eyes had wandered off to follow the waitress, who was glowing and looking back at him from across the now-busy dining room.

"Not fascinating. Necessary, Lord," said Kyle. But he did not believe the younger man had heard him.

After dinner, they moved back to the bar. And the Prince, after questioning Kyle a little longer, moved up to continue his researches among the other people standing at the bar. Kyle watched for a little while. Then, feeling it was safe to do so, slipped out to have another look at the horses and to ask the innkeeper to arrange a saddle lunch put up for them the next day.

When he returned, the Prince was not to be seen.

Kyle sat down at a table to wait; but the Prince did not return. A cold, hard knot of uneasiness began to grow below Kyle's breastbone. A sudden pang of alarm sent him swiftly back out to check the horses. But they were cropping peacefully in their stalls. The stallion whickered, low-voiced, as Kyle looked in on him, and turned his white head to look back at Kyle.

"Easy, boy," said Kyle and returned to the inn to find the innkeeper.

But the innkeeper had no idea where the Prince might have gone.

". . . If the horses aren't taken, he's not far," the innkeeper said. "There's no trouble he can get into around here. Maybe he went for a walk in the moods. I'll leave word for the night staff to keep an eye out for him when he comes in. Where'll you be?"

"In the bar until it closes—then, my room," said Kyle.

He went back to the bar to wait, and took a booth near an open window. Time went by and gradually the number of other customers began to dwindle. Above the ranked bottles, the bar clock showed nearly midnight. Suddenly, through the window, Kyle heard a distant scream of equine fury from the stables.

He got up and went out quickly. In the darkness outside, he ran to the stables and burst in. There in the feeble illumination of the stable's night lighting, he saw the Prince, palefaced, clumsily saddling the gelding in the center aisle between the stalls. The door to the stallion's stall was open. The Prince looked away as Kyle came in.

Kyle took three swift steps to the open door and looked in. The stallion was still tied, but his ears were back, his eyes rolling, and a saddle lay tumbled and dropped on the stable floor beside him.

"Saddle up," said the Prince thickly from the aisle. "We're leaving." Kyle turned to look at him.

"We've got rooms at the inn here," he said.

"Never mind. We're riding. I need to clear my head." The young man got the gelding's cinch tight, dropped the stirrups and swung heavily up into the saddle. Without waiting for Kyle, he rode out of the stable into the night.

"So, boy . . ." said Kyle soothingly to the stallion. Hastily he untied the big white horse, saddled him, and set out after the Prince. In the darkness there was no way of ground-tracking the gelding; but he leaned forward and blew into the ear of the stallion. The surprised horse neighed in protest and the whinny of the gelding came back from the darkness of the slope up ahead and over to Kyle's right. He rode in that direction.

He caught the Prince on the crown of the hill. The young man was walking the gelding, reins loose, and singing under his breath—the same song in an unknown language he had sung earlier. But, now as he saw Kyle, he grinned loosely and began to sing with more emphasis. For the first time Kyle caught the overtones of something mocking and lusty about the incomprehensible words. Understanding broke suddenly in him.

"The girl!" he said. "The little waitress. Where is she?"

The grin vanished from the Prince's face, then came slowly back again. The grin laughed at Kyle.

"Why, where d'you think?" The words slurred on the Prince's tongue and Kyle, riding close, smelled the beer heavy on the young man's breath. "In her room, sleeping and happy. Honored . . . though she doesn't know it . . . by an Emperor's son. And expecting to find me there in the morning. But I won't be. Will we, good Kyle?"

"Why did you do it, Lord?" asked Kyle, quietly.

"Why?" The Prince peered at him, a little drunkenly in the moonlight. "Kyle, my father has four sons. I've got three younger brothers. But I'm the one who's going to be Emperor; and Emperors don't answer questions."

Kyle said nothing. The Prince peered at him. They rode on together for several minutes in silence.

"All right, I'll tell you why," said the Prince, more loudly, after a while as if the pause had been only momentary. "It's because you're not *my* bodyguard, Kyle. You see, I've seen through you. I know whose bodyguard you are. You're *theirs!*"

Kyle's jaw tightened. But the darkness hid his reaction.

"All right—" The Prince gestured loosely, disturbing his balance in the saddle. "That's all right. Have it your way. I don't mind. So, we'll play points. There was that lout at the beer garden, who put his hands on me. But no one would tell me his name, you said. All right, you managed to bodyguard him. One point for you. But you didn't manage to bodyguard the girl at the inn back there. One point for me. Who's going to win, good Kyle?"

Kyle took a deep breath.

"Lord," he said, "some day it'll be your duty to marry a woman from Earth—"

The Prince interrupted him with a laugh, and this time there was an ugly note in it.

"You flatter yourselves," he said. His voice thickened. "That's the trouble with you—all you Earth people—you flatter yourselves."

They rode on in silence. Kyle said nothing more, but kept the head of the stallion close to the shoulder of the gelding, watching the young man closely. For a little while the Prince seemed to doze. His head sank on his chest and he let the gelding wander. Then, after a while, his head began to come up again, his automatic horseman's fingers tightened on the reins, and he lifted his head to stare around in the moonlight.

"I want a drink," he said. His voice was no longer thick, but it was flat and uncheerful. "Take me where we can get some beer, Kyle."

Kyle took a deep breath.

"Yes, Lord," he said.

He turned the stallion's head to the right and the gelding followed. They went up over a hill and down to the edge of a lake. The dark water sparkled in the moonlight and the farther shore was lost in the night. Lights shone through the trees around the curve of the shore.

"There, Lord," said Kyle. "It's a fishing resort, with a bar."

They rode around the shore to it. It was a low, casual building, angled to face the shore; a dock ran out from it, to which fishing boats were tethered, bobbing slightly on the black water. Light gleamed through the windows as they hitched their horses and went to the door.

The barroom they stepped into was wide and bare. A long bar faced them with several planked fish on the wall behind it. Below the fish were three bartenders—the one in the center, middle-aged, and wearing an air of authority with his apron. The other two were young and muscular. The customers, mostly men, scattered at the square tables and standing at the bar wore rough working clothes, or equally casual vacationers' garb.

The Prince sat down at a table back from the bar and Kyle sat down with him. When the waitress came they ordered beer and coffee, and the Prince half-emptied his stein the moment it was brought to him. As soon as it was completely empty, he signaled the waitress again.

"Another," he said. This time, he smiled at the waitress when she brought his stein back. But she was a woman in her thirties, pleased but not overwhelmed by his attention. She smiled lightly back and moved off to return to the bar where she had been talking to two men her own age, one fairly tall, the other shorter, bullet-headed and fleshy.

The Prince drank. As he put his stein down, he seemed to become aware of Kyle, and turned to look at him.

"I suppose," said the Prince, "you think I'm drunk?"

"Not yet," said Kyle.

"No," said the Prince, "that's right. Not yet. But perhaps I'm going to be. And if I decide I am, who's going to stop me?"

"No one, Lord."

"That's right," the young man said. "That's right." He drank deliberately from his stein until it was empty, and then signaled the waitress for another. A spot of color was beginning to show over each of his high cheekbones. "When you're on a miserable little world with miserable little people . . . hello, Bright Eyes!" he interrupted himself as the waitress brought his beer. She laughed and went back to her friends. ". . . You have to amuse yourself any way you can," he wound up.

He laughed to himself.

"When I think how my father, and Monty—everybody—used to talk this planet up to me—" he glanced aside at Kyle. "Do you know at one time I was actually scared—well, not scared exactly, nothing scares me ... say *concerned*—about maybe having to come here, some day?" He laughed again. "Concerned that I wouldn't measure up to you Earth people! Kyle, have you ever been to any of the Younger Worlds?"

"No," said Kyle.

"I thought not. Let me tell you, good Kyle, the worst of the people there are bigger, and better-looking and smarter, and everything than anyone I've seen here. And I, Kyle, I—the Emperor-to-be—am better than any of them. So, guess how all you here look to me?" He stared at Kyle, waiting. "Well, answer me, good Kyle. Tell me the truth. That's an order."

"It's not up to you to judge, Lord," said Kyle.

"Not—? Not up to me?" The blue eyes blazed. *"I'm* going to be Emperor!"

"It's not up to any one man, Lord," said Kyle. "Emperor or not. An Emperor's needed, as the symbol that can hold a hundred worlds together. But the real need of the race is to survive. It took nearly a million years to evolve a survival-type intelligence here on Earth. And out on the newer worlds people are bound to change. If something gets lost out there, some necessary element lost out of the race, there needs to be a pool of original genetic material here to replace it."

The Prince's lips grew wide in a savage grin.

"Oh, good, Kyle—good!" he said. "Very good. Only, I've heard all that before. Only, I don't believe it. You see—I've seen you people, now. And you don't outclass us, out on the Younger Worlds. *We* outclass *you.* We've gone on and got better, while you stayed still. And you know it."

The young man laughed softly, almost in Kyle's face.

"All you've been afraid of, is that we'd find out. And I have." He laughed again. "I've had a look at you; and now I know. I'm bigger, better and braver than any man in this room—and you know why? Not just because I'm the son of the Emperor, but because it's born in me! Body, brains and everything else! I can do what I want here, and no one on this planet is good enough to stop me. Watch."

He stood up, suddenly.

"Now, I want that waitress to get drunk with me," he said. "And this time I'm telling you in advance. Are you going to try and stop me?"

Kyle looked up at him. Their eyes met.

"No, Lord," he said. "It's not my job to stop you."

The Prince laughed.

"I thought so," he said. He swung away and walked between the tables toward the bar and the waitress, still in conversation with the two men. The Prince came up to the bar on the far side of the waitress and ordered a new stein of beer from the middle-aged bartender. When it was given to him, he took it, turned around, and rested his elbows on the bar, leaning back against it. He spoke to the waitress, interrupting the taller of the two men.

"I've been wanting to talk to you," Kyle heard him say.

The waitress, a little surprised, looked around at him. She smiled, recognizing him—a little flattered by the directness of his approach, a little appreciative of his clean good looks, a little tolerant of his youth.

"*You* don't mind, do you?" said the Prince, looking past her to the bigger of the two men, the one who had just been talking. The other stared back, and their eyes met without shifting for several seconds. Abruptly, angrily, the man shrugged, and turned about with his back hunched against them.

"You see?" said the Prince, smiling back at the waitress. "He knows I'm the one you ought to be talking to, instead of—"

"All right, sonny. Just a minute."

It was the shorter, bullet-head man, interrupting. The Prince turned to look down at him with a fleeting expression of surprise. But the bullet-headed man was already turning to his taller friend and putting a hand on his arm.

"Come on back, Ben," the shorter man was saying. "The kid's a little drunk, is all." He turned back to the Prince. "You shove off now," he said. "Clara's with us."

The Prince stared at him blankly. The stare was so fixed that the shorter man had started to turn away, back to his friend and the waitress, when the Prince seemed to wake.

"Just a minute—" he said, in his turn.

He reached out a hand to one of the fleshy shoulders below the bullet head. The man turned back, knocking the hand calmly away. Then, just as calmly, he picked up the

Prince's full stein of beer from the bar and threw it in the young man's face.

"Get lost," he said, unexcitedly.

The Prince stood for a second, with the beer dripping from his face. Then, without even stopping to wipe his eyes clear, he threw the beautifully trained left hand he had demonstrated at the beer garden.

But the shorter man, as Kyle had known from the first moment of seeing him, was not like the busboy the Prince had decisioned so neatly. This man was thirty pounds heavier, fifteen years more experienced, and by build and nature a natural bar fighter. He had not stood there waiting to be hit, but had already ducked and gone forward to throw his thick arms around the Prince's body. The young man's punch bounced harmlessly off the round head, and both bodies hit the floor, rolling in among the chair and table legs.

Kyle was already more than halfway to the bar and the three bartenders were already leaping the wooden hurdle that walled them off. The taller friend of the bullet-headed man, hovering over the two bodies, his eyes glittering, had his boot drawn back ready to drive the point of it into the Prince's kidneys. Kyle's forearm took him economically like a bar of iron across the tanned throat.

He stumbled backwards choking. Kyle stood still, hands open and down, glancing at the middle-aged bartender.

"All right," said the bartender. "But don't do anything more." He turned to the two younger bartenders. "All right. Haul him off!"

The pair of younger, aproned men bent down and came up with the bullet-headed man expertly handlocked between them. The man made one surging effort to break loose, and then stood still.

"Let me at him," he said.

"Not in here," said the older bartender. "Take it outside."

Between the tables, the Prince staggered unsteadily to his feet. His face was streaming blood from a cut on his forehead, but what could be seen of it was white as a drowning man's. His eyes went to Kyle, standing beside him; and he opened his mouth—but what came out sounded like something between a sob and a curse.

"All right," said the middle-aged bartender again. "Outside, both of you. Settle it out there."

The men in the room had packed around the little space

by the bar. The Prince looked about and for the first time seemed to see the human wall hemming him in. His gaze wobbled to meet Kyle's.

"Outside . . . ?" he said, chokingly.

"You aren't staying in here," said the older bartender, answering for Kyle. "I saw it. You started the whole thing. Now, settle it any way you want—but you're both going outside. Now! Get moving!"

He pushed at the Prince, but the Prince resisted, clutching at Kyle's leather jacket with one hand.

"Kyle—."

"I'm sorry, Lord," said Kyle. "I can't help. It's your fight."

"Let's get out of here," said the bullet-headed man.

The Prince stared around at them as if they were some strange set of beings he had never known to exist before.

"No . . ." he said.

He let go of Kyle's jacket. Unexpectedly, his hand darted in towards Kyle's belly holster and came out holding the slug pistol.

"Stand back!" he said, his voice high-toned. "Don't try to touch me!"

His voice broke on the last words. There was a strange sound, half grunt, half moan, from the crowd; and it swayed back from him. Manager, bartenders, watchers—all but Kyle and the bullet-headed man drew back.

"You dirty slob . . ." said the bullet-headed man, distinctly. "I knew you didn't have the guts."

"Shut up!" The Prince's voice was high and cracking. "Shut up! Don't any of you try to come after me!"

He began backing away toward the front door of the bar. The room watched in silence, even Kyle standing still. As he backed, the Prince's back straightened. He hefted the gun in his hand. When he reached the door he paused to wipe the blood from his eyes with his left sleeve, and his smeared face looked with a first touch of regained arrogance at them.

"Swine!" he said.

He opened the door and backed out, closing it behind him. Kyle took one step that put him facing the bullet-headed man. Their eyes met and he could see the other recognizing the fighter in him, as he had earlier recognized it in the bullet-headed man.

"Don't come after us," said Kyle.

The bullet-headed man did not answer. But no answer was needed. He stood still.

Kyle turned, ran to the door, stood on one side of it and flicked it open. Nothing happened; and he slipped through, dodging to his right at once, out of the line of any shot aimed at the opening door.

But no shot came. For a moment he was blind in the night darkness, then his eyes began to adjust. He went by sight, feel and memory toward the hitching rack. By the time he got there, he was beginning to see.

The Prince was untying the gelding and getting ready to mount.

"Lord," said Kyle.

The Prince let go of the saddle for a moment and turned to look over his shoulder at him.

"Get away from me," said the Prince, thickly.

"Lord," said Kyle, low-voiced and pleading, "you lost your head in there. Anyone might do that. But don't make it worse, now. Give me back the gun, Lord."

"Give you the gun?"

The young man stared at him—and then he laughed.

"Give *you* the gun?" he said again. "So you can let someone beat me up some more? So you can not-guard me with it?"

"Lord," said Kyle, "please. For your own sake—give me back the gun."

"Get out of here," said the Prince, thickly, turning back to mount the gelding. "Clear out before I put a slug in you."

Kyle drew a slow, sad breath. He stepped forward and tapped the Prince on the shoulder.

"Turn around, Lord," he said.

"I warned you—" shouted the Prince, turning.

He came around as Kyle stooped, and the slug pistol flashed in his hand from the light of the bar windows. Kyle, bent over, was lifting the cuff of his trouser leg and closing his fingers on the hilt of the knife in his boot sheath. He moved simply, skillfully, and with a speed nearly double that of the young man, striking up into the chest before him until the hand holding the knife jarred against the cloth covering flesh and bone.

It was a sudden, hard-driven, swiftly merciful blow. The blade struck upwards between the ribs lying open to an underhanded thrust, plunging deep into the heart. The Prince grunted with the impact driving the air from his lungs; and he was dead as Kyle caught his slumping body in leather-jacketed arms.

Kyle lifted the tall body across the saddle of the gelding

and tied it there. He hunted on the dark ground for the fallen pistol and returned it to his holster. Then, he mounted the stallion and, leading the gelding with its burden, started the long ride back.

Dawn was graying the sky when at last he topped the hill overlooking the lodge where he had picked up the Prince almost twenty-four hours before. He rode down towards the courtyard gate.

A tall figure, indistinct in the pre-dawn light, was waiting inside the courtyard as Kyle came through the gate; and it came running to meet him as he rode toward it. It was the tutor, Montlaven, and he was weeping as he ran to the gelding and began to fumble at the cords that tied the body in place.

"I'm sorry ..." Kyle heard himself saying; and was dully shocked by the deadness and remoteness of his voice. "There was no choice. You can read it all in my report to-morrow morning—"

He broke off. Another, even taller figure had appeared in the doorway of the lodge giving on the courtyard. As Kyle turned towards it, this second figure descended the few steps to the grass and came to him.

"Lord—" said Kyle. He looked down into features like those of the Prince, but older, under graying hair. This man did not weep like the tutor, but his face was set like iron.

"What happened, Kyle?" he said.

"Lord," said Kyle, "you'll have my report in the morning ..."

"I want to know," said the tall man. Kyle's throat was dry and stiff. He swallowed but swallowing did not ease it.

"Lord," he said, "you have three other sons. One of them will make an Emperor to hold the worlds together."

"What did he do? Whom did he hurt? Tell me!" The tall man's voice cracked almost as his son's voice had cracked in the bar.

"Nothing. No one," said Kyle, stiff-throated. "He hit a boy not much older than himself. He drank too much. He may have got a girl in trouble. It was nothing he did to anyone else. It was only a fault against himself." He swallowed. "Wait until tomorrow, Lord, and read my report."

"No!" The tall man caught Kyle's saddle horn with a grip that checked even the white stallion from moving. "Your family and mine have been tied together by this for three hundred years. What was the flaw in my son to

make him fail his test, back here on Earth? *I want to know!*"

Kyle's throat ached and was dry as ashes.

"Lord," he answered, "he was a coward."

The hand dropped from his saddle horn as if struck down by a sudden strengthlessness. And the Emperor of a hundred worlds fell back like a beggar, spurned in the dust.

Kyle lifted his reins and rode out of the gate, into the forest away on the hillside. The dawn was breaking.

STEEL BROTHER

"We stand on guard."
　　—MOTTO OF THE FRONTIER FORCE

"*. . . Man that is born of woman hath but a short time to live and is full of misery. He cometh up and is cut down, like a flower; he fleeth as it were a shadow and never continueth in one stay—*"

The voice of the chaplain was small and sharp in the thin air, intoning the words of the burial service above the temporary lectern set up just inside the transparent wall of the landing field dome. Through the double transparencies of the dome and the plastic cover of the burial rocket the black-clad ranks could see the body of the dead stationman, Ted Waskewicz, lying back comfortably at an angle of forty-five degrees, peaceful in death, waxily perfect from the hands of the embalmers, and immobile. The eyes were closed, the cheerful, heavy features still held their expression of thoughtless dominance, as though death had been a minor incident, easily shrugged off; and the battle star made a single blaze of color on the tunic of the black uniform.

"*Amen.*" The response was a deep bass utterance from the assembled men, like the single note of an organ. In the front rank of the Cadets, Thomas Jordan's lips moved stiffly with the others', his voice joining mechanically in their chorus. For this was the moment of his triumph, but in spite of it, the old, old fear had come back, the old sense of loneliness and loss and terror of his own inadequacy.

He stood at stiff attention, eyes to the front, trying to lose himself in the unanimity of his classmates, to shut out the voice of the chaplain and the memory it evoked of an

183

alien raid on an undefended city and of home and parents
swept away from him in a breath. He remembered the
mass burial service read over the shattered ruin of the
city; and the government agency that had taken him—a
ten-year-old orphan—and given him care and training until
this day, but could not give him what these others about
him had by natural right—the courage of those who had
matured in safety.

For he had been lonely and afraid since that day. Un-
touched by bomb or shell, he had yet been crippled deep
inside of him. He had seen the enemy in his strength and
run screaming from his spacesuited gangs. And what could
give Thomas Jordan back his soul after that?

But still he stood rigidly at attention, as a Guardsman
should; for he was a soldier now, and this was part of his
duty.

The chaplain's voice droned to a halt. He closed his
prayerbook and stepped back from the lectern. The captain of the training ship took his place.

"In accordance with the conventions of the Frontier
Force," he said, crisply. "I now commit the ashes of Station Commandant First Class, Theodore Waskewicz, to
the keeping of time and space."

He pressed a button on the lectern. Beyond the dome,
white fire blossomed out from the tail of the burial rocket,
heating the asteroid rock to temporary incandescence. For
a moment it hung there, spewing flame. Then it rose, at
first slowly, then quickly, and was gone, sketching a fiery
path out and away, until, at almost the limits of human
sight, it vanished in a sudden, silent explosion of brilliant
light.

Around Jordan, the black-clad ranks relaxed. Not by
any physical movement, but with an indefinable breaking
of nervous tension, they settled themselves for the more
prosaic conclusion of the ceremony. The relaxation
reached even to the captain, for he about-faced with a relieved snap and spoke to the ranks.

"Cadet Thomas Jordan. Front and center."

The command struck Jordan with an icy shock. As long
as the burial service had been in progress, he had the protection of anonymity among his classmates around him.
Now, the captain's voice was a knife, cutting him off, finally and irrevocably from the one security his life had
known, leaving him naked and exposed. A despairing
numbness seized him. His reflexes took over, moving his

body like a robot. One step forward, a right face, down to
the end of the row of silent men, a left face, three steps
forward. Halt. Salute.

"Cadet Thomas Jordan reporting, sir."

"Cadet Thomas Jordan, I hereby invest you with command of this Frontier Station. You will hold it until relieved. Under no conditions will you enter communications
with an enemy or allow any creature or vessel to pass
through your sector of space from Outside."

"Yes, sir."

"In consideration of the duties and responsibilities req-
uisite on assuming command of this Station, you are pro-
moted to the rank and title of Station Commandant Third
Class."

"Thank you, sir."

From the lectern the captain lifted a cap of silver wire
mesh and placed it on his head. It clipped on to the electrodes already buried in his skull, with a snap that sent
sound ringing through his skull. For a second, a sheet of
lightning flashed in front of his eyes and he seemed to feel
the weight of the memory bank already pressing on his
mind. Then lightning and pressure vanished together to
show him the captain offering his hand.

"My congratulations, commandant."

"Thank you, sir."

They shook hands, the captain's grip quick, nervous and
perfunctory. He took one abrupt step backward and trans-
ferred his attention to his second in command.

"Lieutenant! Dismiss the formation!"

It was over. The new rank locked itself around Jordan,
sealing up the fear and loneliness inside him. Without listening to the barked commands that no longer concerned
him, he turned on his heel and strode over to take up his
position by the sally port of the training ship. He stood
formally at attentiion beside it, feeling the weight of his
new authority like a heavy cloak on his thin shoulders. At
one stroke he had become the ranking officer present. The
officers—even the captain—were nominally under his authority, so long as their ship remained grounded at his Station. So rigidly he stood at attention that not even the
slightest tremor of the trembling inside him escaped to
quiver betrayingly in his body.

They came toward him in a loose, dark mass that
resolved itself into a single file just beyond saluting distance. Singly, they went past him and up the ladder into
the sally port, each saluting him as they passed. He re-

turned the salutes stiffly, mechanically, walled off from classmates of six years by the barrier of his new command. It was a moment when a smile or a casual handshake would have meant more than a little. But protocol had stripped him of the right to familiarity; and it was a line of black-uniformed strangers that now filed slowly past. His place was already established and theirs was yet to be. They had nothing in common any more.

The last of the men went past him up the ladder and were lost to view through the black circle of the sally port. The heavy steel plug swung slowly to, behind them. He turned and made his way to the unfamiliar but well-known field control panel in the main control room of the Station. A light glowed redly on the communications board. He thumbed a switch and spoke into a grill set in the panel.

"Station to Ship. Go ahead."

Overhead the loudspeaker answered.

"Ship to Station. Ready for take-off."

His fingers went swiftly over the panel. Outside, the atmosphere of the field was evacuated and the dome slid back. Tractor mechs scurried out from the pit, under remote control, clamped huge magnetic fists on the ship, swung it into launching position, then retreated.

Jordan spoke again into the grill.

"Station clear. Take-off at will."

"Thank you, Station." He recognized the captain's voice. "And good luck."

Outside, the ship lifted, at first slowly, then faster on its pillar of flame, and dwindled away into the darkness of space. Automatically, he closed the dome and pumped the air back in.

He was turning away from the control panel, bracing himself against the moment of finding himself completely isolated, when, with a sudden, curious shock, he noticed that there was another, smaller ship yet on the field.

For a moment he stared at it blankly, uncomprehendingly. Then memory returned and he realized that the ship was a small courier vessel from Intelligence, which had been hidden by the huge bulk of the training ship. Its officer would still be below, cutting a record tape of the former commandant's last memories for the file at Headquarters. The memory lifted him momentarily from the morass of his emotions to attention to duty. He turned from the panel and went below.

In the triply-armored basement of the Station, the man from Intelligence was half in and half out of the memory bank when he arrived, having cut away a portion of the steel casing around the bank so as to connect his recorder direct to the cells. The sight of the heavy mount of steel with the ragged incision in one side, squatting like a wounded monster, struck Jordan unpleasantly; but he smoothed the emotion from his face and walked firmly to the bank. His footsteps rang on the metal floor; and the man from Intelligence, hearing them, brought his head momentarily outside the bank for a quick look.

"Hi!" he said, shortly, returning to his work. His voice continued from the interior of the bank with a friendly, hollow sound. "Congratulations, commandant."

"Thanks," answered Jordan, stiffly. He stood, somewhat ill at ease, uncertain of what was expected of him. When he hesitated, the voice from the bank continued.

"How does the cap feel?"

Jordan's hands went up instinctively to the mesh of silver wire on his head. It pushed back unyieldingly at his fingers, held firmly on the electrodes.

"Tight," he said.

The Intelligence man came crawling out of the bank, his recorder in one hand and thick loops of glassy tape in the other.

"They all do at first," he said, squatting down and feeding one end of the tape into a spring rewind spool. "In a couple of days you won't even be able to feel it up there."

"I suppose."

The Intelligence man looked up at him curiously.

"Nothing about it bothering you, is there?" he asked. "You look a little strained."

"Doesn't everybody when they first start out?"

"Sometimes," said the other, noncommittally. "Sometimes not. Don't hear a sort of humming, do you?"

"No."

"Feel any kind of pressure inside your head?"

"No."

"How about your eyes. See any spots or flashes in front of them?"

"No!" snapped Jordan.

"Take it easy," said the man from Intelligence. "This is my business."

"Sorry."

"That's all right. It's just that if there's anything wrong with you or the bank I want to know it." He rose from the rewind spool, which was now industriously gathering in the loose tape; and unclipping a pressure-torch from his belt, began resealing the aperture. "It's just that occasionally new officers have been hearing too many stories about the banks in Training School, and they're inclined to be jumpy."

"Stories?" said Jordan.

"Haven't you heard them?" answered the Intelligence man. "Stories of memory domination—stationmen driven insane by the memories of the men who had the Station before them. Catatonics whose minds have got lost in the past history of the bank, or cases of memory replacement where the stationman has identified himself with the memories and personality of the man who preceded him."

"Oh, those," said Jordan. "I've heard them." He paused, and then, when the other did not go on: "What about them? Are they true?"

The Intelligence man turned from the half-resealed aperture and faced him squarely, torch in hand.

"Some," he said bluntly. "There's been a few cases like that; although there didn't have to be. Nobody's trying to sugarcoat the facts. The memory bank's nothing but a storehouse connected to you through your silver cap—a gadget to enable you not only to remember everything you ever do at the station, but also everything anybody else who ever ran the Station, did. But there've been a few impressionable stationmen who've let themselves get the notion that the memory bank's a sort of a coffin with living dead men crawling around inside it. When that happens, there's trouble."

He turned away from Jordan, back to his work.

"And that's what you thought was the trouble with me," said Jordan, speaking to his back.

The man from Intelligence chuckled—it was an amazingly human sound.

"In my line, fella," he said, "we check all possibilities." He finished his resealing and turned around.

"No hard feelings?" he said.

Jordan shook his head. "Of course not."

"Then I'll be getting along." He bent over and picked up the spool, which had by now neatly wound up all the tape, straightened up and headed for the ramp that led up from the basement to the landing field. Jordan fell into step beside him.

"You've nothing more to do, then?" he said.

"Just my reports. But I can write those on the way

back." They went up the ramp and out through the lock on to the field.

"They did a good job of repairing the battle damage," he went on, looking around the Station.

"I guess they did," said Jordan. The two men paced soberly to the sally port of the Intelligence ship. "Well, so long."

"So long," answered the man from Intelligence, activating the sally port mechanism. The outer lock swung open and he hopped the few feet up to the opening without waiting for the little ladder to wind itself out. "See you in six months."

He turned to Jordan and gave him a casual, offhand salute with the hand holding the wind-up spool. Jordan returned it with training school precision. The port swung closed.

He went back to the master control room and the ritual of seeing the ship off. He stood looking out for a long time after it had vanished, then turned from the panel with a sigh to find himself at last completely alone.

He looked about the Station. For the next six months this would be his home. Then, for another six months he would be free on leave while the Station was rotated out of the line in its regular order for repair, reconditioning, and improvements.

If he lived that long.

The fear, which had been driven a little distance away by his conversation with the man from Intelligence, came back.

If he lived that long. He stood, bemused.

Back to his mind with the letter-perfect recall of the memory bank came the words of the other. Catatonic—cases of memory replacement. Memory domination. Had those others, too, had more than they could bear of fear and anticipation?

And with that thought came a suggestion that coiled like a snake in his mind. That would be a way out. What if they came, the alien invaders, and Thomas Jordan was no longer here to meet them? What if only the catatonic hulk of a man was left? What if they came and a man was here, but that man called himself and knew himself only as—

Waskewicz!

"No!" the cry came involuntarily from his lips; and he came to himself with his face contorted and his hands

half-extended in front of him in the attitude of one who
wards off a ghost. He shook his head to shake the vile suggestion from his brain; and leaned back, panting, against
the control panel.

Not that. Not ever that. He had surprised in himself a
weakness that turned him sick with horror. Win or lose;
live or die. But as Jordan—not as any other.

He lit a cigarette with trembling fingers. So—it was
over now and he was safe. He had caught it in time. He
had his warning. Unknown to him—all this time—the
seeds of memory domination must have been lying waiting
within him. But now he knew they were there, he knew
what measures to take. The danger lay in Waskewicz's
memories. He would shut his mind off from them—would
fight the Station without the benefit of their experience.
The first stationmen on the line had done without the aid
of a memory bank and so could he.

So.

He had settled it. He flicked on the viewing screens and
stood opposite them, very straight and correct in the middle of his Station, looking out at the dots that were his
forty-five doggie mechs spread out on guard over a million
kilometers of space, looking at the controls that would enable him to throw their blunt, terrible, mechanical bodies
into battle with the enemy, looking and waiting, waiting,
for the courage that comes from having faced squarely a
situation, to rise within him and take possession of him,
putting an end to all fears and doubtings.

And he waited so for a long time, but it did not come.

The weeks went swiftly by; and that was as it should be.
He had been told what to expect, during training; and it
was as it should be that these first months should be tense
ones, with a part of him always stiff and waiting for the
alarm bell that would mean a doggie signaling sight of an
enemy. It was as it should be that he should pause, suddenly, in the midst of a meal with his fork halfway to his
mouth, waiting and expecting momentarily to be sum-
moned; that he should wake unexpectedly in the nighttime
and lie rigid and tense, eyes fixed on the shadowy ceiling
and listening. Later—they had said in training—after you
have become used to the Station, this constant tension will
relax and you will be left at ease, with only one little
unobtrusive corner of your mind unnoticed but forever
alert. This will come with time, they said.

So he waited for it, waited for the release of the coiled

springs inside him and the time when the feel of the Station would be comfortable and friendly about him. When he had first been left alone, he had thought to himself that surely, in his case, the waiting would not be more than a matter of days; then, as the days went by and he still lived in a state of hair-trigger sensitivity, he had given himself, in his own mind, a couple of weeks—then a month.

But now a month and more than a month had gone without relaxation coming to him; and the strain was beginning to show in nervousness of his hands and the dark circles under his eyes. He found it impossible to sit still either to read, or to listen to the music that was available in the Station library. He roamed restlessly, endlessly checking and rechecking the empty space that his doggies' viewers revealed.

For the recollection of Waskewicz as he lay in the burial rocket would not go from him. And that was not as it should be.

He could, and did, refuse to recall the memories of Waskewicz that he had never experienced; but his own personal recollections were not easy to control and slipped into his mind when he was unaware. All else that he could do to lay the ghost, he had done. He had combed the Station carefully, seeking out the little adjustments and conveniences that a lonely man will make about his home, and removed them, even when the removal meant a loss of personal comfort. He had locked his mind securely to the storehouse of the memory bank, striving to hold himself isolated from the other's memories until familiarity and association should bring him to the point where he instinctively felt that the Station was *his* and not the other's. And, whenever thoughts of Waskewicz entered in spite of all these precautions, he had dismissed them sternly, telling himself that his predecessor was not worth the considering.

But the other's ghost remained, intangible and invulnerable, as if locked in the very metal of the walls and floor and ceiling of the Station; and rising to haunt him with the memories of the training school tales and the ominous words of the man from Intelligence. At such times, when the ghost had seized him, he would stand paralyzed, staring in hypnotic fascination at the screens with their silent mechanical sentinels, or at the cold steel of the memory bank, crouching like some brooding monster, fear feeding on his thoughts—until, with a sudden, wrenching effort of the will, he broke free of the mesmerism and flung himself frantically into the duties of the Station, checking and rechecking his instruments and the space they watched, doing anything and everything to drown his wild emotions in the necessity for attention to duty.

And eventually he found himself almost hoping for a raid, for the test that would prove him, would lay the ghost, one way or another, once and for all.

It came at last, as he had known it would, during one of the rare moments when he had forgotten the imminence of danger. He had awakened in his bunk, at the beginning of the arbitrary ten-hour day; and lay there drowsily, comfortably, his thoughts vague and formless, like shadows in the depths of a lazy whirlpool, turning slowly, going no place.

Then—the alarm!

Overhead the shouting bell burst into life, jerking him from his bed. Its metal clangor poured out on the air, tumbling from the loudspeakers in every room all over the Station, strident with urgency, pregnant with disaster. It roared, it vibrated, it thundered, until the walls themselves threw it back, seeming to echo in sympathy, acquiring a voice of their own until the room rang—until the Station itself rang like one monster bell, calling him into battle.

He leaped to his feet and ran to the master control room. On the telltale high on the wall above the viewer screens, the red light of number thirty-eight doggie was flashing ominously. He threw himself into the operator's seat before it, slapping one palm hard down on the switch to disconnect the alarm.

The Station is in contact with the enemy.

The sudden silence slapped at him, taking his breath away. He gasped and shook his head like a man who has had a glassful of cold water thrown unexpectedly in his face; then plunged his fingers at the keys on the master control board in front of his seat— Up beams. Up detector screen, established now at forty thousand kilometers distance. Switch on communications to Sector Headquarters.

The transmitter purred. Overhead, the white light flashed as it began to tick off its automatic signal. "Alert! Alert! Further data follows. Will report."

Headquarters has been notified by the Station.

Activate viewing screen on doggie number thirty-eight.

He looked into the activated screen, into the vast arena of space over which the mechanical vision of that doggie mech was ranging. Far and far away at top magnification were five small dots, coming in fast on a course leading ten points below and at an angle of thirty-two degrees to the Station.

He flicked a key, releasing thirty-eight on proximity fuse control and sending it plunging toward the dots. He scanned the Station area map for the positions of his other mechs. Thirty-nine was missing—in the Station for repair. The rest were available. He checked numbers forty through forty-five and thirty-seven through thirty to rendezous on collision course with enemy at seventy-five thousand kilometers. Numbers twenty to thirty to rendezvous at fifty thousand kilometers.

Primary defense has been inaugurated.

He turned back to the screen. Number thirty-eight, expendable in the interests of gaining information, was plunging towards the ships at top acceleration under strains no living flesh would have been able to endure. But as yet the size and type of the invaders was still hidden by distance. A white light flashed abruptly from the communications panel, announcing that Sector Headquarters was alerted and ready to talk. He cut in audio.

"Contact. Go ahead, Station J-49C3."

"Five ships," he said. "Beyond identification range. Coming in through thirty-eight at ten point thirty-two."

"Acknowledge," the voice of Headquarters was level, precise, emotionless. "Five ships—thirty-eight—ten—thirty-two. Patrol Twenty, passing through your area at four hours distance, has been notified and will proceed to your station at once, arriving in four hours, plus or minus twenty minutes. Further assistance follows. Will stand by here for your future messages."

The white light went out and he turned away from communications panel. On the screen, the five ships had still not grown to identifiable proportions, but for all practical purposes, the preliminaries were over. He had some fifteen minutes now during which everything that could be done, had been done.

Primary defense has been completed.

He turned away from the controls and walked back to the bedroom, where he dressed slowly and meticulously in full black uniform. He straightened his tunic, looking in the mirror and stood gazing at himself for a long moment. Then, hesitantly, almost as if against his will, he reached out with one hand to a small gray box on a shelf beside the mirror, opened it, and took out the silver battle star that the next few hours would entitle him to wear.

It lay in his palm, the bright metal winking softly up at him under the reflection of the room lights and the small movements of his hand. The little cluster of diamonds in its center sparked and ran the whole gamut of their flashing colors. For several minutes he stood looking at it; then slowly, gently, he shut it back up in its box and went out, back to the control room.

On the screen, the ships were now large enough to be identified. They were medium-sized vessels, Jordan noticed, of the type used most by the most common species of raiders—that same race which had orphaned him. There could be no doubt about their intentions, as there sometimes was when some odd stranger chanced on the Frontier, to be regretfully destroyed by men whose orders were to take no chances. No, these were *the enemy*, the strange, suicidal life form that thrust thousands of attacks yearly against the little human empire, who blew themselves up when captured and wasted a hundred ships for every one that broke through the guarding stations to descend on some unprotected city of an inner planet and loot it of equipment and machinery that the aliens were either unwilling or unable to build for themselves—a contradictory, little understood and savage race. These five ships would make no attempt to parley.

But now, doggie number thirty-eight had been spotted and the white exhausts of guided missiles began to streak toward the viewing screen. For a few seconds, the little mech bucked and tossed, dodging, firing defensively, shooting down the missiles as they approached. But it was a hopeless fight against those odds and suddenly one of the streaks expanded to fill the screen with glaring light.

And the screen went blank. Thirty-eight was gone.

Suddenly realizing that he should have been covering with observation from one of the doggies further back, Jordan jumped to fill his screens. He brought the view from forty in on the one that thirty-eight had vacated and filled the two flanking screens with the view from thirty-seven on his left and twenty on his right. They showed his first line of defense already gathered at the seventy-five kilometer rendezvous and the fifty thousand kilometer rendezvous still forming.

The raiders were decelerating now, and on the wall, the telltale for the enemy's detectors flushed a sudden deep and angry purple as their invisible beams reached out and were baffled by the detector screen he had erected at a distance of forty thousand kilometers in front of the Station. They continued to decelerate, but the blockage of their detector beams had given them the approximate area of his Station; and they corrected course, swinging in until they were no more than two points and ten degrees in error. Jordan, his nervous fingers trembling slightly on the keys, stretched thirty-seven through thirty out in depth and sent forty through forty-five forward on a five-degree sweep to attempt a circling movement.

The five dark ships of the raiders, recognizing his intention, fell out of their single file approach formation to spread out and take a formation in open echelon. They were already firing on the advancing doggies and tiny streaks of light tattooed the black of space around numbers forty through forty-five.

Jordan drew a deep and ragged breath and leaned back in his control seat. For the moment there was nothing for his busy fingers to do among the control keys. His thirties must wait until the enemy came to them; since, with modern automatic gunnery the body at rest had an advantage over the body in motion. And it would be some minutes before the forties would be in attack position. He fumbled for a cigarette, keeping his eyes on the screens, remembering the caution in the training manuals against relaxation once contact with the enemy has been made.

But reaction was setting in.

From the first wild ringing command of the alarm until the present moment, he had reacted automatically, with perfection and precision, as the drills had schooled him, as the training manuals had impressed upon him. The enemy had appeared. He had taken measures for defense against them. All that could have been done had been done; and he knew he had done it properly. And the enemy had done what he had been told they would do.

He was struck, suddenly, with the deep quivering realization of the truth in the manual's predictions. It was so, then. These inimical others, these alien foes, were also bound by the physical laws. They as well as he, could move only within the rules of time and space. They were shorn of their mystery and brought down to his level. Different and awful, they might be, but their capabilities were limited, even as his; and in a combat such as the one now shaping up, their inhumanness was of no account, for the inflexible realities of the universe weighed impartially on him and them alike.

And with this realization, for the first time, the old remembered fear began to fall away like a discarded garment. A tingle ran through him and he found himself warming to the fight as his forefathers had warmed before him away back to the days when man was young and the tiger roared in the cool, damp jungle-dawn of long ago. The blood-instinct was in him; that and something of the fierce, vengeful joy with which a hunted creature turns at last on its pursuer. He would win. Of course he would win. And in winning he would at one stroke pay off the debt of blood and fear which the enemy had held against him these fifteen years.

Thinking in this way, he leaned back in his seat and the old memory of the shattered city and of himself running, running, rose up again around him. But this time it was no longer a prelude to terror, but fuel for the kindling of his rage. *These are my fear*, he thought, gazing unseeingly at the five ships in the screens *and I will destroy them*.

The phantasms of his memory faded like smoke around him. He dropped his cigarette into a disposal slot on the arm of his seat, and leaned forward to inspect the enemy positions.

They had spread out to force his forties to circle wide, and those doggies were now scattered, safe but ineffective, waiting further directions. What had been an open echelon formation of the raiders was now a ragged, widely dispersed line, with far too much space between ships to allow each to cover his neighbor.

For a moment Jordan was puzzled; and a tiny surge of fear of the unexplicable rippled across the calm surface of his mind. Then his brow smoothed out. There was no need to get panicky. The aliens' maneuver was not the mysterious tactic he had half-expected it to be; but just what it appeared, a rather obvious and somewhat stupid move to avoid the flanking movement he had been attempting with his forties. Stupid—because the foolish aliens had now rendered themselves vulnerable to interspersal by his thirties.

It was good news, rather than bad, and his spirits leaped another notch.

He ignored the baffled forties, circling automatically on safety control just beyond the ships' effective aiming range; and turned to the thirties, sending them plunging toward the empty areas between ships as you might interlace the fingers of one hand with another. Between any two ships there would be a dead spot—a position where a mech could not be fired on by either vessel without also aiming at its right- or left-hand companion. If two or more doggies could be brought safely to that spot, they could turn and pour down the open lanes on proximity control, their fuses primed, their bomb loads activated, blind bulldogs of destruction.

One third, at least, should in this way get through the defensive shelling of the ships and track their dodging prey to the atomic flare of a grim meeting.

Smiling now in confidence, Jordan watched his mechs approach the ships. There was nothing the enemy could do. They could not now tighten up their formation without merely making themselves a more attractive target; and to disperse still further would negate any chance in the future of regaining a semblance of formation.

Carefully, his fingers played over the keys, gentling his mechs into line so that they would come as close as possible to hitting their dead spots simultaneously. The ships came on.

Closer the raiders came, and closer. And then—bare seconds away from contact with the line of approaching doggies, white fire ravened in unison from their stern tubes, making each ship suddenly a black nugget in the center of a blossom of flame. In unison, they spurted forward, in sudden and unexpected movement, bringing their dead spots to and past the line of seeking doggies, leaving them behind.

Caught for a second in stunned surprise, Jordan sat dumb and motionless, staring at the screen. Then, swift in his anger, his hands flashed out over the keys, blasting his mechs to a cruel, shuddering halt, straining their metal sinews for the quickest and most abrupt about face and return. This time he would catch them from behind. This time, going in the same direction as the ships, the mechs could not be dodged. For what living thing could endure equal strains with cold metal?

But there was no second attempt on the part of the thirties, for as each bucked to its savage halt, the rear weapons of the ships reached out in unison, and each of the blasting mechs, that had leaped forward so confidently, flared up and died like little candles in the dark.

Numb in the grip of icy failure, Jordan sat still, a ramrod figure staring at the two screens that spoke so elo-

quently of his disaster—and the one dead screen where
the view from thirty-seven had been, that said nothing at
all. Like a man in a dream, he reached out his right hand
and cut in the final sentinel, the *watchdog,* that mech that
circled closest to the Station. In one short breath his
strong first line was gone, and the enemy rode their
strength undiminished, floating in toward his single line of
twenties at fifty thousand with the defensive screen a mere
ten thousand kilometers behind them.

Training was strong. Without hesitation his hands went
out over the keys and the doggies of the twenties surged
forward, trying for contact with the enemy in an area as
far from the screen as possible. But, because they were
moving in on an opponent relatively at rest, their courses
were the more predictable on the enemy's calculators and
the disadvantage was theirs. So it was that forty minutes
later three ships of the alien rode clear and unthreatened
in an area where two of their mates, the forties and all of
the thirties were gone.

The ships were, at this moment, fifteen thousand kilometers from the detector screen.

Jordan looked at his handiwork. The situation was obvious and the alternatives undeniable. He had twenty doggies remaining, but he had neither the time to move them
up beyond the screen, nor the room to maneuver them in
front of it. The only answer was to pull his screen back.
But to pull the screen back would be to indicate, by its
shrinkage and the direction of its withdrawal, the position
of his Station clearly enough for the guided missiles of the
enemy to seek him out; and once the Station was knocked
out, the doggies were directionless, impotent.

Yet, if he did nothing, in a few minutes the ships would
touch and penetrate the detector screen and his Station,
the nerve center the aliens were seeking, would lie naked
and revealed in their detectors.

He had lost. The alternatives totaled to the same answer, to defeat. In the inattention of a moment, in the
smoke of a cigarette, the first blind surge of self-confi-
dence and the thoughtless halting of his by-passed doggies
that had allowed the ships' calculators to find them sta-
tionary for a second in a predictable area, he had failed.
He had given away, in the error of his pride, the initial
advantage. He had lost. Speak it softly, speak it gently, for
his fault was the fault of one young and untried. He was
defeated.

And in the case of defeat, the actions prescribed by the

manual was stern and clear. The memory of the instructions tolled in his mind like the unvarying notes of a funeral bell.

"When, in any conflict, the forces of the enemy have obtained a position of advantage such that it is no longer possible to maintain the anonymity of the Station's position, the commandant of the Station is required to perform one final duty. Knowing that the Station will shortly be destroyed and that this will render all remaining mechs innocuous to enemy forces, the commandant is commanded to relinquish control of these mechs, and to place them with fuses primed on proximity control, in order that, even without the Station, they may be enabled to automatically pursue and attempt to destroy those forces of the enemy that approach within critical range of their proximity fuse."

Jordan looked at his screens. Out at forty thousand kilometers, the detector screen was beginning to luminesce slightly as the detectors of the ships probed it at shorter range. To make the manual's order effective, it would have to be pulled back to at least half that distance; and there, while it would still hide the Station, it would give the enemy his approximate location. They would then fire blindly, but with cunning and increasing knowledge and it would be only a matter of time before they hit. After that—only the blind doggies, quivering, turning and trembling through all points of the stellar compass in their thoughtless hunger for prey. One or two of these might gain a revenge as the ships tried to slip past them and over the Line; but Jordan would not be there to know it.

But there was no alternative—even if duty had left him one. Like strangers, his hands rose from the board and stretched out over the keys that would turn the doggies loose. His fingers dropped and rested upon them—light touch on smooth polished coolness.

But he could not press them down.

He sat with his arms outstretched, as if in supplication, like one of his primitive forebearers before some ancient altar of death. For his will had failed him and there was no denying now his guilt and his failure. For the battle had turned in his short few moments of inattention, and his underestimation of the enemy that had seduced him into halting his thirties without thinking. He knew; and through the memory bank—if that survived—the Force would know. In his neglect, in his refusal to avail himself of the experience of his predecessors, he was guilty.

And yet, he could not press the keys. He could not die properly—*in the execution of his duty*—the cold, correct phrase of the official reports. For a wild rebellion surged through his young body, an instinctive denial of the end that stared him so undeniably in the face. Through vein and sinew and nerve, it raced, opposing and blocking the dictates of training, the logical orders of his upper mind. It was too soon, it was not fair, he had not been given his chance to profit by experience. One more opportunity was all he needed, one more try to redeem himself.

But the rebellion passed and left him shaken, weak. There was no denying reality. And now, a new shame came to press upon him, for he thought of the three alien vessels breaking through, of another city in flaming ruins, and another child that would run screaming from his destroyers. The thought rose up in him, and he writhed internally, torn by his own indecisions. Why couldn't he act? It made no difference to him. What would justification and the redeeming of error mean to him after he was dead?

And he moaned a little, softly to himself, holding his hands outstretched above the keys, but could not press them down.

And then hope came. For suddenly, rising up out of the rubble of his mind came the memory of the Intelligence man's words once again, and his own near-pursuit of insanity. He, Jordan, could not bring himself to expose himself to the enemy, not even if the method of exposure meant possible protection for the Inner Worlds. But the man who had held this Station before him, who had died as he was about to die, must have been faced with the same necessity for self-sacrifice. And those last minute memories of his decision would be in the memory bank, waiting for the evocation of Jordan's mind.

Here was hope at last. He would remember, would embrace the insanity he had shrunk from. He would remember and be Waskewicz, not Jordan. He would be Waskewicz and unafraid; though it was a shameful thing to do. Had there been one person, one memory among all living humans, whose image he could have evoked to place in opposition to the images of the three dark ships, he might have managed by himself. But there had been no one close to him since the day of the city raid.

His mind reached back into the memory bank, reached

back to the last of Waskewicz's memories. He remembered.

Of the ten ships attacking, six were down. Their ashes strewed the void and the remaining four rode warily, spread widely apart for maximum safety, sure of victory, but wary of this hornet's nest which might still have some stings yet unexpended. But the detector screen was back to its minimum distance for effective concealment and only five doggies remained poised like blunt arrows behind it. He—Waskewicz—sat hunched before the control board, his thick and hairy hands lying softly on the proximity keys.

"Drift in," he said, speaking to the ships, which were cautiously approaching the screen. "Drift in, you. Drift!"

His lips were skinned back over his teeth in a grin—but he did not mean it. It was an automatic grimace, reflex to the tenseness of his waiting. He would lure them on until the last moment, draw them as close as possible to the automatic pursuit mechanisms of the remaining doggies, before pulling back the screen.

"Drift in," he said.

They drifted in. Behind the screen he aimed his doggies, pointing each one of four at a ship and the remaining one generally at them all. They drifted in.

They touched.

His fingers slapped the keys. The screen snapped back until it barely covered the waiting doggies. And the doggies stirred, on proximity, their pursuit mechs activated, now blind and terribly fully armed, ready to attack in senseless directness anything that came close enough.

And the first shells from the advancing ships began to probe the general area of the Station asteroid.

Waskewicz sighed, pushed himself back from the controls and stood up, turning away from the screens. It was over. Done. All finished. For a moment he stood irresolute; then, walking over to the dispenser on the wall, dialed for coffee and drew it, hot into a disposable cup. He lit a cigarette and stood waiting, smoking and drinking the coffee.

The Station rocked suddenly to the impact of a glancing hit on the asteroid. He staggered and slopped some coffee on his boots, but kept his feet. He took another gulp from the cup, another drag on the cigarette. The Station shook again, and the lights dimmed. He crumpled the cup and dropped it in the disposal slot. He dropped the cigarette on the steel floor, ground it beneath his boot sole; and walked back to the screen and leaned over for it for a final look.

The lights went out. And memory ended.

The present returned to Jordan and he stared about him a trifle wildly. Then he felt hardness beneath his fingers and forced himself to look down.

The keys were depressed. The screen was back. The doggies were on proximity. He stared at his hand as if he had never known it before, shocked at its thinness and the lack of soft down on its back. Then, slowly, fighting reluctant neck muscles, he forced himself to look up and into the viewing screen.

And the ships were there, but the ships were drawing away.

He stared, unable to believe his eyes, and half-ready to believe anything else. For the invaders had turned and the flames from their tails made it evident that they were making away into outer space at their maximum bearable acceleration, leaving him alone and unharmed. He shook his head to clear away the false vision from the screen before him, but it remained, denying its falseness. The miracle for which his instincts had held him in check had come—in the moment in which he had borrowed strength to deny it.

His eyes searched the screens in wonder. And then, far down in one corner of the watch dog's screen and so distant still that they showed only as pips on the wide expanse, he saw the shape of his miracle. Coming up from inside of the Line under maximum bearable acceleration were six gleaming fish-shapes that would dwarf his doggies to minnows—the battleships of Patrol Twenty. And he realized, with the dawning wonder of the reprieved, that the conflict, which had seemed so momentary while he was fighting it had actually lasted the four hours necessary to bring the Patrol up to his aid.

The realization that he was now safe washed over him like a wave and he was conscious of a deep thankfulness swelling up within him. It swelled up and out, pushing aside the lonely fear and desperation of his last few minutes, filling him instead with a relief so all-encompassing and profound that there was no anger left in him and no hate—not even for the enemy. It was like being born again.

Above him on the communications panel, the white message light was blinking. He cut in on the speaker with a steady hand and the dispassionate, official voice of the Patrol sounded over his head.

"Patrol Twenty to Station. Twenty to Station. Come in Station. Are you all right?"

He pressed the transmitter key.

"Station to Twenty. Station to Twenty. No damage to report. The Station is unharmed."

"Glad to hear it, Station. We will not pursue. We are decelerating now and will drop all ships on your field in half an hour. That is all."

"Thank you, Twenty. The field will be clear and ready for you. Land at will. That is all."

His hand fell away from the key and the message light winked out. In unconscious imitation of Waskewicz's memory he pushed himself back from the controls, stood up, turned and walked to the dispenser in the wall, where he dialed for and received a cup of coffee. He lit a cigarette and stood as the other had stood, smoking and drinking. He had won.

And reality came back to him with a rush.

For he looked down at his hand and saw the cup of coffee. He drew in on the cigarette and felt the hot smoothness of it deep in his lungs. And terror took him twisting by the throat.

He had won? He had done nothing. The enemy ships had fled not from him, but from the Patrol; and it was Waskewicz, *Waskewicz*, who had taken the controls from his hands at the crucial moment. It was Waskewicz who had saved the day, not he. It was the memory bank. The memory bank and Waskewicz!

The control room rocked about him. He had been betrayed. Nothing was won. Nothing was conquered. It was no friend that had broken at last through his lonely shell to save him, but the mind-sucking figment of memory-domination sanity. The memory bank and Waskewicz had seized him in their grasp.

He threw the coffee container from him and made himself stand upright. He threw the cigarette down and ground it beneath his boot. White-hot, from the very depths of his being, a wild anger blazed and consumed him. *Puppet,* said the mocking voice of his conscience, whispering in his ear. *Puppet!*

Dance, Puppet! Dance to the tune of the twitching strings!

"No!" he yelled. And, borne on the white-hot tide of his rage, the all-consuming rage that burnt the last trace of

fear from his heart like dross from the molten steel, he
turned to face his tormentor, hurling his mind backward,
back into the life of Waskewicz, prisoned in the memory
bank.

Back through the swirling tide of memories he raced,
hunting a point of contact, wanting only to come to grips
with his predecessor, to stand face to face with Waskewicz. Surely, in all his years at the Station, the other must
sometime have devoted a thought to the man who must
come after him. Let Jordan just find that point, there
where the influence was strongest, and settle the matter,
for sanity or insanity, for shame or pride, once and for all.

"Hi, Brother!"

The friendly words splashed like cool water on the
white blaze of his anger. He—Waskewicz—stood in front
of the bedroom mirror and his face looked out at the man
who was himself, and who yet was also Jordan.

"Hi, Brother!" he said. "Whoever and wherever you
may be. Hi!"

Jordan looked out through the eyes of Waskewicz, at
the reflected face of Waskewicz; and it was a friendly
face, the face of a man like himself.

"This is what they don't tell you," said Waskewicz.
"This is what they don't teach in training—the message
that, sooner or later, every stationman leaves for the guy
who comes after him.

"This is the creed of the Station. *You are not alone.* No
matter what happens, *you are not alone.* Out on the rim
of the empire, facing the unknown races and the endless
depths of the universe, this is the one thing that will keep
you from all harm. As long as you remember it, nothing
can affect you, neither attack, nor defeat, nor death. Light
a screen on your outermost doggie and turn the magnification up as far as it will go. Away out at the limits of your
vision you can see the doggie of another Station, of another man who holds the Line beside you. All along the
Frontier, the Outpost Stations stand, forming a link of
steel to guard the Inner Worlds and the little people there.
They have their lives and you have yours; and yours is to
stand on guard.

"It is not easy to stand on guard; and no man can face
the universe alone. But—*you are not alone!* All those who
at this moment keep the Line, are with you; and all that
have ever kept the Line, as well. For this is our new im-
mortality, we who guard the Frontier, that we do not stop

with our deaths, but live on in the Station we have kept. We are in its screens, its controls, in its memory bank, in the very bone and sinew of its steel body. *We are the station,* your steel brother that fights and lives and dies with you and welcome you at last to our kinship when for your personal self the light has gone out forever, and what was individual of you is nothing any more but cold ashes drifting in the eternity of space. *We are with you and of you, and you are not alone.* I, who was once Waskewicz, and am now part of the Station, leave this message for you, as it was left to me by the man who kept this guard before me, and as you will leave it in your turn to the man who follows you, and so on down the centuries until we have become an elder race and no longer need our shield of brains and steel."

"Hi Brother! You are not alone!"

And so, when the six ships of Patrol Twenty came drifting in to their landing at the Station, the man who waited to greet them had more than the battle star on his chest to show he was a veteran. For he had done more than win a battle. He had found his soul.

Numerical Checklist of DAW BOOKS
NEVER BEFORE IN PAPERBACK

All DAW books are 95¢ (plus 15¢ postage and handling if by mail)

DAW BOOKS are represented by the publishers of Signet and Mentor Books, THE NEW AMERICAN LIBRARY, INC.

THE NEW AMERICAN LIBRARY, INC.,
P.O. Box 999, Bergenfield, New Jersey 07621

Please send me the DAW BOOKS I have checked above. I am enclosing
$_____(check or money order—no currency or C.O.D.'s).
Please include the list price plus 15¢ a copy to cover mailing costs.

Name_____

Address_____

City_____State_____ Zip Code_____
Please allow at least 3 weeks for delivery